THE LAST STAGE OF GRIEF IS MURDER

TAM BARNETT

Boldwood

First published in Great Britain in 2026 by Boldwood Books Ltd.

Copyright © Tam Barnett, 2026

Cover Design by Head Design Ltd.

Cover Images: Shutterstock

A CIP catalogue record for this book is available from the British Library.

Paperback ISBN 978-1-83633-072-1

Large Print ISBN 978-1-83633-073-8

Hardback ISBN 978-1-83633-071-4

Trade Paperback ISBN 978-1-80656-183-4

Ebook ISBN 978-1-83633-074-5

Kindle ISBN 978-1-83633-075-2

Audio CD ISBN 978-1-83633-066-0

MP3 CD ISBN 978-1-83633-067-7

Digital audio download ISBN 978-1-83633-069-1

This book is printed on certified sustainable paper. Boldwood Books is dedicated to putting sustainability at the heart of our business. For more information please visit https://www.boldwoodbooks.com/about-us/sustainability/

Boldwood Books Ltd, 23 Bowerdean Street, London, SW6 3TN

www.boldwoodbooks.com

For Dad and Paula, my indefatigable champions.

PROLOGUE
IVOR

April 2025

The shrill cuts through my sleep like a chainsaw screaming on rusty metal. Phone alarm. I switch it off in my pocket.

Cranking my eyes open, the dew is glittering on the grass, every blade a tiny diamond reflecting the clear spring sky above. If this park bench were a hotel room, the view would get five stars.

I rise gingerly into a sitting position, lead marbles lurching from one temple to the other in my head, icy morning air stinging my nostrils. The vertigo begins to settle.

Stillness and silence. Good.

Blinking, I take in the view again. A dark pattern of tiny pawprints is the only blemish on the glistening lawn stretching out in all directions around me.

The key to beating any hangover is not to underestimate it. Unzipping my backpack, I pull out a two-litre bottle of Evian and four ibuprofens. Agua mineral and anti-inflammatories –

the breakfast of champions. Sharp pain blinds me for a second as the glacier-cold water hits the roof of my mouth and brain freeze turns the lead marbles into stabbing shards. But it soon washes away with the pills.

Now, and only now, does victory feel assured. Getting to my feet, I gather up the carpet of empty lager cans under my bench and tip them into the litter bin along the path. Their tinny clang is not in keeping with the distant chirp of birdsong and whirr of early-morning traffic.

Sitting back down, I check the time. 6.07 a.m. Excellent. Right on schedule.

Off in the distance, two overly healthy women clad in offensively neon leggings and white fleeces run along a path brushed in weak sunshine. Their breath chugs out in front of them and disappears over their heads like they're a pair of racing steam trains.

I pull out a wet wipe and little bottle of Listerine from my bag; I may have slept alfresco but I'm no scruffbag, thank you very much. Scrub and gargle done, I throw the remnants back in my bag along with the woolly hat I'd been wearing through the night. Cold air sucks the heat away from my scalp; I leave my coat on and tuck my leather-gloved hands under my armpits.

Looking past those two women, I focus on the all-important house at the far end of the park – upstairs curtains still closed, as expected. Still a while to wait, but I can't risk being noticed by the commuting masses. A man in a black beanie hat lying horizontal, snoring and belching with a coterie of Heineken cans for company may draw attention. A dull young man, minty of breath and clean of face, enjoying the robins and chiffchaffs in his parka? Much less memorable.

It isn't long before the world does begin to go by. More

joggerati, dogwalkers, parents holding on to reusable coffee cups for dear life as children tear about on scooters.

As soon as this is done, I am going to have the most wonderful pint. Not a warm, frothy can slurped and burped down in the park. A carefully picked, artfully poured beer, consumed on licensed premises at a small round table as I rest into a comfortable, cushioned chair.

It is life's greatest pleasure, I would argue – a pub-bought pint. The back corners of my mouth tingle at the mere notion of it. That first gulp alone: it's a counselling session, hour's massage, loving hug and warming fire all in one. The voluptuous curve of the glass against your lip; the crisp bite as the liquid hits the tongue; the sparkle against the insides of your cheeks, like a febrile crowd; the unique tang that takes you back to your first ever sip; the exquisite, extinguishing cool as it slips down; and the way it hits the stomach, protecting you from the inside out.

Oh yes, I will very much deserve my first pint later today.

At 6.43 a.m. I refocus on that house in the distance. The curtains will open bang on time – he's pathetically predictable. I squeeze my fists into tight rocks, the black leather squeaking as it strains over my knuckles.

6.44 a.m. Still closed. It's a good job I've got excellent vision, a lesser mortal would need binoculars to see all the way over there, and that would not suit my need for discretion.

A buzz builds in my chest. This is happening. I count down the seconds.

His alarm must go off at 6.45 a.m. every day, then he must get straight out of bed and rip open the curtains like some sort of programmed droid. I mean, who wakes up hellishly early and thinks... what I need now is more daylight?

Ah! There it is. Red and white drapes flung wide to reveal a topless man, with his arms spread, about two hundred metres away from me.

I get to my feet, sling my bag over my shoulder and trot towards the topless man.

He doesn't know it, but he's just thrown those curtains open for the very last time.

4 MONTHS EARLIER...

1
IVOR

December 2024

Wow!

Wow wow wow!

She looked incredible. Well, it's Becky... of course she looked incredible. Teeth white like untouched snow, lips full and alluring behind cherry gloss, skin soft and pristine, taking me back to the billion kisses I have peppered her mouth and cheeks with before. And those almond-shaped eyes, forest green, impossible not to get lost in... looking straight back at me!

The waft of her rose perfume alone was a fix. I'm an addict deprived too long, determined to make this relapse last forever.

It's been so painful being apart. Life is nothing without her. Part of me tried to pretend I could survive, but that was a scurrilous lie. Becky is my life.

Looking around the artisan coffee shop, I wonder if anyone else noticed the sparks flying as we drank our piping hot cortados. Probably not. Everyone's face down in phones and laptops, as if that's a reasonable substitute to having a personality. Go to the pub, amigos! Much more fun.

It was Becky's choice to go for coffee rather than proper drinks. To be fair, I'd have met her on the slopes of Mount Etna, mid-eruption, if she'd asked. Feel a bit bad for not admitting to the couple of looseners I had beforehand, especially when she asked. But I was nervous – no way I'd have given my best performance sober.

I can't mess this up now I've got a second chance. I can't, I won't.

Should I have reached out and held her hand when she put it in the middle of the table? I'm so rubbish at reading signals. Maybe I should have. Next date, I'll hold her hand, hold her cold palm against my own to warm it up, just like always.

Those small, beautiful hands. How I've missed them! Missed how we used to lace our fingers together, intertwined on my crummy sofa, whispering in each other's ears, laughing as my lips brushed her neck. But the good times are roaring back!

I want to go around giving every one of these doppio dummies a high five. No, a high ten!

Everything me and Becky have been through, the misunderstandings, the break-up, it's all in the rear view. Now we can speed off into the sunset. That's what an adult relationship looks like, that's true love. You overcome your obstacles and you're a stronger couple on the other side.

Just being one-on-one again, talking, sharing air and thoughts and time... Tears come to my eyes. The pain, the dark thoughts, the guilt, all banished forever.

There's a young couple at the till as I get up to leave.

'Allow me!' I holler, whipping out my debit card and slapping it on the PIN machine before either of them knows what's happening. It bleeps to confirm the payment. 'Have a great day!'

Skipping out into the freezing winter grey, I zip up my parka and stroll past shops bustling with bargain-hunters. The post-Christmas sales in full swing, the decorations still up, rows of white tinsel and twisted lines of fairy lights swaying in the breeze between buildings.

I play back every last detail of mine and Becky's conversation.

Hope I listened enough, didn't talk too much. I really tried.

A bolt of dread jolts me as I'm slipping my debit card away again. Did I make sure I paid for our drinks, didn't make her fork out? My mind races back to the start. She got there first, was in the queue and then...

Oh no, it's all good! The chirpy barista man tried to get me to sign up to some coffee club mailing list, but I graciously declined and tapped the reader. Absolute chancer.

OK, then what happened? We sat down, she talked about her parents. I have not missed them! She was really kind about Tesco. That was very Becky – trying to encourage me by bringing up that old performance review, the one where I got the pay rise. Couldn't believe she remembered that – almost made me well up again!

I should apply to be on The Traitors; they all love sitting at tables and crying at the drop of a hat too.

But that celebration of each other's achievements, it nourishes like nothing else can. Starved for so long, the sudden feast of time shared is delectable.

She laughed, as well, when I told her about how I'd tried to order the new Arsenal shirt as a Christmas present to myself, accidentally ended up buying the women's one, but how I'm going to keep it anyway. Joy whizzes around my chest like the golden trail of a live sparkler as I replay that laugh.

At the end, did she say she'd text me or did I say I'd text her? It's a blur. I'll text her anyway.

Some people say being in love is discovering you feel a way you've never felt before for someone, like it's a bolt-on, a bonus to your existing life. I've never felt like that about Becky. It isn't that she made a bad thing better. For me there is nothing before her. She hasn't enhanced my life, she hasn't even transformed it, she is the beginning; all that went before is an empty, black absence of anything. At times, this last eight months have felt like that. Lost, alone, nothing.

But then she texted, wanted to meet up, reconnect, and bosh... I have a second chance at living.

I need a beer!

I'm not too far from London Bridge, which means The George – one of several pubs that claims to be the capital's oldest. No matter the historical wrangling, it is a marvellous place in which to imbibe.

Best of all, I can nip into Greggs on the way. Steak bake, sausage roll, salted caramel doughnut. Mmmm! That bakery chain is Britain's greatest ever enterprise. Never mind doctors, nurses and Western medicine, Greggs has saved my life a hundred times after big nights out.

Then finally, I shall sit in the pub and craft the perfect follow-up message to get me and Becky back together for good.

If life gives you lemons – make limoncello.

2

BECKY'S DIARY

Saturday 26 June 2021

Good job I'm writing this down, so it's preserved as a statement of public record...

I. Am. Never. Chaperoning. Cam. Again.

Actually, it's not really public record, since no one else will ever read this. But at least I can read it back and remind myself that playing third wheel on a first date is a truly appalling way to spend a Saturday.

I'm sorry but if you are so unconvinced by a man that you have to bring your friend along, then things are already off to a bad start. And this bloke had enough red flags to cover a golf course.

He was fifteen minutes late for the cinema, which meant we missed the trailers – red flag number one. Then he still insisted on buying a suitcase-sized box of popcorn at the kiosk, which he didn't share with me OR Cam – red flag number two. THEN he chose salted rather than sweet – red flag number three. And this was all in the first five minutes of knowing the guy!

The film was all right – some mad horror thing set on a ship being circled by human-eating piranhas. The fact I can't even remember the title says it all. Cam seemed invested, although she might have just been gasping and grabbing her date's arm to flirt. That's definitely her style.

They started whispering to each other at one point, then both disappeared saying they were 'off to the loo' – definitely went for a sneaky kiss at the very least. I mean, aren't we past that kind of cinema behaviour? We're twenty-one, for goodness' sake. Also... if you're willing to run off alone with the man mid-film, why insist I come along in the first place? But no, Cam left me there, watching endless fish chomp through endless bodies, and without enough mobile signal to otherwise distract myself. I didn't even dare snaffle any of her date's discarded popcorn – don't know where his hands have been. It was the first film I'd been to see in the presence of fellow human beings since the latest lockdown. First cinema trip since the start of the pandemic last year actually, so there was a novelty in that. Might have been useful to have the two-metre distancing rule still in place too, protect Cam from Captain Tragic.

After the film, the three of us went to Franco Manca for pizza. I had the salami one with chilli oil, and a side of cheesy garlic bread with pesto. To be fair, the food was de-lish! If only the conversation had been anywhere near as appetising. Cam kept asking him questions that he answered with monosyllabic answers – another red flag. Then he launched into a twenty-minute monologue about how his football or rugby or tiddlywinks team – I wasn't really listening – should have won a thing but didn't, or something.

Thankfully there was phone signal at the restaurant. Looked up a few things I could get Dad for his birthday, not that he'll like any of them. Is it too pathetic and silly to buy him a wine voucher? Probably.

Note to self: need to get the present to him by Wednesday latest, as they're away on the actual day. So typical, making it all about

Amy's death day rather than Dad's birthday. It'll have been 14 years ago this time round, and they still insist on going away every time that date comes up... but they don't invite me. Oh no, never mind my grief, I was just Amy's twin sister for goodness' sake, I can mourn on my own time.

Anyway, eventually Cam's blithering date finished delivering the sports news and we asked for the bill. I was intrigued to see how he'd handle that particular juncture after his popcorn fail, and do you know, he tried to pull the same trick again, cheap bastard. He asked the waitress to charge one third to his card, which she did, and then he indicated for me to pay the rest on behalf of me and Cam. 'Becca, would you mind?' he said. Becca! If you can't even get my name right, mate, I ain't coughing up for dinner. I should have been paid to endure that painfest! And I felt angry for Cam as well, putting up with this wet wipe who's only concerned with hearing his own voice and protecting his own bank balance. So I did something. Something SO not me. Something a bit outrageous. And it left my heartbeat pounding in my ears and my whole body burning in latent anxiety that the world might swallow me up at any second. I took the PIN machine off the waitress, held it up to my ear like I was answering a phone call and said, 'Hello?' Then I passed it back over to him and said, 'Sorry, I think it's for you.'

Cam went scarlet with embarrassment, of course. But young Romeo was so confused, he ended up paying rather than admit he didn't understand my joke. Hilariously low intellect – yet another red flag. The waitress smirked, at least. It took about ten minutes for my head to stop swimming from the boldness it had taken to do it. Or maybe it wasn't boldness, just pure indignation. Ha! Kind of proud of myself either way. Plus... free pizza! Win-win!

I took him in a little more as we walked away from the restaurant. He did have nice hair, a blond fringe sweeping down and across, a bit like Justin Bieber had it for a while. And he's quite tall and athletic. But honestly, his chat was so, so bad. No one wants to be top of the singles chart, but Cam can do better. I'm not saying he's boring, but I'd rather hang out with Crabbe and Goyle!

He walked us back to his flat rather than our place – how many red flags is that now?! Then he asked Cam upstairs. She looked at me – didn't give my eyes enough time to scream 'no!' – and then turned back to him and said, 'Sure'. It was at least amusing as he beamed, but then lost his smile quick when he saw me follow Cam up the path after them. There's no way I was letting this feckless gorm get her alone for any length of time. Cam was definitely in thrall to being on a date – far too susceptible to even the tiniest level of attention, but by tomorrow she'll have sobered up from all that and be grateful I cockblocked her, so to speak.

We went into this dull man's flat and sat on his stiff, uncomfortable sofa for an hour or so watching old repeats of *Married at First Sight*. The pair of them made out for about two minutes as well, during which time I contemplated setting myself ablaze and backflipping out of the window. But then the bloke's flatmate came in and saved me from my fiery defenestration.

The second lad was nicer. He spotted the Hufflepuff logo on my jumper and we chatted about the Deathly Hallows for a bit. By far the highlight of the evening. I think his name was Ivor.

It got to ten o'clock and I told Cam it was time we left. She gave in and we ordered an Uber. She said in the taxi home that she'll be messaging her date again, but I bet a million pounds she doesn't.

And there it is – my cringeworthy day out.

Why are boys so useless?

No, wait! I'm WAY too old for teenage diary clichés. What about...

Why are MEN so useless?

Yeah, much better.

3

IVOR

January 2025

There's a foot stomping on my head. I prise open an eye. No one's there, but the stomping persists.

I breathe out, heat catching my lips, last night's whisky come back to haunt me. Waiting for the world to stop wobbling as I lie on my side on the sofa, I focus on a pint glass perched on the windowsill, filled with small birds' feathers.

What happened last night? New Year's Eve. I don't think I even made it to the bongs. Heavy one at a dingy bar with my best mate, Noz.

At least I got home. Was it in an Uber? Yeah, I came to in the back of a car, being told I was home, then fell out of the back seat to find myself face-to-face with my front door.

What did we drink? Beer, obviously, whisky, yes... even a little bit of Auld Lang's Wine if memory serves.

I spotted a feather on the floor of the club too, didn't I? Brought it back and dropped it in the glass with all the others before passing out.

I shut my eyes again and exhale through my nose. Thought of the whisky wrings my stomach like a Chinese burn.

Technically it wasn't my fault, the big boozy end to the year. I'm deeply sad and hurt. Four days since I saw Becky and sent her that text. And... nothing.

She's definitely read the message – those two little blue ticks on WhatsApp have snitched on her.

That needy, unquenchable insecurity that clings to any fledgling relationship has returned now we're on the cusp of getting back together. It's more than returned, actually. It's found its old plot of land in my mind, built a towering skyscraper and is casting mocking shadows over every positive thought I had about our coffee date. What happened to Noz too, by the way? He was kissing that girl with the boobs. Think he was pretty far gone as well. And she *must* have been to be snogging him.

I scrape my phone off the coffee table, maybe that will shed more light on the evening.

There's a message waiting for me.

Becky! She's finally texted back!

Jolting up far too quickly, my world spins like I'm on the waltzers for a second before settling. I open the message:

> BECKY
>
> Mum and Dad have told me everything about Amy. I will always love you.

The weight of the last few days vanishes through a heart-shaped trap door. She's replied! And she's told me she loves me! My eyes brim as I look again at those feathers in their glass. This year has started brilliantly – murderous headache and tsunami of nausea aside.

Moving to lie down again, I tap the screen to call her and move the phone up to my ear.

It rings... and rings... and rings.

Hmm, must be on silent. I hang up. My phone says it's 2.30 p.m. Her message came through just before midnight.

Shit.

Should I text her?

No need to rush. Right now, I just need to outlive this hangover.

My goodness, some food would help; it'd help so damn much. But the Greggs close enough to deliver is closed on New Year's Day. I made that mistake last January 1st.

Domino's, I choose you! I need your dough, your cheese, your weird salty disks of meat, and I need them now. I order my usual on the app – Pepperoni Passion.

Skull still pulsing, too much blood pumping around too small a space, I shut my eyes again. If only my brain wasn't so big, taking up all that room...

I must drift off again because the next thing I know, the doorbell is buzzing. I force myself to my feet and collect my shallow cardboard box of happiness from the takeaway boy in his logoed uniform. It still feels wrong to be standing up, but the opportunity of being vertical allows me to top up my glass of agua mineral and pop a couple of ibuprofens. I stumble to the bedroom, crawl under the duvet and devour three slices in no time. That Domino's smell, they should trademark it. The mozzarella is gooey and soft, the sauce tangy and hot, the pepperoni moreish with a spice that lingers on the tongue. Heaven.

I imagine Noz telling me he's never seen someone have so much fun in bed with twelve inches of Italian sausage.

Confidence grows that I may survive the day – I try another call to Becky. Still no answer.

Right, stop being such a Desperate Dan and message her,

Ivor!

So I do:

IVOR

> Hey babe, I'll always love you too. You got a
> sec to chat? x

Plucking out a fourth cheesy triangle of goodness, I wolf it down, vitality expanding with every chomp.

Another half hour passes as I eat and rehydrate, reclining in my lovely warm bed. Why isn't she replying? Maybe she's as hungover as me, in need of someone to look after her. I ring again, to no avail.

Next idea isn't very *Pride and Prejudice*, but I don't know what else to do. I've been so disciplined about not checking up on her recently. But maybe it's OK now we're back on. Should I give in? There's no way I can stop myself. I could spend the next eight hours wrestling with the moral quandary, but sooner or later, if she doesn't reply, I'm going to look. Let's cut out the middleman of time.

I open the Find My Friends app.

It's as I feared – she's at her mum and dad's.

I inhale another slice of pizza. OK. She's not answering calls; maybe her parents have told her she's not to answer her phone while she's there. That'd be very them.

It's hard to put into words how much more alive I feel than I did before that Domino's arrived.

Alternative plan. Women like spontaneity, right? Becky certainly does. She burst into tears when I shocked her with that trip to Budapest – in a good way, obviously.

I will go to her – a knight in shining armour – surprise her, convince her to come out and play, spend what's left of the day together. An extravagant demonstration of how ready I am for us to start this year right, to be there for her, to be fun and single-minded in thinking about her.

Wetting my hair in the bathroom sink, I look in the mirror. Stubble's OK, eyes not too dark.

More agua mineral down the hatch, I tug on a fresh-ish pair of jeans, and gargle with mouthwash. Let's rock 'n' roll!

Risking having to talk to Becky's parents so I can surprise her? That really is true love.

4

IVOR

January 2025

Becky's parents. Hate is a strong word. But I despise them.

The first interaction I ever had with Phillip Burrows, upon my arrival at this mansion, was for him to berate me for not wearing chinos to a Sunday lunch. Who does he think I am, a member of the Cambridge University Rowing Club? I have never worn chinos. But the illustrious Phillip Burrows judged me on my jeans. He'd rather wear asbestos than denim.

The lady of the house is no better. Audrey. Becky has told me that dear old Aud insisted her daughter be underfed for several months one year, in the hope she'd grow slower and still fit into last year's school uniform come September.

This couple live in a house the size of Russia that backs on to Wimbledon Park, but their penny-pinching makes Ebenezer Scrooge look extravagant.

Walking down their drive – which feels longer than most airport runways – I pray Becky answers and not them. I take in the expanse in front of the house on my endless hike to the front door. Overgrown shrubs, grass not mown, three stone water features with no water flowing forth; the front garden is a shambles. Has been ever since I started visiting this creepy place. The Burrowses flat-out refuse to hire a gardener. So much of their life is a contradiction – they live in luxury, they won't pay to maintain it; they value status, they never buy anything new; they lost a daughter, they don't care about their remaining one.

Eventually I complete my required step-count for the whole of January and reach the house.

The front door alone sums them up perfectly, the size of it making 10 Downing Street look like a hobbit hole, but the chipped paintwork is giving crack-den chic. Black paint-flecks literally flutter to the floor as I clank my knuckles against it.

I wait and pray for Becky to open up instead of her parents.

Good news… neither Phillip nor Audrey opens the door.

Bad news… neither does Becky.

I bow my head. 'Hello, Jules!'

It's the Burrowses' housekeeper, Julie – forgot she might be bopping about. She is the one upper-class asset the Burrowses do seem to indulge in. But I'd bet my house – if I had one – that they pay her minimum wage and make her stay late. That's my theory for why she's so dour, anyway.

'Hello, Ivor,' comes her patronising, snobbish welcome – warm as a Victorian family portrait.

'Here to see Becky.' I step up to the threshold, but Jolly Julie doesn't budge, her dyed black hair, black blouse and black trousers all very much in keeping with her magnetic personality.

She shakes her head. 'Rebecca isn't here.'

I roll my eyes. 'Yes, she is!'

Pushing the door open properly, I strut into the swanky hall with its white-tiled flooring. On an old, oak table in the middle of the space stands an empty vase that's almost big enough for me to sit in. My heart soars, strangely, at the familiar objects – the ostentatious setting that tells me... I'm back in Becky's life.

It's fair to say Julie isn't coping with my triumphant return. Her face looks like a wet Monday morning. 'Ivor, you can't... She's not here. Mr and Mrs Burrows will not want to see you...'

'Please, Julie, just go and tell her I'm here?' I ask gently – too gently, given the proof in my pocket that she is definitely home. 'If Becky tells me to go, then I'll go. But I'm not leaving until...'

Julie doesn't wait for me to finish, striding off instead through a pair of glass doors at the far end of the hall.

I stand there for a few seconds like a lemon. Could just charge up to Becky's room and invite myself in. That's where we usually took refuge. Hmm, maybe too intense, especially given I've already travelled fifty-five minutes across London on a whim to surprise her. Was it Aristotle who said, 'Patience is bitter, but its fruit is sweet'? I'm being modest – it definitely was Aristotle.

Keeping the peace, I try the door to my right and it opens. Excellent! Becky's dad's library. It's my second favourite room in the house. I'd missed the smell of it. Tobacco, ancient novels and polished wood. I take in one of the great bookshelves with its countless spines of leatherbound volumes, then wander over to a mahogany cabinet and open the door.

Eureka! Inside are four crystal tumblers and a decanter full of cognac. Knew he kept the good stuff in here.

Dare I partake? He already hints about my past life every chance he gets, I shouldn't give him fresh ammunition by purloining any alcohol.

That thought survives about 1.2 microseconds.

Screw it! They only leave the bottle there for show. This maple-coloured tipple deserves to go to a belly that will treasure it.

Pouring a decent measure into one of the glasses, I knock it back and marvel at the fruity burn. I pour an equally generous second helping and settle into an antique chaise-longue perpendicular to all the books, facing forwards to the front windows.

If Laurence Llewelyn-Bowen were here, the first thing he'd do would be to turn the furniture to face the grand old books, not the jungle of a driveway.

Looking round the room, all the same Burrows-trademarked contradictions flood back – the appearance of wealth with none of the requisite vigour to keep up the veneer. Everything's shabby and dated: the scuffs on the drinks cabinet, the dust on the sun-bleached spines of the books, the way the furniture creaks as if it's moments away from collapsing. Photos galore of Becky and her late twin sister Amy as little girls, but barely anything since Amy died.

At least their expensive cognac is going to a good home. I sit back. What should Becky and I get up to this evening? What would she like best? Could suggest we stay in and watch a film in her room. Cosy and cute. Or we could find some cheap tickets to one of the pantos, that'd be fun. Could just go to the pub nearest here like we used to when…

'Ivor!'

I snap round. Phillip and Audrey are in the doorway, glaring as if I've just run around the mansion naked. Calm down, dears, this isn't *Saltburn*.

'I'm here for Becky,' I say, conciliatorily.

'She's not here!' Phillip snaps, marching over in his cream and brown checkered shirt, straggly grey hairs flapping around his ears as he grabs my arm in a bid to yank me up.

I shrug myself free and down the rest of my drink, fearing he'll take it.

'Why would you think she's here?' Audrey demands.

'Just do.'

It's always been odd looking Phillip and Aud in the face. They are Becky's parents – she has her mother's almond eyes, her father's full lips.

But in terms of personality and outlook on life, she couldn't be less like them.

Phillip now notices I've been helping myself to the good stuff. Snatching the tumbler, he thuds it back in the cabinet and shuts it before adjusting the worn leather strap on his watch.

'That'll need washing,' I inform him helpfully, suddenly realising I've just sipped from a glass that would not pass a hygiene test in any licensed premises.

Audrey comes and sits next to me on the chaise-longue. The heavy bags under her eyes aren't quite hidden by her foundation – she looks exhausted. 'Ivor, she is not here.' Her tone is a little more tender, not that she's any keener for me to stay than her husband. Her soapy perfume swamps me as she angles herself towards me, dressed in a typically bright lilac jacket, matching pencil skirt and white frilly blouse.

I shake my head and get to my feet. All that Aristotle patience nonsense has been subsumed by cognac. I make for the ornate staircase in the middle of the hall. Julie has been standing just outside the library, listening in. She's indignant now on behalf of her masters: 'Rebecca isn't here!'

'No, let him go.' Phillip says as he too returns to the hall and sees me climbing the sweeping staircase. 'Thieving fool.'

Reaching the end of the musty corridor, I take a deep breath and knock on her closed bedroom door. 'Becky... Becky... it's me. I got your message. You OK?'

The three musketeers catch up and crowd around me like I'm a rat they're determined to trap.

Audrey looks quite tearful. 'Ivor... she's not here.'

'Aud, there's no point pretending that—'

'She's not here!' Phillip shouts, his sagging face puce and shuddering with rage. 'Open her door. Go on! Open every door in the house. Check the shed, the cellar, the tumble dryer. She's not here.' The last three words are delivered between gritted teeth with deadly venom.

I pull down the handle to the room and push it open.

No Becky.

Back out into the corridor, I spiral. The three of them watch as I go door to door, swinging in, finding no Becky, then backpedalling out and on to the next door. It's a risk, but I even push open the door to Becky's sister's room. The family have kept it exactly the same ever since she died. I don't go in, I'm not a monster, but can see from the doorway a small single bed, pink duvet with rainbows on, a cuddly Tigger from Winnie the Pooh propped against the pillows. But no Becky.

All rooms on the upper floor explored, I go downstairs and repeat the process. There's an eerie silence from the occupiers as I charge around, invading their privacy a little more with every room I enter. Why are they even letting me do this? The longer I stalk, the more the horrible thought bubbles up that they are happy for me to look in every room, because it makes me look stupid... because they know Becky truly isn't here.

Reaching the kitchen, I stare out into their back garden. Beyond the fence is Wimbledon Park. She couldn't have disappeared off into the park, could she? No, not without her phone. And yet she really isn't here.

'Please, Ivor,' Audrey says when the three of them follow my tracks to the kitchen. Her tired eyes are brimming with tears.

'Where is she?'

'Do you think we'd tell you?' her dad snarls.

Storming back into the hall, it's time for the Hail Mary pass.

'BECKY!' I scream, back arching, throat straining, echo bouncing off the magnolia walls.

Nothing.

I look at the three of them, huddled in the kitchen, as distressed as I am confused.

'Apologies, my mistake,' I mutter, feeling my cheeks burning. I heave open that big front door again and wander back onto the gravel driveway.

As I start the gruelling retreat towards the front gates, I pull out my phone and open the Find My Friends app again.

Becky Burrows is at this address. Or at least her phone is.

I try calling her again. No response.

I need a beer.

5

BECKY'S DIARY

Saturday 3 July 2021

I did it. I successfully went on a date. And one of my own this time, rather than third-wheeling. So relieved it's over. Not because it was bad – actually quite the opposite! It was FUN!! I was terrified of something going wrong or me doing something stupid and putting him off. I don't think I did. I'm home in bed now and feel... the best I have in months! That's the relief.

Ivor had got his housemate to get my number off Cam, then he'd texted me this cute little message making a joke about my Hufflepuff jumper and asking if I'd be free any time.

I haven't been on a date since me and Dillon broke up. A woman in her early twenties and I haven't been on a single date in 18 months. Must never admit that out loud.

Anyway, Ivor was nothing like his housemate. The vibes I'd got from him in the two minutes we shared in their flat had already hinted he'd be nothing like the other guy. (I called it btw, Cam decided not to arrange another date with that walking red flag. Knew she wouldn't.) Ivor says he's in the process of getting his own flat, says he only knew that bloke from an internet advert and doesn't really like him either. Should be in his new place by next month.

Anyway anyway… MY date! Love writing that out. My date.

PULL YOURSELF TOGETHER, BECKY, HA HA!

So – his key details…

Name: Ivor Ruvelle O'Foyle (But doesn't speak with an Irish accent, sounds pretty cockney to me. Love his middle name too. Feels like it would be from an old wizarding family or something).

Age: 28.

Lives: With Mr I-only-pay-for-my-own-popcorn in Finchley. But about to move out, as already discussed.

Works: At local Tesco.

Family: Mum died giving birth to him (His middle name is actually her first name passed down. Love that too!). No brothers or sisters. Brought up by his dad but seemingly not that close now (Felt like a sore topic… didn't pry).

Likes: Arsenal, pubs, Greggs (He mentioned Greggs several times, so funny!).

Dislikes: Not sure, really; he was very positive the whole time.

For a first date, I reckon I found out quite a lot, thank you very much. So, what did we do…?

He'd suggested we meet at the Duke's Head pub near Putney Bridge, but the weather was so nice I kind of twisted his arm into going for a walk along the river in the sunshine first. Could tell he wasn't convinced, but it was nice that he was chilled enough to go with it.

That's how I'd describe him, I reckon. Chilled. He was so easy-going. We talked and we walked and then eventually we got back to the Duke's Head and sat outside there and it was the least awkward conversation I can ever remember having. I'd spent days fretting, thinking we'd run out of chat after like five minutes, and then sit in silence for another hour chewing the sides of our mouths until they bled, then head home.

It could not have been less like that! Gah, I don't even know what we talked about. But he asked great questions and – even better! – genuinely listened. Men never listen, like actually listen and understand. Not that I know all the men. But at work you can tell they don't. And look at Dad!

But Ivor did. And it was effortless. He made me laugh so much too. He's got this cheeky grin and super-quick sense of humour. I got light-headed at one point, I laughed so hard. It wasn't even that funny. I'd admitted – very uncoolly – that I'd done some sketches of Hogwarts and stuff but that I wished I was better at drawing, and he said, 'Don't worry, Becky, I can't draw a curtain.'

You see… not that funny. But we'd built up such a head of steam being silly and saying stupid stuff that it absolutely KILLED me!

He was cute too. He's quite tall and spindly, not muscly, but with nice teeth and brown eyes. That was another thing – he had great eye contact. Kind of intense but in an electric, exciting way.

What else did we talk about…? I told him I was thinking of leaving Costa because the pay's rubbish and it's dull and everyone's rude. That I want to be a veterinary assistant but need to save up for the course. He was very encouraging, said he knows a couple of bars looking for staff and that he could put a good word in, if I'd like.

He supports Arsenal so we talked about them. He seemed so surprised when I said we never watched football when I was growing up, so I didn't support any team. He said he'd have to take me to a game sometime. I'd never thought about watching a full game of football at a stadium before but now he's suggested it, it might be super-exciting.

He asked about Mum and Dad… knew he would. Kind of said I

don't get on with them but they're OK. To be honest, I didn't really want to think about them on my sunny day out. (Did I mention I was on a date?! Ha!) But he seemed genuinely interested, not in a nosey way, more in a concerned, caring sort of way. So I went on a rant about how they'd ditched me on Dad's birthday just to go away together and didn't even try to rearrange so I could see them another time and how that is typical of how little they think about me and treat me like an afterthought ALL THE TIME. Obviously, I didn't go into any of how Dad's birthday is the same date as Amy's death day.

I'm cringing thinking about how much I went on about Mum and Dad now. Ivor was so patient while I did, especially given he obviously doesn't like his dad either. Urgh, but he didn't go on about it for ever and ever. Was he sitting there thinking I was a self-obsessed narcissist? It didn't feel like it. Plus, to give myself some credit, self-obsessed narcissists don't worry about coming across as such, do they?

I think that's the overriding thing. It doesn't matter what I said, how I came across, whatever goofy comment I made or feeling I admitted to, nothing put him off.

He made me feel like all he wanted was to learn more about me, and the more he learned, the more he liked me. So accepting, it was lovely. That's what being with someone should feel like.

Dillon used to be like that, I suppose. When we were first going out, at least. But then came all the... well, let's not go there. Maybe that's why I've been so anti-meeting anyone new, in case they made me feel the way he did, towards the end. But I've been stupid. Of course, not all boys are like that. I'd forgotten what it was like to be out in a romantic setting with someone who just makes you feel wanted – pure and simple.

Rom-coms make me cringe but that bit in *Bridget Jones* keeps coming to me since I got home. When Colin Firth tells Renée Zellweger he likes her just as she is, and it catches her off guard. Ivor didn't say that, obviously, but that's how the whole date felt. He liked me just as I am.

Didn't tell him about Dillon. We didn't really get on to exes, thank goodness. I wonder how long things will last between me and Ivor? And how many women has he been with? Is he always like this on first dates? Or did he genuinely have as good a time as me? And if he did, then what's stopping us going out proper?

Calm down, it's been one date!

Oh my word! And there was this amazing moment when we were walking, before the pub. There was this bush outside one of the houses facing out on to the river, and it was kind of rustling a bit but with no one around. Ivor noticed it as we went past and looked, and there was this TINY little sparrow that'd got stuck somehow, like tangled, in a vine or something inside the bush. And it was flapping and flapping but couldn't get free. So Ivor held the branches apart while I unwrapped this knot around it, and all of a sudden, the sparrow shot out and flew away. It was so nice to have helped it! And Ivor spotted it had shed one of its breast feathers, so he picked it up off the floor, said we should keep it, and put it in his pocket. Bless, ha ha!

By the time we left the pub, I'd had loads to drink. He offered to buy me a glass of champagne when we first ordered. Cute but... yuk! Made it clear I don't like bubbly. But I did polish off four Kopparbergs, I think, and he'd had at least one more pint than me. Having to concentrate really hard now to make sure my handwriting is legible lol!

Also avoided Cam on my way into the flat so she wouldn't start quizzing me and then pass judgment if I slurred a word.

It wasn't my fault! Ivor wouldn't let me pay for anything all afternoon and evening – just kept buying us drinks. Then he got the bus with me to make sure I got home OK.

The only tiny awkward moment was when we got to the flat and we both stood there and for a horrible split-second I thought he was going to pressure me into inviting him up. But it wasn't that at all. Instead, he said he'd had a great day and would love to meet up again. I tried to play it cool, told him that would be nice.

Nice?! It would be AMAZING!

I keep checking my phone like I'm 14. He hasn't messaged. It is only like an hour since he left, to be fair.

Bet he doesn't ever reply. Maybe I should have invited him in. Is that why he listened to me and bought me drinks, so I'd have sex with him? And then I didn't. Maybe I should have. Feels too soon though. Regardless of how good a first date is, if you've got a spark then it should carry on to a second.

Urgh no, I'm starting to feel gloomy again. He definitely just wanted sex. No way he's going to message. I need to toughen up; if I want a boyfriend I'm going to have to be a bit more, I don't know, free. Just all feels a bit gross and icky. That's why it HAD worked with Dillon, friends first is such a better policy. But I don't have any friends I want to date. Need more boy friends if I want to get a boyfriend. Maybe what today's shown is that I am finally ready for another relationship after Dillon, at least.

Sucks though. I don't want a random boyfriend. I want to see Ivor again.

It's gone midnight. Time for bed. Need to stop thinking about him. Maybe I should go on dating apps. But then most guys on there will definitely just want to shag and move on. Or is that just Tinder? Cam uses Hinge. Maybe I should try that. I'll ask her tomorrow.

All right seriously, bedtime.

LATE-NIGHT UPDATE:

Ivor texted me asking to meet again!!!! I can't believe it!!! He said he had the best time and can't stop thinking about me. I feel exactly the same!!! I've already texted him back saying as much. Oh my word!!!! I can't believe it!! I'm so so so happy!! I thought I'd misread everything but I hadn't!! He DID really like me!!!

Oooo… he's typing…

Now he's asked if we can meet for dinner next Thursday. Should I reply to him tomorrow? Play it cool? No! He's been forward and honest and keen. I'm going to be the same. Yes Ivor, I will meet you for dinner. Yes yes yes!

6

IVOR

January 2025

The train beer has to be one of the most majestic beers one can indulge in.

Not ones bought on a train, they're a scam. I mean a four pack, bought at a little station supermarket, in anticipation of a long rail journey.

You find your seat, get comfy, cans in front of you. And that's it. Technically you're being very productive – you're hurtling across the country far faster than you could accomplish the task by running. So no one can criticise you. Yet you also have a beautiful excuse to achieve nothing. So you sit, time suspended between set-off and destination. And what better way to spend that perfect purgatory than to drink.

As I say, majestic.

The fact Noz is sitting opposite is less majestic. Why, oh why, did I invite him, last night?

No one was more amazed than me that a mere six hours after fearing death by hangover yesterday, I found myself back at a pub. But I needed to talk to someone about the weird trip to Becky's parents' place. Her phone apparently being there but not her.

And Noz is always up for a drink.

We went to one of our favourite little runs of watering holes in Stoke Newington. There's The Red Lion, The Auld Shillelagh and The Clarence Tavern. The R.A.C., we call them to amuse ourselves – helping to fix us every time we're facing a break-down. Total walking distance between all three? Less than ten minutes.

It was Noz who had the lightbulb moment, quite late in the evening in the stylish surroundings of the Clarence. I didn't know where Becky had gone... but maybe she got an Uber to somewhere and had forgotten her phone, he'd suggested.

Embarrassingly I am still logged into her family's Uber account. I don't use it that much. Yes, I did on New Year's Eve, but they were extreme circumstances. The circumstances being I was extremely ready to go home.

Anyway, Noz suggested I see on the app whether she'd booked an Uber anywhere. Fat chance I thought. But then... there it was! A ride logged for all the way down to Sandbanks in Dorset, ordered around midnight on New Year's Eve – just after she'd texted me. I know exactly where she's gone to stay. So I'm heading down to surprise her.

My one error? In the drunken excitement of discovering where she'd gone – and the fact it was Noz's bright idea to check – I said he could tag along for the train journey.

Finishing his first beer he lets out a belch that echoes around the carriage, making the little train table between us vibrate.

Raising the empty can in his hand like an Oscar, he shakes

his head in rhapsody. 'Tell you what, that's like a bruised dick...
you just can't beat it.'

My eyeroll is savage. Leave them wanting less, that's Noz's
approach to comedy. But what he lacks in maturity, he makes up
for in waist circumference. I'm not saying he's obese, but he cut
his finger once and camembert oozed out.

He's got a penchant for cringeworthy T-shirts, too. Today's
offering – a blue crew neck that barely covers his paunch with
the words 'Orgasm donor' emblazoned on it in big white letters.

What I do like about him is that he's straight-talking and
loyal. Sometimes, I think he's quite lonely, even though he'd
never admit it. And he did buy the train beers – four each – to be
fair. M&S Belgian lagers too! Mr Moneybags.

'What are you planning to do when you get there?' Noz asks.

'More importantly, what are you going to do while I'm seeing
her?' I retort.

'Watch the Arsenal at a pub, find myself a hottie.'

'Being bald doesn't make you Jason Statham,' I say.

'You're bitter coz I pulled on New Year's Eve and you didn't.'

This is a topic he already pontificated on at length last night
in Stoke Newington. I roll my eyes again. 'I'm getting back with
Becky, I don't need another—'

'That girl in the club... her boobs were incredible, weren't
they?' he interrupts, proud as punch. 'The kind of boobs that
could turn tides, never mind heads.' He opens a new beer,
glancing wistfully out of the window.

'Life isn't all about girls in clubs with big boobs, Noz.'

'What do you even mean? Of course it is,' he says, aghast.
'Sometimes I feel like I don't know you at all.'

'You're jealous because I'm getting back with Becky and
therefore won't be coming to the pub as much.'

'You're jealous coz your manhood's so small women call it a childhood.'

I snort. He can have that one, at least he's not expecting to join me seeing Becky. I take a large swig from my beautiful lime green can.

'What if I end up staying over with her?' I wonder out loud.

'That's the kind of positive thinking we need!' Noz says, pointing at me.

I continue to sup as the fields and stations fly past, lager soothing the nerves. Good old lager. This is an audacious demonstration of love and commitment by anyone's standards. I probably do drink a bit more than most, but not drinking is like driving with the handbrake on. Life's just easier, happier, makes more sense when you can drink. I could stop tomorrow if I needed to, but why? Why actively choose to be more miserable, less carefree? I don't get violent, I don't hurt anyone, I feel better, so the choice is always a simple one when offered a nice friendly beer... cheers, prost, santé, cin-cin, salud!

After a lull in conversation, the sound of Noz's third can popping open rings around as he asks: 'What if this family kick you out while you're still trying to get your trousers off?'

I frown. 'They won't kick me out. Me and Becky used to go down a lot.'

'But that's enough about your sex life,' he says with a chuckle. He really is a walking aubergine emoji. Definitely won't be telling Becky that I had a travelling buddy.

'The Montagues were always way kinder to me and Becky than her actual parents.'

'The Monty-whos?' Noz roars at the posh name, drawing derisory looks from two women sitting on the adjacent table.

'Montagues,' I repeat, knowing he heard right the first time.

'Becky's family and the Montagues go way back. They were the other family there when, y'know...'

'Becky's sister died?'

'Amy, yeah. They're still in that house where it happened, up on the cliffs overlooking the beach. That's the address Becky got her Uber to. I've been loads of times. I told you all this last night.'

'Do you want to call ahead to the Minty-Poos—'

'Montagues,' I correct him.

'Mingey-screws,' he uncorrects. 'Why not phone them, make sure she's there?'

'Don't have their numbers.' I swipe my hand sideways to rule out his pessimism. 'Plus, I want it to be a surprise for Becky. She must have booked the Uber, then realised she'd left her phone behind when she got into the cab. Bet she'd had a row with her parents. No other reason she'd be so desperate to get away at such short notice. Plan is: show up, let her vent about her mum and dad, get back together officially, both head back to London, film a fly-on-the-wall documentary for ITV2 showing how in love we both are.'

Noz takes a huge, rattling snort in at the back of his nose before swallowing the resultant grotty gunge down his thick-set throat. 'So she got this Uber, at midnight on New Year's Eve from Wimbledon to Sandbanks. How much did that cost?'

'£480. Again... as I told you last night.'

'Bloody hell!'

'Well it's her dad's money, not hers.'

'Still think your plan's a bit mad,' Noz says, swatting away some of the butterflies building in my stomach about how happy Becky will be to see me.

'It's romantic!' I spit, earning me my own stare from the judgmental women over from us, sipping little G&T cans.

'What's mad is coming along anyway, even though you're not part of the plan!'

'I bought these beers! You'd be bored shitless if I wasn't here.'

I don't reply. He's hurt. That's why I don't say no to him, he gets all sad when I hint at him not having more of his own life. It's too close to the bone.

'Don't care, anyway. As I say, going to find myself another hottie.' He scratches at his groin and looks over at the two women, who take one glance at him and both throw a disgusted side-eye out of the window on their side of the carriage. Poor Noz – the libido of a sire, the amorous acumen of a dodo. The rest of the journey is conducted in silence, which is quite helpful. Gives me a chance to plot what I'll say when I get there.

We get off the train – or 'alight', as the lady on the tannoy insists on calling it – and Noz mutters about going to find a pub to watch the Arsenal game. I offer him my fourth – and last – can as a sort of olive branch. Feels counterintuitive to give away beer, like turning down a pay rise. But I want to be on good form when I see Becky, not sloppy.

This has to go well. It's only the rest of my life at stake.

7

IVOR

January 2025

I buy a packet of gum at the WHSmith in Bournemouth station to get rid of the beers on my breath.

A middle-aged lady with wrinkled lips asks if I've got a spare cigarette as I'm leaving the shop. Rude much! What's the point of me remembering to moisturise once every eight to twelve weeks if people still think I have skin like a smoker's?

Shaking off the impertinence, I head to the rank outside and get in a yellow taxi. '3 Rochelle Drive, please.'

The driver glances in his rearview mirror; he's thinking I don't belong on Rochelle Drive. You couldn't be more right, good sir, but today is no normal day – so step on it!

Thank goodness for my Christmas bonus. I've done fewer hours, gone out with Noz more and now got a train and taxi, and still should come up OK by the time the January wedge goes in. Living the high life, me! I give a little chuckle in the back of the cab, earning me a second glance from my driver. I wonder if he charges extra for his condescending looks. Hope not.

Suppose I could have used the Burrowses' family Uber account again, but it's good to pay your own way once in a while.

The clouds are heavy and daylight's dwindling by the time I get to the massive, wood-panelled gates at the end of 3 Rochelle Drive. There isn't much breeze though, unusually. Becky loves it down here, aside from the coastal wind that pulls her hair in a hundred different directions all at once and makes selfies impossible.

I press the buzzer next to the large gates. This gaff must be worth £5million, easy. It'll be one of the Montagues who answers, most likely, not Becky, but that's OK.

Hmmm... no answer. I buzz again, for like thirty seconds. There isn't a camera, just a speaker, so there's no way they could have seen it was me and chose to ignore it.

I go up to the gates – there's no handle, you just have to wait for the mechanism to kick in and then they swing open. I shoulder barge the wood a couple of times: the two mocking halves remain unmoved. I'm no rugby player.

Maybe they've gone out for food, or a walk? Or what if the buzzer isn't working? Noz's scepticism rings in my ears... Am I mad? Is this a barmy plan?

Well, if Plan A was barmy, Plan B is sneaky.

Becky and I used to wander down to the beach from the house and the quickest way was via the cliffs in front of the Montagues' mansion. It sounds dangerous but the path is pretty simple. Wes Montague, the husband, had some steps put in around and down in front of the balcony so he could walk straight from his home to the shore. They also put in a little memorial to Becky's twin sister, Amy, part-way down – on the spot where she fell and died aged seven. Bit morbid, if you ask me.

The Montagues own the cliffs all the way down to the beach.

I can go in reverse, from the base back up to the property that way. If the Montagues are in, I can go to the front door, knock, tell them the main gate was open, the buzzer wasn't working, something like that.

If they're not in, I'll have to wait until I see them and Becky come back, then go all the way back around, hoping the buzzer is actually working and buzz again, so it doesn't look like I was lying in wait in their garden.

Would I attempt this if I was sober? Who cares? I'm doing it.

Gloom and chill closes in as I round on to the beachfront. I put my leather gloves on. The whisper of gentle waves, the stench of brine, it brings back a thousand memories with Becky. She was the one who taught me the alternative route in the first place. And we hadn't just used it to get down to the beach then either, we'd relied on it if we'd been out late and didn't want to wake the Montagues. The ascent is more gruelling than the tumble down the cliffs, I can tell you.

Slipping behind a row of beach huts, I prepare to go from public bystander to illegal trespasser. Third hut along, yellow stain on the concrete. Bingo. This is where the chain-link fence separating the cliffs from the beach is weakest. It's about 5ft high where the mesh dips lowest. Wes Montague would bring a little stepladder and navigate over the top with minimal fuss. Alas, I have no such apparatus, so launch myself at it. It seems flimsier and yet harder to breach than when me and Becky used to do this. I refuse to admit it's because I've put on weight.

I refuse... because I am in denial.

Finally rolling over the top with all the elegance of a beached whale, I land on soil replete with tiny, pointy stones. But I am over! Brushing most of the detritus off my cheek and side, I look upwards at the ascent. I'm coming, Becky!

She won't appreciate the comparison, given she's such a

Harry Potter girl and isn't much into *The Lord of the Rings*. But the rudimentary steps Wes Montague has fashioned up to his property remind me of Cirith Ungol.

It's so dark now, the sky almost completely given up for the night. And yet all the steep incline ahead offers is denser tree cover and even less light.

I turn on my phone's torch and peer up into the copse and barely visible steps. The way ahead swallows my phone's light, returning nothing.

Pull yourself together, Ivor.

I move forward, focusing hard on the mossy, jaggedly arranged railway sleepers – my slippery staircase – trying to ignore the ravenous gulp of the blackness ahead.

My goodness, it's going to be good to give Becky a hug. I can't wait to tell her in person how much I love her too. Glad I didn't have that extra lager either. The trees around me as I ascend are blocking out any last vestige of light beyond my pathetic, milky mobile torch. Phone in my right hand, my left hand is more useful, helping me feel my way up each steep, slimy plank of wood, my breathing growing wheezier and more pathetic with each fresh lurch upwards. It can't be too much further – I know I'm unfit but this is horrendous, lungs like two camel skins filled with battery acid.

When Becky and I used to stumble up here in the middle of the night half-cut, all I remember is the giggling and the kissing, not the passing out due to lack of oxygen.

Amy's memorial, please let me get to there. Then I'm on the home straight. One last stretch after that and you're into their garden on ground level.

I puff louder. This is embarrassing. I don't even smoke – despite what that woman in the station appeared to think.

OK, first thing when I get back to civilisation, I need to do more exercise or, like, join Asthmatics Anonymous? This is just... Oh thank goodness! There it is. My torchlight catches the nearest pillar of Amy's memorial a few steps further up the slope, emerging from the darkness like I'm in a submersible coming across a shipwreck on the ocean floor.

The railway sleepers end and the ground levels out like a small natural shelf in the cliff. Standing up straight and sucking in as much air as I can, I curve right, towards the four stone pillars of the memorial. The large square is underpinned by a set of stone slabs. At the centre of the pillars and stone flooring is a bird table. I can't see it straight away, but still holding my phone torch forward, I clump forwards and the bird table comes into view. Staggering into it, I lean on the outer rim to catch my breath.

My heart stops.

There's someone on the floor, less than six steps ahead.

Mouth ajar, eyes open, reflecting my phone's torch.

It's Becky.

8

BECKY'S DIARY

Saturday 31 July 2021

Can't stop smiling! Actually, smiling is an understatement, even a Cheshire Cat grin would be an understatement.

Ivor said he loved me! Only the second man to ever say that to me. Well, except Carl at work when I fixed the lock on the disabled loo. But I don't think he meant it quite the same way.

Ivor meant it. No pressure, no hinting from me. I wasn't expecting it myself. But it felt so right.

First, he surprised me by saying he'd bought us two tickets to London Zoo to celebrate four weeks since our first date. That's not a thing, lol. Cute, though. He said considering how much I like animals, he thought I'd enjoy going. So thoughtful and lovely! I didn't have the heart to tell him I've been a hundred times. But this was probably the best visit.

Then he held my hand all the way around the zoo. He always makes me feel like he's so proud we're together. It was mega busy because of the holidays but that's fine. Got some super-hilarious pictures of the penguins and there was a baby tiger I wanted to take home with me, she was so shy and just the most adorable little bundle licking her tiny paws. Made me think of Amy, the little cuddly Tigger she used to have, how she used to suck the paws of it whenever we were in the car.

Ivor arrived with coffees and chocolate cookies from Greggs (of course!) and bought us lunch too. Eating food there was a change from when I usually come – think I've got a smidge of Dad's aversion to spending money! Gross, I know. Ivor sneaked in a hipflask with whisky in, too. I don't really like the taste but it felt so naughty sneaking sips every so often. Was quite tipsy by the time we left. He seemed sad the giraffe house was off-limits, and a lot of the bird cages were being cleared out too. That wasn't a surprise to me, I'm on their mailing list. They've already warned us loyal patrons that a few things will be closed for the rest of the year.

Then we went back to his new place (he moved his stuff out of that boring man's flat and into a one-bedder near Finchley Central last week) and he said it right there and then on the sofa. 'I love you, Becky.'

How many dates have we been on? Five? Yes, we've seen each other six times in total, and been on five dates. That's not very long. Most men would be counting in months or decades before they said the L-word, not five dates.

What makes it even better is that there didn't seem to be any ulterior motive. We still haven't done the dirty deed. That side of things is all moving naturally, tantalisingly, sexily (ha ha, is that even a word?) towards the bedroom, shall we say. But he never makes me feel like we have to, or that it's all he's here for. Even after he'd said he loved me, I started thinking, 'Oh yeah, here we go, he's probably wearing those stripper trousers and is about to rip them off without further warning'. But he didn't. He just kept talking and looking at me with those kind, soft brown eyes as I stroked my hand against the sandpapery stubble of his cheek. Our faces were so close together we could have touched foreheads, if we hadn't been so intent on keeping eye contact. He said he'd never felt like this before, and that I complete him, and fill up his whole life, and he can't think about anything else when I'm not there and he doesn't want to come on too strong or make me feel I have to stay around if I don't feel the same, and that maybe he should be playing it more cool, but life's too short, so he needed to tell me.

It was all I could do to not burst into tears!!

I told him I felt the same. I'd been so worried he wouldn't feel that way, so hadn't wanted to think about it too much up to that point, but I reassured him that my heart was singing from the exact same song sheet. Don't think I put it quite so poetically in the moment but he seemed to relax more after that.

We had a music channel on the TV in the background and as we were holding each other that Keane song, 'Somewhere Only We Know', came on. Felt special. Looking into each other's eyes as we listened.

Then we lay there, kissing.

It was perfect.

We're still learning so much about each other, but even the fact he had the bravery and courage to say all those emotional things, and in such an articulate way, you could tell he'd been thinking about it.

Why don't I do that? Why couldn't I have been the one to say all those lovely things and make my partner so happy? Why do I keep everything in? I still haven't told him I dated Dillon. Ivor admitted he'd never had a girlfriend (which, honestly, I don't understand!) and I made out I hadn't had a partner either. It's not like I've got a plethora of exes, strewn across the battlefield of love (is that the cleverest thing I've ever written or the cringiest? Maybe both).

But yeah, it's not like I've had a lot of boyfriends, but I did have Dillon. There's no fun time to talk about that, though. And, to be honest, my parents, Amy, everything else, it's as much a part of Dillon's life as mine. Both of us there that day, both of us forbidden to talk about it ever again. Both told to lie to police, say we weren't there, didn't see anything. It was all an undercurrent that brought us closer as teenagers, the only other person in the world who understood what I was going through.

But with Ivor, it's nice to be completely removed from everything. A truly fresh start. So not bringing up Dillon and knowing Ivor hasn't got any idea of the rumours online about my parents – that suits me. Long must it continue. He very much lives in the moment, does Ivor. Live today, spend today, drink today. Tomorrow will look after itself. It's exciting. The opposite of my parents, where everything is tied back to Amy.

I do not understand why someone as kind and giving as him wants me. When we do have sex, will I find out he's a deviant? To be honest, he treats me so well and makes me feel so happy that he'd have to have a pretty wild kink for me to say no. How did we end up here? Let's move on, diary...

OK, he isn't rich or earning a million pounds an hour, but frankly, that's a good thing. I do not want to be super-well-off and live like Mum and Dad and judge everyone and everything by what they wear and who they associate with. I want to laugh, I want to connect, I want to be able to be me, and Ivor just allows me to do that without any effort whatsoever.

It's not even like he's after my parents' money, either. He lets me rant on about them, always listens and gives thoughtful answers. But one of his ideas was that I should stop taking their money, using their accounts for trains and Ubers, cut off the monthly top-up they give me for rent. I should halt it all and then I'd feel more independent, less like an unloved shadow of my sister. He wouldn't say that if he was money-grabbing.

Nope, I have to face it. I've found a man with no flaws. One who gives me confidence to be me.

I LOVE YOU, IVOR RUVELLE O'FOYLE!

And after all that kissing this evening, I cannot stop thinking about taking the next step. Like, I wish he was here RIGHT NOW!

But I must wait until Tuesday. Three whole days. It's too long, I tell you!

I'm going to text him now. Tell him it might be nice if I stay over on Tuesday night…

Right, I've sent it, I've bloody done it. With a winky-face emoji and everything. Gah, I feel so bold!

He's replied! 'Can't wait' and a hearts-for-eyes emoji.

Is it Tuesday yet?!

Life's so exciting when you go out and make things happen for yourself!

Watch out world, Becky 2.0 coming through!

9

IVOR

January 2025

Everything's juddering, like a plane hitting a runway with no wheels.

I open my eyes. I'm on the floor, shivering so violently my joints could buckle.

Unbearable cold crushes in from all sides, the hissing chill of the wind knifing me through my bomber jacket.

Knees squashed up to my chest, arms strapped around them – where am I?

I try to raise my head; the movement is agony, neck muscles set in concrete. How long have I been stuck curled up like this? Fighting the tension, I look around. The beach promenade stretches out in both directions, Bournemouth pier twinkling in the distance.

It's nighttime, no one's around. The glow of a street lamp further along the seafront provides just enough light to see the two steps down to the sand ahead of me. The relentless crash and heave of the sea is a black, infinite wall beyond.

It was Becky.

Another rush of wind sees me drop my head back between my knees.

I touched her, held her head. She was... hideous. Not Becky at all. A doll, a nightmare, with Becky's face, contorted and empty.

My fists are tight shut, the leather of my black gloves stretched taut over white knuckles. Something is sticking into my right palm. I open the hand and strain to make sense of what I'm seeing. The glint of a necklace – a small silver bear pendant.

Was she wearing that? No, it was caught in her fingers. Why did I take it?

This can't be real.

Hand shaking uncontrollably, I push the necklace into my pocket and retrieve my phone. 4 a.m.? I've been here hours. Details circle, swoop, then disappear again behind the all-consuming horror of that face. Wide, staring eyes, chestnut hair muddy and matted, limbs bent and snapped like twigs on a forest floor, in the exact same place her sister died.

I ran back down the cliff steps at one point. Have I been here ever since?

Wake up, please. Please! This can't happen. Not her. Anything else in the world. Not her. This isn't real.

I scream at the ground – voice paper-thin, mocked and drowned out by the white noise of the sea. A flush of nauseating heat sweeps through me, the trembling intensifies. I hammer my head backwards against the pebble-encrusted wall I'm leaning against. Harder. Harder. Harder.

Wake up, Ivor. Wake up!

The pain sharpens. I don't wake up. Instead, sobs billow out. My chest bobs out of sync with my jittering limbs.

We met up for coffee. She loved me. This can't happen...

Letting out another yelp, my voice breaks. Slamming my head back as hard as I can, the thud snaps my teeth together in a skull-shuddering crack. My hair feels wet as it presses into the stone and catches the wind, and a trickle snakes down my neck. It's not until I attempt to slap the feeling away that I realise quite how deep the split in my scalp is. I let the blood fall, embrace the warmth as it soaks into my collar and wait for the four or five beaches in front of me to wobble back into a single view.

Maybe I should walk into the waves. They can sting me, numb me, then take me. There is no life without Becky. She brought me to this beach for the first time on a blazing day in May. We drank Strawberry and Lime Kopparbergs, cooked chicken on a throwaway barbecue. She told me she was the happiest she'd ever been. Her loving eyes reflecting the sunset back at me.

Eyes that bore no memory of me tonight.

* * *

It takes three hours to walk back to Bournemouth station. The balls of my feet throb from pounding the pavement, itchy hot as if held over a Bunsen burner.

I scout the precinct, bustling with head-down commuters. I'm in luck – there's a row of payphones.

Coins in. 999 dialled.

'Hello, which emergency service do you need?' comes the operator's question.

'Police,' I say in a quiet voice.

The phone rings again and another operator picks up. 'You are through to police, what is your emergency?'

'There's a dead body on the cliffs below 3 Rochelle Drive.'

'Who is this speaking?'

I hang up and board the next train back to London.

Part of me did want to walk into the sea. One day I might.

But I owe Becky something first – I need to find out who killed her.

STAGE 1 – DENIAL

10

IVOR

January 2025

Her face is torture. No, worse – it possesses me, infects every thought. Eyes wide, mouth locked open, on the exact same spot her sister died. What was once Becky gone, replaced with that monstrous husk. Three days, that image has owned me.

Maybe it wasn't her. I could have been hallucinating, it could have been the ghost of her sister, or it could have been another person, but because I was there looking for Becky my mind made a leap it shouldn't have.

I slip my phone out of my work trousers and check Becky hasn't texted.

No message. I put it back into my uniform and stare at the Tesco shelves in front of me, the chill from the coolers not helping me kick this murky hangover. I check my phone again immediately before catching myself, huffing and shoving it deeper into my pocket.

A nasty, dramatic snarl charges down the aisle. 'Are you broken?' Floor manager Trish stomps over and peers up at me, tiny tyrant that she is. 'Veg crates take five seconds, what are you staring at?'

'Sorry,' I grunt, heaving the cauliflowers up, then the tenderstem broccoli.

Trish stays a second longer, her pupils enormous as they glare through her Coke-bottle glasses. Then finally, disdainfully, the eyes of Sauron move on to their next victim.

Finding a body in the exact same place that Amy's twin sister died must be significant. I keep thinking about that – a scream among so many others clamouring for attention in my mind. And there was no hint Becky wanted to kill herself or was unhappy when we met for that coffee. So, maybe it wasn't her. I spent the train journey back to London determined to work out what happened, but if I can just get a reply from her to all my messages then I can leave that body at the Montagues' to the authorities.

Checking my phone yet again, there's no new text, but I look at that message she did send me.

BECKY

Mum and Dad have told me everything about Amy. I will always love you.

That hits so different now. What did she find out? What did it do to her? Surely, she couldn't have decided to kill herself based on one—

'What do you think you're doing?'

I snap back into the store, worried I've been caught once more by the supermarket Stasi. Trish isn't looking at me though, she's turned her ire on a new girl – I think her name's Sophie – by the lettuce, opposite.

Poor Sophie freezes, lips twitching, no words forming. She looks petrified, like she's never been shouted at before. Her

Tesco fleece also appears to have been ironed – typical, misplaced conscientiousness of a newbie.

Such an attempt to impress matters not to Trish. 'You bring the old loose-leaf bags to the front. How many times! The freshest ones to the back. Basics. What is wrong with you?'

Sophie splutters an apology that Trish dismisses as she marches off. The trainee's eyes fill and she turns back to the shelves, hiding away from the world. I think this is her first week.

'Don't worry, the first twenty years are the hardest,' I say, stepping over and nudging her with my elbow.

She looks at me, tears streaking down both cheeks, then her eyes dart away again as she tries and fails to sustain a half-smile. She's got brown hair, similar to Becky's but combed more neatly. She's smaller too, very petite.

'Forget the lettuce, you just need to know how to avoid *her*, then life's dandy. I only got caught today because...'

Hmm, can't go around telling people what I found in Sandbanks.

'...because I had fourteen cans of very strong lager last night. Not on top form today.'

She titters. Did she think that was a joke?

Her eyes shuffle up to meet me again. 'Thanks.'

I want to give her a hug, tell her she's doing fine. Don't want to overstep, though.

'Wait there,' I tell her.

I whizz down the aisle, turn left towards the tills, taking the last left before them. There are ways to steal from a supermarket and ways not to steal, and success is almost exclusively determined by knowing where the CCTV cameras are. I lean into a shelf, my back to the nearest camera. No way they can see me slipping an individual pack of Kleenex tissues up my fleece sleeve.

You'd think I'd have learned that from my years working here. But it was Dad, and his limitless appetite for taking what wasn't his, that taught me such dark arts. I don't use the trick often, promise!

Returning to the veg aisle via the sweets shelves too, I pass her the tissues. It's a good call – her eye make-up is a little messier, as she's brushed away more tears in my absence.

'Did you just... take these?' she whispers.

I shrug.

'Won't we get in trouble? Like, isn't it illegal?'

Her accent sounds local, maybe more east London than north, but it's soft and friendly.

'Illegal? Illegal is making an employee cry three days into the job over a bag of lettuce. Oh, and you'll need this too.'

I pass her the tube of Smarties.

She looks at me as if I might be five bob short.

'Not many people bother to iron their uniform. Thought you looked smart.'

She lets out a little snort of laughter. 'Oh. Thank you!'

Her stare lingers on me. I swivel and trot back to my crates, checking my phone en route.

No messages.

I finish at 4 p.m. and purchase my evening beverages from a nearby off-licence. The first one is opened before I've even made it back onto the street. The relief is enormous, a rapture. I drain half the ice-cold can in one go.

My mind spirals back around that abysmal, indescribable horror in Sandbanks during the ten-minute walk home. There's no making sense of it: we met up, she texted me saying she loved me, she got an Uber to the Montagues' without her phone, then I go to Sandbanks and...

I check my phone again.

Urgh! Stop it, Ivor!

Becky is my soulmate. More than that, if it's possible. My soul belongs to her. The body I found – it can't have been Becky. I can't put them together. They are not the same. I keep thinking about the beautiful, smart, funny woman I met for coffee; how I'm going to take her back to Budapest; how we're going to find a place of our own; how we'll start trying for a baby again.

I almost bump into a middle-aged couple as I approach my door, lost in a reality that makes so much more sense than the sick delusion my mind keeps trying to tell me I'm now trapped in.

Unlocking my front door, I look down at my feet and spot a perfect white feather. Putting my two light blue plastic bags from the off-licence down on the pavement, I pluck the feather up – another one for Becky's collection. I pop it in my pocket, pick up my bags again and shoulder-barge the door open.

'Mr O'Foyle?' a female voice calls from a distance.

I look right to see that couple I'd almost bumped into. Both tall, a woman with shoulder-length, plum-coloured hair and a bald man with droopy jowls and salt-and-pepper stubble.

'Yeah...?' I mutter, suspiciously. I glance down at my bags; thankfully it's impossible to see from the couple's vantage point that my grocery shop is solely liquid.

'I'm Detective Chief Inspector Schwarz and this is Detective Inspector Bird,' she says.

'That's nice,' I say as they reach me, though I'm not sure why.

'We just tried your door and thought you were out. How serendipitous. May we come in?'

11

IVOR

January 2025

They're here about Becky. Even a Spurs fan could work that out.

But they don't know *I* know.

'What's this all about?' I ask as we clamber up the stairs.

'Best we sit down first,' the female detective says.

'Am I in trouble?' That's the sort of thing a nonplussed person would ask, isn't it?

'Just some questions... and some news,' her male colleague says.

I show them into the lounge, cringing at the scruffiness that surrounds us. Crisp crumbs in crevices of the sofa, red wine stains on the carpet, long-forgotten pizza menus poking out from under the coffee table.

Ah, screw it, who are they going to report me to, Stacey Solomon? They'll survive.

I need time to think, time to breathe. 'Tea or coffee?' I offer.

They both say coffee, and I disappear into the kitchen with my bags of beers. Urgh, I really want another one. But it'd look odd to sup in front of law enforcement. I cover the noise of me cracking a fresh can by asking if they want milk and sugar, then take a deep slug of Heineken as the kettle heats.

I pull the little white feather that had been lying outside my front door out of my pocket, hold it between my thumb and forefinger and kiss it.

What if these two officers are here to say Becky's still missing? That would mean she wasn't found at the Montagues. I could help them. We can work out where she is together. Get her back to London. Pick up where we left off before New Year's.

I check my phone to see if she's messaged. Nothing.

Maybe it's not about her at all – it could be regarding Dad, an old break-in, my prints found, my face on a security camera.

Draining my second can, I cover the slow scrape and pop of a fresh one by coughing theatrically. A thespian I am not.

Steam shoots out of the top of the kettle as it clicks off, so bloody efficient. I thought these things were never supposed to boil if you watched them!

Better make myself a coffee too – but not before one last glorious gulp.

Did they say they wanted milk and sugar? Sod it, they're getting both.

I carry three mugs into my lounge with its bare walls, oversized TV, underused PlayStation 5 and single beyond-retro paper lantern lightshade.

'Mr O'Foyle, I think it's best you sit down,' DCI What's-her-face says as I pass her and her sidekick their drinks.

I stop hovering in front of them and drop into a seat opposite. 'What's this all about?' I demand.

'Mr O'Foyle, are you the ex-boyfriend of Rebecca Burrows?' the woman asks.

'Not really ex... we're getting things back together.'

'I'm so sorry to tell you that Ms Burrows was found dead on Friday at a property in Dorset.'

The urge to go back into the kitchen, shut the door and keep drinking grabs me by the shoulders, shaking violently.

'This must be incredibly hard to process,' the woman adds.

Getting up again, I walk to the windowsill, pull the feather back out of my pocket and drop it into the glass. It's starting to rain outside, umbrellas go up, coat hoods are pulled tight over damp hair. 'I forgot if you both wanted milk and sugar. I hope it tastes OK.'

The female detective is speaking behind me. A man crosses the wet street with his whippet, he hasn't got a coat or an umbrella, he hasn't even zipped his fleece up. And yet his skinny dog has a red gilet-style coat on. It's nice when a pet owner cares more about their pet than themselves. Becky would appreciate that about him.

'Mr O'Foyle...'

Turning back into the room, both detectives are staring at me.

The woman stands up and walks towards me, putting her hands on my shoulders as I look off to the side.

'Mr O'Foyle, we understand this must be extremely difficult, but we do need to—'

'She always wanted a dog but her parents wouldn't let her.' I don't know why I say it. It's what I'm thinking. Glancing at the detective, 'She's confused.'

'Sorry,' I add.

'Maybe sit down, Mr O'Foyle, then we can—'

'Ivor.'

'Ivor,' she says, understanding. 'Sit down, let's have our coffees.'

She smells nice, like bath salts or something. She puts her

arm around me, having to reach up slightly to rest her palm on the top of my shoulder, and ushers me back to my berth.

'Sorry,' I say again, desperate to focus on absolutely anything except what she has just told me.

The female officer retakes her seat too. The man next to her clings to his mug – bored, unconcerned. Bet he's a Spurs fan.

I want my beers. Should have put them in the fridge, they'll be warming up on the counter.

I accidentally make eye contact with the female detective as I contemplate going back into the kitchen to tuck the cylindrical soldiers up in their chilly barracks.

Brushing her plum-coloured fringe out of her eyes, she gives me a small, comforting nod. 'We won't stay long, Ivor. Do you have any friends or family who you could stay with tonight, given this is such a shock?'

'I've got a mate.'

'OK, good. I'd phone him once we've gone, if you can.'

I tell them I will. Those words the woman said before hover in my mind but won't land. 'Ms Burrows was found dead' 'Ms Burrows was found dead' 'Ms Burrows was found dead'. I still think they're wrong. The revelation, the confirmation even, would crush me if it was real. I wouldn't be able to sit here and engage with them if I truly believed them. It's all going to be some horrendous mix-up. They'll get a call in a minute from some colleague telling them to apologise and stand down, Becky's been found safe and well. That's what's going to happen.

But it doesn't happen straight away.

The pair ask a lot of questions... How Becky seemed, mentally, in the weeks before; when did I last see her; had she ever suffered with depression.

That third question comes from the awkward male detective, with his icy-blue eyes and paunch stretching the buttons of his grey shirt as he sips at the steaming coffee I'm ready to throw back in his face.

'She wouldn't kill herself,' I state, determined to convince him with my glare alone.

'We're still trying to ascertain the precise circumstances,' the woman says.

'Who found her?'

'Officers got a tip-off about the whereabouts of the body,' she explains.

'From who?'

'We don't know yet. When did you last speak to her?'

'She texted me on New Year's Eve. I replied the next day, but she didn't get back to me. I'd been trying to get in touch with her ever since. I went round to her parents' but she wasn't there.'

'What did her last text say?' asks the woman.

I get my phone out and show her.

> **BECKY**
>
> Mum and Dad have told me everything about Amy. I will always love you.

She takes out her own phone, holds it up as if ready to take a photo of my screen, then glances at me for permission. I nod, and she takes a picture of our WhatsApps.

'What did you say your name was?' I enquire.

'I'm Detective Chief Inspector Tina Schwarz and this is Detective Inspector Lee Bird. But look, we'll leave you now, Mr O'Foyle—'

'Ivor,' I correct.

'Ivor, sorry,' she says, twitching her head towards the door as she looks at her colleague and gets to her feet.

'One last thing, Ivor,' Lee Birdbrain states as they head towards the stairs. 'Did you and Becky ever have a way of tracking each other's phones? Like Find My Friends or something? We've not been able to find her phone yet.'

Should I pretend I don't? Will they demand to see how often I checked her location and get suspicious?

Too little time, never lie in a hurry. Learned that the hard way the last time I had law enforcement in my flat, interrogating me about Dad's burglaries.

'We did, yeah.' I get my phone out again, knowing what it will say. I tap on the app and let them see as I find her name. No location comes up – of course it doesn't, the battery's surely died at this point. 'Sorry.'

'No worries,' Tina Schwarz says with a tiny grateful smile. She hands me a card with her direct number, in case I think of anything else. They leave.

Back in the kitchen, I finish my long-neglected beverage and open another, storing the remainder in the fridge – finally.

Noz shows up about an hour later – with more beer. He came round last night and I thought he was going to give me a tough time for never getting back to him in Bournemouth, leaving him in the lurch, but he didn't care at all. I shouldn't be surprised, I once uninvited him from a trip to Budapest at the last minute so I could take Becky instead and he took that on the chin too.

Last night, I couldn't bring myself to tell him what I might have found at Sandbanks. Tonight, however, I run him through everything. Finding a body, blacking out, coming to on the promenade, calling police. The full director's cut of the worst day of my life. He sits, picking at his cuticles, looking about as comfortable as a teenager at his own parents' sex therapy session.

'Did you give the necklace to the detectives, the one you found?' he asks.

'I can't, they'd know I was there,' I explain, the pendant burning a bear-shaped hole in my jeans pocket. It's not left my possession at any point.

'And police say they still haven't found her phone?' Noz confirms.

I shake my head, checking my own phone on impulse then putting it back on the table.

'But it's at Becky's parents' house, isn't it? That was the whole thing, you could see she'd got the Uber to Sandbanks but she'd left her phone behind.'

I shrug. 'So?'

'So why haven't her parents handed it over? If police reckon there might be some clue on her phone and can't find it, they'd definitely have asked the parents if they had it.'

I take an enormous sip from a green can of strong Polish lager which has a Buffalo as the logo. 6.5 per cent – proper beer. One of the selection Noz brought round. 'Maybe her parents can't find it either.'

'Bollocks!' Noz jeers. 'Your daughter's just died in suspicious circumstances, the fuzz are asking about her phone, you'd turn the house over.'

'What's your point?'

'They're withholding the phone. Hiding it.' He takes a hearty slurp of his own can then stretches his massive pan hands out as if to say why can't you see it?

I stay staring at him, not in the mood for guessing games.

He grunts, impatient yet smug. 'There's something on that phone that Becky's parents don't want police to see.'

12

BECKY'S DIARY

Friday 8 October 2021

What a whirlwind! If you'd said ten days ago, I'd spend the majority of this week in Budapest, I'd have said you were mad. Completely and utterly mad. But that's what happened.

Ivor's had this holiday booked in for months with a mate of his. He'd always wanted to go because he'd heard the beer was really cheap, lol (to be fair it was!).

Anyway, I asked him about it one night last week while we were out at a pub near his. (Note to self, don't let him take you to The Mitre again, vibey it ain't, unless your vibe is old men leering at you, carpet that sticks to your shoes and warm white wine.)

So, Ivor is telling me how excited he is, then he goes, 'you should come'.

I was like... I'd love to, but I'm broke. As soon as I said it, I knew he'd think I was hinting that he'd have to pay. So I also pointed out I had work. Plus... what would his mate say? I kept trying to say I couldn't, but once Ivor had the idea, he was like a dog with a big juicy bone, adamant I wouldn't have to pay for anything. I felt so bad because he's not a billionaire. But I must admit, it was SO SO NICE to have him be really enthusiastic and insistent I go. He's so laissez-faire about most things, which is great in its own way, but I got this sort of unique thrill from seeing him in full control, not accepting no for an answer, taking the reins – all out of a sincere desire to spend time with lil' old me. Honestly, my heart!

So there and then, that night, we booked me on to his flight, and he wouldn't even let me pay for that.

Had to be a bit bad with work… said it was a family emergency. Which it technically was, the emergency being that my boyfriend (which is basically family) wanted to whisk me away for an impromptu romantic getaway. Call 999!

Carl was very understanding, the company even sent a condolence card, it was waiting in the flat when I got back… feel a tad guilty.

But it was worth it! I'd never been to Hungary, never been anywhere near there. My verdict… SO FUN!

We popped from cheap bar to cheap bar – but when I say cheap, I don't mean The Mitre cheap, I mean the drinks were cheap. Honestly, Ivor was so generous, he would not stop treating us to a shot here, a glass of wine there, a cocktail, a beer, another shot. We partied and talked and let our hair down. He wouldn't let me pay for our meals, either. They were good value and all delicious (we had these chicken wraps with humous and peppers at one place that changed my life). But he was militant about paying.

We went to these ornate, pretty thermal baths, we ate constantly, we'd run back to our room for sex, we'd do more drinking. We walked around the parliament building for about three seconds before realising it was far less fun than all the other things Budapest had to offer. We had the BEST day looking around Budapest Zoo. The gorillas were the highlight, they were so gregarious and cheeky, coming right up to us, huge dark brown eyes and twitchy noses, chomping on nuts and sort of playfighting with each other. Took so many videos of them!

The weather was glorious and hot. Came back with more colour than I got through the whole summer at home.

It was honestly the most happy, carefree, silly adventure I can remember. We talked about so many stupid things. I love it when you spend long enough with someone that you get past all the normal day-to-day stuff and get weird. That's when you really lay down roots.

I asked him the funniest thing he'd done drunk. He said he'd once got home from a night out, found a pen and paper, handwritten a letter to Greggs telling them they needed to start selling chips, googled their head office address, sealed and stamped the envelope, then gone BACK out at 3 in the morning to post it. Hilarious! So Ivor!

We went to a karaoke bar and he sang 'Somewhere Only We Know' (officially our song at this point) – sweet.

I didn't think about work or Mum and Dad, and we talked so much. I keep waiting for there to be a problem, but there isn't anything.

We are definitely closer and stronger for the time away.

There was one night we were sitting in a bar called... hmm... can't remember. But it had a nice outdoor terrace. He had a large beer, I was taking a breather with a strawberry mocktail. He started being a bit shy and bashful out of nowhere, said he'd got something to tell me. I was thinking to myself... here we go, this is where he admits he's got a secret second family or thirty-seven STIs. I've never seen him look so serious... or scared. Then he told me.

He's been to prison.

In his early twenties he was arrested alongside his dad over a load of burglaries, and he tried to lie to protect his dad, but police took it to trial and he was found guilty. I couldn't work out the details exactly, it was so much to take in at once, but it sounds like he didn't get much time for the burglaries, it was the lies to police that got him in more trouble, because he'd done that as an adult, whereas the burglaries were done as a teenager. He said he was so ashamed of the burglaries, how it still upsets him that he was part of taking things from innocent families, how he started getting himself really drunk every night so his dad and his mates wouldn't take him any more. But he still tried to protect his dad by lying to police later down the line. He said he'd understand if I didn't want to be with him any more, but he wanted to be honest. He was genuinely distraught at being a part of this gang, you could tell he felt so guilty, and then also was so embarrassed that he'd spent four years in prison. He hardly made eye contact, just sat drinking his beer, looking at the ground, and saying it all. When he'd got it all out, he glanced up, head still bowed. I don't think I'll ever forget that look. It was as if he was bracing for me to end it. I've never seen him cry before, either, but as he was waiting to see what I'd do, I could tell even with the dim lights of the outdoor bar, there were tears.

I grabbed his hand and told him it made absolutely ZERO difference. If anything, it just helps explain why he hasn't got more of a dating history. He was literally not able to date. There's such a stigma attached to being a criminal, but knowing Ivor, I totally believe him when he says how much he regrets going along with his dad's plans. His dad's still in jail, apparently.

So there it is, I know his biggest secret, and I still feel EXACTLY the same. Even over the next couple of days, as I had time for it to sink in, nothing changed. If anything, Ivor beats himself up too much about it, it's his dad who was the ringleader and bullied him into everything. It sounds like Ivor's dad has always made him feel extremely guilty about the fact Ivor's mum died giving birth to him, and used that to manipulate Ivor and undermine his confidence. Horrible really. Still... kind of nice to know I'm not the only one with controlling, cruel parents. What a pair we are!

So yes, all in all, Budapest was super-duper!

I will say this… I thought Ivor drank a lot at home. In a foreign city with cheaper prices… he was on a new level. I barely drank half as much as him and yet he was the one feeling spritelier and raring to go again each day. His poor liver!

We're already talking about which other cities we could jet off to next.

Gah. What a time to be alive! Such a shame I've promised myself I'll never get married. I think I'll be with Ivor forever, but the idea that it will boil my parents' blood that we don't go about it the traditional, respectable way makes the whole thing that little bit sweeter still.

I did think about Amy a bit while we were away, weirdly. When I was with Dillon, he'd obviously known Amy, they'd been friends too, so I knew what she thought of him, albeit as children. But this is the first time I've had a boyfriend she hadn't met. I found myself pondering whether she'd like Ivor. That's the kind of conversation twin sisters would have, isn't it? Swapping opinions and highs and lows of their dating lives. Made me sad that opportunity has been taken away. But deep down I think she'd really like him. It was nice to feel that, at least.

Had to sober up quick when I got home yesterday though. Cam had left two letters on the kitchen table for me. One was the condolence card from Costa. I could tell from the handwriting that the other one was from Mum.

Letters from Mum are NEVER pleasant. Emotional nunchucks flying all over the shop the moment you open them.

She can't just message me like normal parent, nooooo! Her and Dad don't trust phones because they know they save a record of past conversations. They'd rather write on good old-fashioned perishable paper. Which is stupid really because I could keep hold of the paper just the same if I wanted to. Museums show off parchments that are centuries old, but for some reason Mum is a million times more mistrusting of there being a digital trail of her cryptic messages than a physical one.

The purpose of this letter?

They want to meet Ivor.

I hadn't mentioned him at all until a couple of weeks ago but then, feeling extra confident, Becky 2.0 and all that, I ignored the Brian-Blessed-sized voice screaming 'NO' in my head and told them I was dating someone. I'm a grown woman, for goodness' sake. Why should I live in fear of having a partner and admitting as much to my parents?

Well, I know the answer… Amy.

It is ALWAYS about Amy.

Mum didn't put it so blatantly, but basically, they want to suss Ivor out. Her phrase was 'with our family's past we can't be too careful about the characters with whom we choose to share our lives, Rebecca'. Literally used the word 'whom'. That's all poxy middle-class speak for 'bring your boyfriend over so we can judge him mercilessly because we don't want anyone knowing the truth about Amy'.

And then the most infuriating line. Right at the end…

'Your father and I both think you'd still be better off back with Dillon.'

I ripped that stupid letter into a dozen pieces and threw it in the bin.

They're going to hate Ivor. It's one of the biggest reasons I love him.

Wish I had the bravery to tell him the secret they've been forcing me and the Montagues to keep all these years. Best not to say, though. I don't even want to think about what they'd do to me if they knew I'd finally told the truth.

13

IVOR

January 2025

There's something on that phone that Becky's parents don't want the police to see. Noz's deduction paints every thought in a thick sinister coat.

I never believed Becky would kill herself, I told DCI Schwarz as much. I'm still waiting for them to call back confirming they got the ID wrong, that Becky is missing, not dead. Are the police open-minded about such other theories? Also, do they know about Becky's sister falling in the exact same spot? They must do.

Becky didn't talk much about her sister, understandably. But something had got her looking into the death again, she said as much when we went for coffee. And then her message...

Mum and Dad have told me everything about Amy. I will always love you.

I need to know more about what happened when Becky's sister died.

Noz leaves my flat just after 2 a.m. and I'm still – just about –

seeing few enough versions of my phone screen to send a message to Becky's old friend Cam.

IVOR

Police think Becky's dead. Need to talk to you.

I hit send and let my head crash onto the cushion at the end of the sofa.

* * *

Today's shift was an absolute slog, a bit like an ultra-marathon, only harder. Ultra-marathon runners don't have to put up with Trish snapping and grimacing all day.

I'm not saying she's a drag, but her blood type's B-negative and her star sign's Cancer.

Ho-hum, I survived despite her best efforts. Showed the new girl, Sophie, how Trish likes the flower buckets arranged, despite Trish leaving her no instructions on how to do it – no doubt hoping that'd give her a good excuse to shout at the newbie again. It was exquisite to watch her inspect every last petal in those bouquets before having to begrudgingly admit Sophie had done an 'OK job'. The relief on the poor girl's face was a picture.

Now I'm off to meet Cam. Get some answers.

Her reply was waiting for me when I crowbarred open a sorry eyelid at 6.55 a.m. Grotesque time to be awoken.

In hindsight, my text to her could have been a little less brutal. Won't be getting job offers at the Samaritans any time soon. But she wants to meet... tonight.

It's days like this I rue the shower being broken. I could have done with one before work, and definitely could do with one before meeting Cam. Becky was always getting on at me to get it sorted.

If the police – or I – do find her alive somewhere, I will make sure to get that sorted. It's the least she deserves. Where could she be? And why haven't the police got back to me yet saying they got the body wrong at the Montagues? There is one explanation for why they aren't calling to say they were wrong – but it's impossible to contemplate. Too big, too scary, just... no.

Cupping water in my hands at the sink, I try to throw it over my hair a couple of times, scrub a towel over my head, then douse myself in enough Sure deodorant to stop every single pore on my body from ever perspiring again.

I inhale a Greggs en route to the pub – no steak bakes so went cheese and onion. Destination is the Railway Tavern in Clapham. Can't face drinking tonight – will stick to lemonade.

Cam's here early. It's her eyes I see first – pained, shell-shocked... staring at me. Wandering over to her table, she gets up and hugs me, neither of us knowing what to say.

Her overgrown bleached bob looks exactly as odd as it always did. She leans back away from me and tears fill her eyes.

I nod at the bar. 'What d'you fancy?'

'Oh, I've already got... sorry.' She nods down at a pathetic little half pint of cider on the table.

'No worries,' I state, wandering off to look at the taps on my own. Ah yes, I'd forgotten that about Cam. She's what Noz calls a T-rex in a tux – deep pockets, short arms.

This is going to be awkward as hell. My lemonade plan drains into the drip tray behind the bar as I order a Heineken instead.

Who only buys a half, by the way? What? Is she piloting a plane full of children straight after she's seen me? Is she conducting open-heart surgery later this evening? Just buy a full pint, for goodness' sake.

Cam wants the full lowdown. I relay everything that happened yesterday with the detectives and nothing that happened three days earlier when I was in Sandbanks.

She sips her tiny tipple and shakes her head constantly like a windscreen wiper.

'And how are you doing?' she asks when I finally grind to a halt. 'If you don't mind me saying, you seem kind of... OK?'

I tap the side of my beer, letting the plump of my index finger pick up the condensation, then drain what's left in the glass. 'Fancy another?'

She nods. 'Pint of Aspall, please.'

Oh yeah, of course she wants a full pint now I'm offering! Unbelievable! I agree without displaying outward displeasure, of course – good Englishman that I am.

The bar is round the corner from our table, so I order two double Bells, slam them back, then return with our pints.

Slumping back down, I take a huge gulp to chase away the smell of spirits on my breath.

'Seriously, Ivor...' she speaks into the silence '...you must be devastated, but...'

'I still reckon they might have mixed up the identities,' I say.

Her eyes bulge. 'What? How?'

Shrugging, I take another sip of beer and realise I don't have an answer. 'I...'

'Ivor, if two detectives tell you they've found someone's body, they've found that person's body. They wouldn't come round to see you if they weren't a thousand per cent sure.'

'I'm just not convinced,' I mutter, wishing she'd drop it.

'Oh, Ivor. You know the stages of grief, the different emotions you have as you process loss? The first one's denial.'

If she already thinks that, based on the detectives' words alone, she'd be screaming from the rooftops if she knew I came across the body that I initially thought was Becky myself.

'Is that why you said you needed to chat?' she asks. 'Because I am here to help you through this, yeah? We can help each other!'

Shaking my head, I force more beer down. 'That's not why I texted.'

'Maybe it's deep down, subconscious. Part of you must know she's gone, and you want to talk about it.'

I really should have got a third shot of Bells at the bar. 'You're not listening, Cam.'

Affronted, she frowns at me. 'What then?'

'I need answers,' I say. 'Like... what do you know about Becky's sister? I've found a couple of old news articles that report her falling from the balcony at that same house, but Becky seemed to be looking into something. Whoever it is they've found there, that's weird for it to happen in the exact same place as Amy died. And Becky was on to something with it.'

I hold out my phone and show her Becky's last message.

Cam's mouth drops open. 'You don't think...?'

'Her parents still have her phone. I'm asking myself 'why', if they're not hiding something.'

'Can you imagine!' Cam whispers, shock and sadness twisting into excitable, unedifying scandal. 'Surely they wouldn't kill both of them the same way at the same place?'

'You think they killed Amy?' I clarify, heart banging against my ribs.

'I... hopefully not. But that was always the rumour... right?' Her eyes don't say hopefully not, they yearn for outrage and disgrace.

The longer we talk, the more I remember why she and Becky drifted apart – Cam's too gossipy and utterly unfeeling. I get the sense that if she won the lottery, the first thing she'd do would be to pay to have her car number-plate changed to XOXO. Thank goodness she went on a date with that bloke I was living with when she did though; if they'd met up a month later, I'd have moved out, and then would never have crossed paths with Becky.

'What rumour about Amy?' I demand.

'Ivor... please tell me you heard!'

I repeat my question.

'There were always question marks over the mum and dad. Why did they take so long to report the body, why did they refuse to speak to police until they had a solicitor? There's a forum online somewhere – people looked into it and hinted the parents were somehow involved.' She gets her phone out and taps at it. She hasn't even touched her cider while my beer's already half gone. I hate people who nurse pints. Get drinking, will you!

After a couple of huffs, shakes of her head and extra taps on her screen, she cries: 'Here!'

Passing me the phone, I scroll through post after post on a webpage, a forum where all the posts are timestamped as being from about a decade ago. It starts with someone asking if anyone's heard of the 'Amy Burrows case', then a pasted version of the BBC story I'd found when I looked up the death myself. Then a list of suspicious details, like Cam said. Apparently, Phillip and Audrey were alone in the house with Amy, while Becky was out with the Montagues – the family that own the house – and their son. Why? Why had they wanted to get Amy alone? They said they were in the room with the balcony, and yet didn't have time to reach seven-year-old Amy before she was up, onto the bars and over them, which seems odd since the lounge isn't that big. Someone even posted a blueprint of the house to prove how unlikely the Burrowses' story is. Other details are relayed too, none of them damning by themselves, but all chipping away at the official narrative.

By the bottom of the conversation, all the posts are adamant... 'Parents did it. Open and shut'... 'Why aren't these two in custody?'... 'If it's true they have a second daughter, she needs taking off them NOW'.

'Can't believe you didn't know this was a thing,' Cam says, finally taking a tiny sip of her beverage. 'You seriously never looked it up?'

'Why would I? Becky said her sister fell from a balcony and died, that was it. She was always honest about how horrible her parents were. But she never hinted they were involved in that.'

'Maybe she didn't want to admit it even to herself,' Cam theorises. 'But weren't you curious? I swear I looked it up the second she told me about her family. I'm such a true crime girlie.'

I wish Cam would say girlie less, and pay for rounds of drinks more.

'What did Becky tell you?' I probe.

She blows her cheeks out. 'Same as you, I guess. None of the conspiracy theories or anything. But it definitely played on her mind. Not day-to-day, but deeper, in like, her psyche, y'know?'

'How d'you mean?'

'Like, whenever she was upset or not coping, that'd be where her mind went. She'd mention still missing her sister and despising her parents, it was kind of like there was a hand under the surface, dragging her down, causing a lot of pain, creating a lot of obstacles for her, mentally.'

I don't like the way she's talking about Becky in the past

tense, I don't like the way she's able to speak so articulately about Becky when she's only just decided her friend is dead, I don't like how what she's saying makes total sense and resonates securely with the Becky I knew.

'That's why I can't stop thinking about her phone,' I admit.

'What do you reckon's on it?' She splutters with a full mouth of cider, letting some of it spill out of her mouth and slap back on to the sticky pub table. What a waste.

'I was going to ask you,' I tell her.

'We hadn't spoken much in yonks, sorry.'

I nod. 'Probably a stupid question, but did Becky have a necklace with a bear pendant on?'

'Not a stupid question. We shared jewellery all the time. But no, a bear... no. Why?'

Because I prised it from a cold, dead hand when I found that body earlier this week.

'Another thing the police asked me about,' I lie.

'Ivor, are you sure you're OK? I know how much you loved Becky. Have you cried or let it out at—'

'I'm fine.'

She sips her cider, more than happy to return to the gossip mill. 'So, what would the parents' motive be?'

A passing barman leans in to collect my empty glass, which I hand up to him, giving a quick 'thank you'.

'Maybe she found out they did kill Amy,' I say back to Cam, hating myself for contemplating that Becky might be dead. 'Becky threatened to call police. They couldn't let that happen, took her phone off her and then...'

Her eyes bore into mine, as if each fresh second is convincing her more and more that this worst-case scenario may be real.

'Even if they did kill Amy...' she starts, 'why would they kill their other daughter in the exact same place, when that literally links them to both deaths?'

It's a great question. Certainly not one I have the answer to. Piecing everything together feels like plaiting fog right now.

Becky's phone might have answers though. That's why her disgusting, deplorable parents are hampering the police investigation by hiding it.

I need that phone.

STAGE 2 – ANGER

14

IVOR

January 2025

I've got Dad to thank for my rock-solid confidence in being able to break into any property undetected.

Of course, when Dad was in his pomp, home security systems weren't as sophisticated or cheap for families to buy. It must be much harder to rummage under plant pots for a spare key when there's a nosy Ring doorbell recording your every move.

Thankfully, the Burrowses aren't the kind to invest in such newfangled tech witchcraft. I sneaked into their house unbeknownst to them numerous times when me and Becky were together. Getting them out of the place long enough now for me to find Becky's phone, however – that could be a challenge.

It hasn't been showing up on Find My Friends for days. What if they've thrown it in the river, or battered it to smithereens? All its truths lost forever.

But that leads to another thought... if they haven't done that yet, they will do soon, and I need to retrieve it before they do. At the very least, I must try. For Becky.

I looked up the stages of grief after what Cam said, and all it did was make me mad. I can't be condensed down into an inevitable sequence of emotions. How dare she dismiss my theory that Becky is still out there, to fit her own pop psychology? But then, as I read on and my fists clenched tighter I realised I was starting to slide into the next emotion exactly how the model would predict – anger. I don't care about getting angry though, what I care about is losing the final vestige of me that still believes Becky is alive. At least in denial there was hope. As the hours slip by, I can feel that ebbing away, replaced by an ever-growing blaze of pure, white-hot fury that this could happen to her, to me, to us. And with every spark of this new-found rage, Becky's parents' faces flash up in my mind.

I smoulder through another day at Tesco... plotting. Dad would never just hit a house. He'd do his homework, he'd watch the place for weeks, get to know the rhythms of the family. It was one of the worst things about it. The more he made you sit and observe their routines – when they left in the morning, which night they took the kids to swimming, how long they were away every Sunday afternoon – the more you liked the family, the more you'd feel sorry for what Dad was about to make us do. I don't need to spy on the Burrowses to know their habits. But will they keep them up now Becky's dead? I'd be amazed if they did. But then, knowing the Burrowses as painfully well as I do, I'd sort of be amazed if they didn't, too.

My mind probes the plan again. Today would be the best of the week to test whether their routines still hold. They always used to go out on Thursdays. Hmm, if I were to nip into the staff kitchenette briefly, skewer off one of my testicles with a fork and present it to Trish like a cake pop, would she let me leave early so I can go and check if Phillip and Aud are in? I am tempted.

Should I really be contemplating breaking in? Going back to the bad old days with my dad... it makes me feel sick. But then those families were victims, whereas the Burrowses might be the opposite. This wouldn't be burglary, more like a sneaky, unofficial warrant. And if Becky is dead, and they have something to do with it, then the very least of their worries will be me breaking in. I can't even imagine what I'll do to them if it turns out they—

A squall echoes down the aisle. Trish is having another very public rant at new girl, Sophie. Poor Sophie, she's so timid. I found out yesterday she's a Gooner too. How dare Trish bully her... over stale sarnies on the reduced shelf, of all things.

'I've seen dead snails move quicker!' she cries, cheery as a chokehold. Her eyes contort in such a way as to insinuate she has never had the misfortune of looking down on such a worthless amoeba as Sophie before.

'Why don't you show her how to do it, rather than humiliating her?' I call over, causing a couple of customers to glance up from their baskets. Standing up from my stool, I wander over. Trish tilts her head up to glare at me, her frog-like swollen second chin stretching to enormous proportions.

'Keep your beak out,' she orders.

'No one learns from being shouted at,' I say calmly as I reach them, meeting Sophie's eye for a second, to say... you're not alone.

'Don't get lippy!' Trish bays. 'Not exactly employee of the month yourself, O'Foyle. She's picking up your shoddy habits.'

Oh, Trish, you've caught me on the wrong day, I'm afraid.

'My girlfriend's just been found dead,' I state with conviction, diction crisp, like a court clerk announcing the arrival of the judge. 'Your bullying is aggravating my fragile mental state. I'm going to need the rest of the day off and will be reporting you to the area manager concerning your cruel behaviour towards me and my colleagues.'

The frog's mouth gawps open, squashing that bulbous second chin back into a graspable clump. She says nothing.

I give Sophie a soft punch of the arm as I stalk past to the exit.

Fuck Trish.

And fuck the Burrowses.

* * *

I head to Finchley Central tube station, turning down the chance to purchase any adult refreshments on the way. I imagine Noz throwing his hands up in disgust at my self-discipline, but the reasons are threefold.

One: while on the Underground I need to send that very important email to my area manager – CC'ing in Trish – outlining some of her most heinous comments, and I want to make sure that information is articulate, clear and accurate.

Two: on the off-chance my hunch about the Burrowses is proved right, it will serve me well to stay sober as I navigate their empty house.

Three: shit, I swear there was a third point, but it's gone. Well, the other two points are very good.

Swept along by the evening rush hour, I swap to the District Line at Embankment and hurtle towards south London. Hustled and bustled by endless worker droids zipping in all directions once off the tube, I take a second to drop a bit of change into a beggar's battered Starbucks cup by the lifts. No one else seems to notice he exists, all too busy mistakenly thinking their lives are of any importance. The homeless man says his name is Dennis, I tell him my name too and bid him a good evening.

My mood is then temporarily dampened by one of those charity muggers accosting me as I leave the station.

'Excuse me, sir,' the twerp begins, holding his little clipboard and making sure to lean into my line of sight. 'Do you mind me asking your age?'

I come to a halt, trying to work out what good cause he's flogging. 'Thirty-two,' I say.

'Ah,' the man replies, already turning away in search of fresh prey.

'Why?' I ask loudly, tapping him on the shoulder.

'Oh no, don't worry, sir,' he says, smiling but oozing the feeling that I'm now wasting his time. 'We only want to speak to men over forty today so...'

'Men over...'

What the actual fuck?

Not only did he interrupt my evening uninvited, then he insults me by suggesting I look a million years old. If he didn't work for a charity I'd sue him. Maybe I still will.

First a woman at Bournemouth station asks if I've got a cigarette, now someone accuses me of being Methuselah himself. What is it about stations that ages me so?

Shaking the insult off, I make the most of the well-earned breaths of fresh, cool outside air as I resume my progress towards Wimbledon Park. Under normal circumstances, arriving via the entrance gates to Becky's parents' home-slash-mansion-slash-hiding-place-for-her-phone would do just fine. But not today.

Twilight's giving up as I reach my position. It's 5.30 p.m. Even if they are going out, they won't have left yet. I sit on a park bench a long way back from the property but even from this distance in the deadening January evening, I can see two lights on upstairs in their home. I zip up my Tesco fleece and breathe into my hands, wallowing in the winter chill.

Ever since I've known the Burrowses, they've attended a bridge club on Thursday nights. Why anyone would deliberately choose to play the card game bridge in a world where Uno also exists, I do not know. But that is their Thursday drill, and they would stick to it even if Putin was dropping hydrogen bombs on SW19 and the rest of the city was hiding in nuclear bunkers.

Now, a large part of me is thinking: they've just found out their one and only surviving daughter has died, they won't contemplate bridge tonight.

But here I am, watching those two lights in the windows across the way, transfixed.

Memories drift by of my own times in that grand abode.

Those Thursday nights were some of the happiest of our lives. Her parents would order a taxi from an expensive firm to pick them up at precisely 6.40 p.m. every time. And after that, Becky and I knew we had the place to ourselves, all fourteen rooms of it.

We'd walk around naked, blare Oasis across both floors, make ham and cheese toasties in an ancient Le Creuset frying pan Becky was forbidden from using. She was rebelling, growing, proving to her parents, and herself, that she was enough. That actually, the kind of things her parents would tut at were not things to feel guilty about at all, that she could create her own moral compass and rules, that enjoying yourself isn't a sin. Never did she seem to grasp that more than on Thursday nights.

I smash my right fist into the wood panels of the bench I'm sitting on, over and over, until it's dragged the breath out of me. Inspecting my knuckles, they're bloody and deepening purple.

It hurts so much.

Not my fist.

Becky.

I peer up at the house again and panic. Those two upstairs lights are out. I check my phone – 6.33 p.m. Shit! Is this happening? I need to see it; I need to see the taxi leave.

Usain Bolt would be proud of the pace I set as I fly across the grass. Surely, they're not keeping up with bridge? Who would be that callous? That's got to be evidence of their involvement in itself, hasn't it?

Reaching the wall at the back of their property, I pull myself up and hang there, looking in: no lights on in the house at all now. When Becky and I sneaked in the back entrance late at night, she'd give me a leg over, and I'd then unlock the rusty gate from the inside. Today, pure adrenalin sees me claw my way up and over, unassisted.

Then I'm still.

I wish my ears were ten times the size – King Charles levels of gargantuan – just for a few seconds, as I wait for a clue as to the Burrowses' movements, but all I can hear is the pump of my fretting heart. What if they catch me? What if police are watching the house because they know the parents have been lying about the phone? I'll be arrested. I'll be a suspect.

I take another of those lovely fresh, deep breaths of clean air. Don't be silly, there's no way...

A car door slams.

Then another one.

I race towards the sound coming from the front of the property.

Reaching the edge of the front driveway, half-hidden behind wheelie bins, I watch as a BMW leaves a trail of dust thankfully

thin enough to confirm that the Burrowses are being chauf-
feured off the property the same way they are every Thursday.

What the actual fuck? Just when you think they can't stoop
any lower! Monsters.

A second thought strikes: the house really is empty. I can
break and enter if I still have the nerve...

Of course I do.

15

BECKY'S DIARY

Sunday 17 October 2021

It was fine, I suppose. Ivor hasn't gone off me instantly, which is what I expected to happen.

Thank goodness he didn't react how I'd dreaded he might. Because my parents certainly did, judged him the millisecond he walked through the door.

I hate them. Hate hate hate them.

'Us men usually wear chinos on Sundays.' They were literally Dad's first words, before he'd even deigned to shake Ivor's hand.

And Ivor had made a real effort, bless him! He'd put on his best jeans, cleaned his trainers and even found a checked short-sleeved shirt to wear. OK, it was a bit creased. But why should we even have to worry about things like that? Wearing a pair of burgundy trousers on a certain day of the week is the opposite of what society should be worrying about.

I don't know what's worse. Dad's patronising nonsense. Or Mum not saying a single word to Ivor as he introduced himself. She stood with this weird half-smile as if trying to surreptitiously pass a pineapple, but in my head I could hear her mind screaming: 'Dillon's a far better match.'

Ivor could sense the animosity, the icy snobbery I despise so much. But he kept trying, kept making conversation, attempting to laugh off Dad's mean jokes and jibes.

He listened, really listened, while Mum talked about all her lame garden plants and flowers, as if she does any of the work on them herself. And yet the moment he mixed up two types of tree, she howled with laughter as if he was a simpleton.

I shot back that they haven't ever got any bird tables or nut bags for squirrels on the lawn, so what's the point in having all the trees, if they aren't encouraging animals into the garden.

Mum tutted and wandered off. I've argued about that with her a hundred times before – I mainly brought it up to show her they aren't allowed to bully Ivor the way they do me.

I kept touching his arm, holding his hand, trying to tacitly reassure him that I love him, regardless of these two fire-breathing Horntail dragons I'm somehow related to.

At least there was booze. Thank goodness for that… No way he'd still be with me if we'd been forced to stay sober too. Fortunately, the posh classes are just as dependent on alcohol as everyone else. They just use huge goblets and put juniper berries in their G&Ts in an ostentatious attempt to hide it.

So we sat and drank Malfy Gin Originale with Fentimans Valencian Orange tonic – Fever-Tree has gone down market, they've decided – and looked out onto the back garden. This has always been their absolute favourite thing to do with guests, get them looking out of the conservatory window, flaunting the tiny glimpse of the Wimbledon tennis courts across the park.

Then lunch was excruciating! Why did I agree we'd go round? WHY? It's like having a deadly peanut allergy and agreeing to a satay sauce facial. No good was ever going to come from it.

Ivor got more of a roasting than the lamb joint. Asked every question under the sun about his work, his hobbies, his background.

Things deteriorated, albeit silently... when he reached over for the decanter of red wine. Up until that point, Julie had been serving all the food and drinks. But in most families, pouring your own fresh glass would mean nothing. It would, if anything, be a sign that you didn't like being waited on, the same way I've always hated being waited on by Julie, a sign that you don't think you're better than anyone else, that you're not above menial tasks. But as Ivor reached for that decanter, I could sense Dad's gaze. As if Ivor's faux pas had proven Dad right in everything he believed to be true about this young man's behaviour and lifestyle, in the same way that everything that Dad believes to be true is, in good time, proven right.

In that infinitesimal moment, I knew, or at least I accepted I knew, all was lost.

In a strange way it made the subsequent crescendo less painful. There had never been any combination of words or sequence of actions that could have redeemed him in my parents' eyes.

But yes. The finale...

We'd discussed it in advance – Ivor's time in jail. He was very nervous about admitting it, tried to talk me into hiding it from them. But I'm tired of lying and hiding and faking for other people's benefit. I won't live in fear of them!

So, as they probed into his employment history, my heart began to race, knowing that – for me, not for himself – he was going to tell them everything. I couldn't look at them as he came out with it. I watched, smiling and nodding at him every time he glanced my way, my hand gripping his under the table.

He finished by saying his own dad is still in jail.

And then...

Heavy silence. A silence so dense that not only noise, but light and time appeared to bend around it, both of us suspended in endless, soundless condemnation.

But as I say, it almost didn't bother me by this point. If they'd been positive and welcoming at first, and then that goodwill had been shattered by Ivor's admission, then maybe it would have felt like we'd lost something. But he never had a chance, so whether he'd set up a charity for orphans or blown up a double-decker bus full of puppies, they would have treated him with the same disdain. Because he doesn't earn much. Because of his accent. Because he doesn't wear chinos on Sundays. Because he is not Dillon. Because they do not trust anybody any more.

Their seabed-low opinion of him was cemented long before he admitted to his time in jail.

Silence continued to swirl. Mum cut her lamb up into smaller and smaller pieces.

My next move was very Becky 2.0. I grabbed the decanter too and poured myself another glass of Barolo. My insolence and loyalty to Ivor exploding in Dad's spiteful eyes.

We left as soon as Julie had cleared away the cut glass bowls scraped clean of Eton Mess.

On the tube back to Finchley, I couldn't stop apologising. I genuinely thought he was going to say it was over. But he was so reassuring.

He put his arm round me, nuzzled his head into my neck and told me to stop worrying. Words can't describe how relieved I felt as he kissed me with those wine-tinged lips.

I guess I had given him such a stiff warning about my parents, not just in the moments before we arrived, but in every conversation we've ever had about them, that he wasn't expecting a royal welcome.

(Sidenote… I wonder if Meghan Markle now thinks the phrase

'royal welcome' is like some kind of ironic British slang for a terrible welcome. Lol.)

But Ivor seemed to let the day roll off him. Considering he'd been so worried about how I'd react about his time in jail, I liked how little he cared about my parents' opinions. He's a keeper, all right! The one thing he did want to do was go to a pub once we were back in Finchley. I was so emotionally drained, I just wanted to crawl under a duvet and watch some YouTube. But how could I deny him after making him spend the day on the rack?

It did prove sort of useful in the end too. (We went to somewhere called The Tally Ho near his flat btw, quite nice.) As I whinged and moaned and apologised some more, he did start to open up about his dad. Not loads, but admitted how ashamed he was of him, and that at least my parents provided for me and even if they did judge and didn't like him, that at least they were doing that because they wanted the best for me.

Sadly, he's dead wrong.

That would have been the moment, if any, to tell him what really happened to Amy, to help him understand what Mum and Dad are truly like. But I didn't have the energy.

He's so trusting and content living in the moment, I doubt he'll ever go looking to see why internet forums still accuse Mum and Dad. Maybe that's the answer – leave the pair of them and Amy behind, forge our own path. Well, not leave Amy behind. I miss her all the time, even now. But leave that day behind.

Another thing that's just occurred to me. They acted like Ivor going to prison was an abomination – if police knew what happened to Amy, then Mum and Dad would have been jailed. The hypocrisy is dizzying!!!

I let Ivor keep talking in the pub. I was on the Diet Cokes, he was knocking back Heinekens so his thoughts and conversation did begin to unravel towards last orders. But I also spied an opportunity. He's met my parents. Quid pro quo, Clarice! Time to meet his dad. After I raised the idea, he stumbled over an attempted rebuttal, which obviously meant I'd won the debate. I made him put the date in his phone for a week on Tuesday, when we're next both off. I'm kind of excited. Will Ivor look like him, sound like him, will they have a similar sense of humour? I'm not saying it's going to be all happy families but maybe Ivor will see actually his dad's not a total swine, especially now he's seen how cold my parents are.

Me meeting his dad is something he's been very very VERY wary of. But it's been almost four months together now, that's a fair enough relationship length to justify being introduced to him. Especially since I grasped the nettle today. So, a week on Tuesday, I will finally meet the one, the only, Jeff O'Foyle and make up my own mind. He can't be that bad, surely!

Will report back.

16

IVOR

January 2025

Getting into Phillip and Audrey's house without using the front door is second nature. Used to do it all the time if me and Becky had planned to stay at her's but had stayed late at a hostelry without her key.

Their taxi disappearing in a puff of dust, I return to the back of the house.

The first time I came here they sat me down and tried to point out Wimbledon tennis courts – which I could barely see – and Audrey went on and on about trees and plants, all the while completely ignoring how neglected the garden was.

Even in the darkness now, you can see it's shabby. Phillip insists on doing all the pruning himself, which leaves the shrubs overgrown, the lawn patchy and the fence – which is flanked by tall ash trees – looking like it's given up on itself. To be fair, I'd give up on myself if I lived with the Burrowses. But why live in a sprawling house with a mega garden yet not pay for it to be maintained? Classic Burrows behaviour.

The orangey G&T they served me that day was nice though, I will at least state that for the record.

They never hid a key outside, but Phillip always left a small rectangular window unlocked in case he got locked out himself. It's not the largest one on the south-facing wall of the home, in fact it might be the smallest. But it was always big enough for me to heave myself through, even under the influence.

The catch is that the human cat-flap is about 9 ft up the wall.

A moss-ridden garden bench rests against the same wall, further along the patio. Plucking leather gloves out of my jeans pockets – Dad would never head to 'work' without gloves – I drag the slimy bench over, wincing as the wooden legs scrape against the stone.

Once in position I wait, ready to react or flee if a neighbour's light flicks on, disturbed by the commotion. No movement follows, however, leaving me alone, the only noise being the small pant of my own breath in the shadows.

Next, I clamber onto the bench, now below the correct window, and put one steady foot on the back beam. Then the other.

The trick is getting your fingers under the rubber seal of the frame while balancing on the thin strip of wood. I place a hand on each lower corner of the window, curl my fingers under and heave.

Nothing.

I try harder but sway and lose my footing, letting the flats of my heels slap back on to the bench's main seat. Another second's silence to check there's still no suspicion from over the fence.

Nope. Just more appallingly unfit panting from yours truly. That sprint across the park when the Burrowses' lights had gone out is the most exercise I've done in months. Now I have to burn more calories to get inside! Joe Wicks would be struggling at this point.

Hoisting myself up onto the back beam again, I push my thumbs harder into the rubber seal and lean back, letting the frame hold my whole weight in position.

No give.

I leave my thumbs and fingers where they are, adjust my feet on the ledge, then yank my arms harder. There's a cracking sound as the rubber comes away from the base, jolting me backwards off the bench and on to my bum on the patio slabs. It hurts.

But!

The window's opened.

Feet back on the slats, I survey the challenge above. I did do it myself once or twice, very drunk, if I remember right. But I was fitter back then. More often, Becky would give me a push to help me through. I'm far less confident about hauling myself up solo like a marine these days. I'm no Commando – the only way I'll earn that title is if my pants are caught on the way in and ripped clean off.

Horrid memories crowd in. Dad staring at a similar window, hoisting me up, growling under his breath for me to get through it before someone notices.

Stop it – this isn't amoral. This is for Becky. Not burglary, but bravery.

I curl my hands onto the inside of the window as if hanging from the edge of a cliff. My unimpressive arms are not going to endure four or five attempts at yanking my butterball body upwards. I either do it, or I stay stranded outside forever – and probably get eaten by a hungry fox, too exhausted to fend the bugger off.

Dad's voice hisses again. *Just fucking go, you stupid arsehole.*

Deep breath. I get both feet on the back of the bench, squeeze my hands to test the grip is true. And leap.

It's a good leap. Before I know it, my shoulders are resting on the window edge and I'm clawing at the inside of the wall, locating a new nook to cling to as my trainers find some friction on the outside, inching me upwards, and in another second my chest is through the gap, and I'm slipping further and further, tumbling head-first onto the toilet seat like some confused dry baby being born in reverse.

Dazed, I lie on the tiled floor, half-expecting to hear footsteps stampeding towards the noise. Not that they should, Julie will have knocked off by now.

No sound approaches.

Shuffling into a more comfortable position leaning against the wall, I let my puffing level out as my eyes acclimatise to the new shade of darkness.

As soon as this door is opened, an alarm will detect movement. That will give me sixty seconds to reach the closet under the stairs and tap in the correct code. Otherwise, all hell will break loose, sirens will blare, lights will flood the whole property and wider Borough of Merton... I think a text is even sent to Phillip's prehistoric phone, alerting him. It's the one strand of modern technology I need to navigate. And if they don't have the same old stupid code they always did... then I'm screwed.

But I bet you ten Heinekens they haven't changed it.

On my feet, I make my dash, as the metronomic pulse of the alarm bleeps through the house. Into the hall, round the stairs, I open the door to see the small rubber keypad illuminated green against the wall.

I tap at it firmly. 1-7-0-7.

The pulse of the alarm stops and is replaced with... nothing.

Mission accomplished.

1 July 2007. The date of Amy's death. Morbid one to choose. But it was never going to be anything else.

Relief descends; I'm shaking.

I never used to shake when me and Becky sneaked in together, we used to turn the alarm off, giggle, whisper, kiss and creep into the kitchen to open a fresh beverage.

Maybe I should start this visit with a pitstop.

No. No sloppiness, no relaxing. I need that phone. That is the only thing that matters.

My own phone torch on, I head out of the closet and make for Becky's bedroom. It's locked, but the key left in the door twists smoothly and it swings open.

I stop.

My concentrated beam is eerie, only striking any one tiny area at a time. Yet every last thing it hits is trauma.

Her bedspread, her trainers, her desk, her sketches, her wardrobe, her books. It's Becky, everything in here is Becky. But there is no Becky. There's just me, surrounded by blackness, with this tiny ray of light on the past. Gripping the phone tighter, I picture tearing the room apart.

Why are they keeping her room like this? She's not here! It's pretending, acting like everything is fine, when the world has ended. Fuck her parents for leaving it like this. Does it not break their hearts to see her room without her in it? I would have ripped it all out. It means nothing, it's a mirage, a relic. And why the fuck have they still gone out tonight? How dare they? I would have...

My dad squeals at me again. *Stop stalling, you imbecile.*

Squeezing my spare hand into a fist, I hit myself in the jaw... and again. A final slap to the temple bounces me back into the room.

What would Dad do?

Her desk first: no phone. Her drawers: no. Under the bed: no.

I chuck her duvet into the air, letting it fall back down. A waft of her smacks me, that mix of sweet perfume and lemon shampoo.

I fall to my knees. I can't do this. Her smell's still on these sheets, her shoes are still out how she'd left them. I literally couldn't be closer to Becky, alone in her bedroom, sticking my head into every last corner of who she was. And yet Becky isn't here. I'm finally realising it now – she isn't anywhere any more.

I scream. Fuck who hears. I pound the carpet, fists like boulders. This is torture. This is literally the most painful thing I could be doing, bringing her back to life in the emptiest way.

I scream louder, praying it'll hurt, praying it will make me feel better or worse or anything, praying it will distract me for a split-second so I can forget I'm in her bedroom while she will never be in it again.

And why haven't I cried yet? What is wrong with me? The guilt of not getting upset sticks to my goose-bumped flesh like molten tar. I've screamed, I've drunk, I've woken up in icy sweats, but I haven't wept. Why?

Moving on to her bed and pulling the duvet over my head, I think about all the times we spent here, trying to stay quiet as we got as close as it's possible for two people to get.

I turn on to my stomach and breathe her in, staying like that until I'm no longer able to pick out her scent, as it brutally recedes without permission.

You've come this far, Ivor. Don't waste it.

Maybe Becky does still exist somehow. I am here for her, after all. I've promised her I'll find out what happened. Come on. Picking up my hunt, the phone continues to elude me. So weird. If she booked an Uber on it but then left it by accident, it'd surely be in here...

But it's not going to be where she left it, is it? That's the whole point. Her parents are hiding it! They aren't going to have it out on show, are they?

And with that thought, I know exactly where it will be.

I leave Becky's room, making sure to shut the door and re-lock it upon my exit, and cross the landing to Phillip's study.

Phone torch still shining, I swing around the already open door and focus at a large black box on the floor – the family safe.

Becky never understood why her parents insisted on having such a monstrosity in the house. They didn't keep jewellery in it, or cash, or fake passports and a revolver. It appeared to be full of old bank statements and not much else. But if they're keeping hold of her phone, it will definitely be in there. I know this rotten clan too well.

And what's more, if they haven't changed their house alarm code, I bet another ten Heinekens the numbers for the safe are the same too. Six numbers on this occasion, so it will be the full date of Amy's death, not the truncated version.

I kneel down and prop my phone in position so that it shines up at the dial. Amy died on the 1st of July. I twist the dial to zero, then to 1, back to zero, forward to 7. The year was 2007. I twist the dial to 20, technically next it should go back to zero but they ran out of digits so it just ends with the seven. I spin the knob to the final number.

Click. Open she swings.

Boom! Where are all these Heinekens I'm now owed?

Snatching up my torch, I peer inside and 10,000 volts crackle through me.

There it is! Becky's phone. I knew it, I knew it, I knew it!

Honestly, if the lighting was a bit better in here, this whole evening would be worthy of the Ocean's Eleven franchise. Add a tense film score, George Clooney smirking in admiration from the landing, it'd be a blockbuster.

Picking the phone out, I slam the safe shut again and spin the dial.

I freeze.

The faint sound of crunching car tyres grows in the distance.

An engine cuts out, a car door slams.

Clacks of a key rattling in a lock echo through the house and directly up my spine.

The creak of the heavy front door opening buries me in the mire.

They're home.

17

IVOR

January 2025

Why are they back already? They stay all evening at bridge. Always.

My brain's cramping.

Cemented to the spot, my ears strain for the tiniest hint of a foot on the stairs. If they do start coming, I'll rush back to Becky's room.

It's hard to stop my breathing galloping away from me. There's more at stake than just being caught trespassing. They might realise I've got the phone, they might call the police. Man skulking around dead girlfriend's family home... it doesn't scream innocent. Detectives would start investigating me, wasting resources that desperately need to be directed towards unravelling what really happened. A whole alternate life plays out, one where I never find out the truth, a trial, an unsympathetic jury, a life sentence, labelled a murderer forever, Becky's actual killer never caught.

And yet why should I cower? They're the ones hiding her

phone. They're the ones who ran her self-esteem into the ground. They're the ones who seem to be lying about their first daughter's death, too. If anyone is involved, it's them. I know it! How dare I be left to feel guilty for anything, next to these two?

I can hear Dad's cackle in my ear. He was never so careless as to get caught in someone's house. *You couldn't even steal a living, stupid sod.* That's what he'd say.

There's a faint clatter downstairs – maybe from the kitchen.

Turning my phone torch off, I shuffle to the door and keep my keen ears peeled. They aren't talking, it's silent except for the clanking. I risk a step out onto the landing – it'll make it easier to dash back to Becky's bedroom if I can see one of them coming towards the staircase.

More noise from the kitchen, as if one of them is knocking glasses together. There's a faint popping noise I know all too well, they're opening a bottle of wine.

Something isn't right. What is it? The initial surge of abject fear has passed, my mind able to grasp the present more fully. Why haven't they turned any lights on? The hall lamp's off, there's no glow coming from the kitchen. And why aren't they talking? They should have noticed the house alarm wasn't triggered when they got in, should be speculating as to whether they'd forgotten to set it, or why it's broken. And where's the sound of the taxi retreating up the endless driveway? I heard the car approaching before anything else, but didn't hear it go.

I'm contemplating another shadowy step towards the staircase when a head moves into view, dark but clear on the ground floor. A fresh spike of terror and a millisecond's gasp thankfully go unnoticed as I watch the silhouette saunter across the hall and into the Burrowses' main lounge.

That wasn't Phillip or Audrey Burrows. Is that... their housekeeper, Julie? She looked like she was holding a bottle of wine and a plate of something. She disappears into the far room, still turning no lights on, but then a silvery sheen leaks round the doorframe and the sound of canned laughter from the TV fills the house.

Is she just helping herself to the house and its contents? I contemplate creeping downstairs, wandering in and asking her if she needs a hand with the wine. Hmm, which of us would be liable for the dry-cleaning bill if she shat herself on the sofa cushions?

I never liked Julie. I once accidentally pronounced quinoa as kwi-noah while she was serving it up for dinner, and she looked at me as if I'd just got a swastika tattooed on my nose.

Right. What now? At least it isn't the lord and lady of the house. Need to get the hell out of dodge and find a lovely, peaceful pub in which to pore over what's on Becky's phone. I'll go out through the back door in the kitchen – it'll make less noise.

I move my feet, inch by inch, towards the top of the staircase, with its polished mahogany banister sweeping round, the dramatic centrepiece in the cavernous front hall. But even my tiny steps feel like they tear through the house, giving me away with their duplicitous, high-pitched squeak. I kneel, drawing another unbearable creak from the old floorboards. Undoing my laces, I slip off both shoes, stretch back up and attempt to slide my feet flat along the carpet. This is successful until I reach the top step, gently place my left heel on to the second step, and quickly lift it up again as even the small touch of pressure elicits an agonisingly loud groan from the wooden frame.

I stand, one foot planted, the other in mid-air, my shoes tucked under one arm, Becky's phone still grasped in that hand, the stress keeping my other arm locked out at my side. I might as well be the little teapot – short and caught out. But after about a minute standing statue-still – a minute that feels like a decade – cool relief seeps in. She didn't hear. The reprieve doesn't last long though. Because there is no way I can get down all of these stairs without blowing my cover.

The upstairs corridor and landing stretch out in both directions, so dark I can't see the doors at either end. I lower myself into a sitting position on the landing, still able to spy on the entrance to the room Julie is using. A calmness ebbs through me again as I grow in confidence that I'm not going to be caught. Not for now, anyway. It gives me time to think.

I know what code Becky's phone password will be. Only the fear that it will beep and alert the hungry housekeeper downstairs stops me busting it open here and now. There must be something incriminating on there for her parents to have lied to the police about it. Once I find it, do I go straight to law enforcement? But then they'll demand, 'how did you come by this information?' or 'how did you come to be in possession of Ms Burrows' handset?'... because that's how law enforcement talk. Maybe I find out what's on the phone, sneak it back into the safe, then tell the police I have a suspicion, even though I'll know damn well what the truth is. But should I risk breaking in again after tonight's close shave? I could post the phone to the police maybe.

Ideas, plots, conspiracies and painful, palpable memories of Becky congeal. All I want is for her to open her bedroom door, beckon me over and hold my hand as I enter. Then she'll shut the door, tell me to ignore Julie, and we'll lie on her bed, foreheads touching, and discuss how we're going to renovate my flat, finally get the shower fixed, start trying for a baby again. I want my ordinary life back, with my extraordinary woman. And yet here I am, skulking around her abominable parents' house looking for clues, because she's...

There's movement. I check my own phone, Julie's been in there over an hour.

The tinny noise of the TV cuts out, as do the soft slivers of light. Then she's walking back across the hall, wine bottle seemingly empty. More bumping and bashing in the kitchen, the sound of a tap gushing – she's cleaning up after herself, leaving no trace.

Still working in the almost pitch black, she walks back towards the front door. It looks like she's got four more bottles under her arms. Is she stealing lots of tasty booze off the Burrowses? If she is, then my estimation of her will be going up exponentially. She awkwardly grapples with the handle as her armpits remain pinned down over the beverages. The latch eventually comes free and she opens the front door, stronger moonlight confirming the plonk she is most definitely purloining. Then she stops, snaps round.

I lean back as far as I can, out of sight.

Has she seen me? Did she hear me somehow?

I imagine her eyes pinned to the top of the staircase, daring herself to come up and make sure the coast is clear. I plead my pounding heart won't give me away, but it thuds all the louder. Her footsteps move back away from the front door, clipping against the floor.

This is it, she's coming.

But the noise dies away as she walks back through the ground floor of the house.

A succession of beeps echo through the walls.

The alarm! She's setting the alarm!

A loud droning blare warns the house that the alarm is about to go live. I lean forward again and watch her trot back through the open front door. She swings round, bottles still clamped to her person, leans in, yanks the handle shut, and ten seconds later, I can hear the most splendid sound as her car tyres crunch over gravel, quieter and quieter, until I am left alone with only the occasional shrill bleep of the house alarm for company.

I need a beer.

18

BECKY'S DIARY

Tuesday 26 October 2021

I feel so guilty. Meeting Ivor's dad was horrible. Every time I think about it, I want to crawl out of my own skin and die.

I can see why Ivor really didn't want me to meet him. I was so adamant: if he had to meet Mum and Dad, I had to meet Jeff. I should have listened. Urgh, what a stupid, pathetic, immature girl. Why is he with me?

His dad's at Belmarsh. We got the train from London Bridge to Plumstead, a station I'd never even heard of before, and Ivor was a bit off already. Not annoyed, but like, nervous… reticent is probably the best word. It made the journey quiet and awkward, like we'd had a fight even though we hadn't.

He insisted on going into a pub near the station, said it was 'his ritual' before seeing his dad. If it were me and I was expecting something to be horrific I'd just want it out of the way, so at this point I felt like he was stalling. This is at like 11 in the morning, by the way. You shouldn't drink in the morning unless you're at an airport or a music festival, they're just the rules. I let it slide, and we went in for one, but when he suggested a second, I flat-out refused and dragged us both back on to the road.

The prison wasn't very nice when we got there. Not sure what I was expecting. I knew it wouldn't be hotel vibes, but it immediately made me feel sorry for Ivor having to live there for so long. It is bleak! Not quite Azkaban bleak, but I can see where J.K. Rowling got her inspiration for prison guards that suck the soul out of you, because everything felt so grey and unnerving. The weird, varnished brick walls, the echoey, unfamiliar noises, the cracked window and flickering light at reception as we reached the visitor area.

But maybe it's not supposed to be inviting. If you were tempted to commit crime before, a day-visit to a jail is an effective deterrent, I'd say.

When we got through to the chairs and tables, the air was thick with detergent. It was like sucking in chilli flakes, prickling my throat.

By this point, Ivor was silent and pale as a sheet. Not sure what was hitting him harder, preparing to see his dad or being back in this place. Honestly, I've never seen him anything like it before.

I didn't know what Jeff looked like, obviously, but then Ivor yanked me sideways and we were staring down at a man chained to the table in front of us, his long black straggly hair flopping over the back of the seat. The man looked up and I could tell – they have the same downturned eyes. Not that he held them the same way. Ivor's are relaxed and easy, creasing at the corners from smiling. This man's were stern, set in stone.

He told Ivor he was late and called him something nasty. I can't remember exactly what now, but it was pretty mean, so I half expected his wrinkly, cross face to smirk, like it was father-son banter. But he didn't. Instead, he turned to me, and without missing a beat added: 'You could have at least brought me someone easy on the eye.'

To me, it was so obviously an insult for the sake of it, almost ready-prepared. Like my dad with his chinos jibe.

But Ivor snapped. SUPER-protective, telling his dad he could insult him but that it was out of order to speak about me like that.

Jeff – this man I'd just met who honestly looked like he was about 150 years old, his skin so haggard and shoulders so hunched – did smirk now. And when Ivor was finished telling him off, his only response was: 'So she wears the trousers. Doesn't surprise me.'

Then we sat there while Ivor tried to make conversation. And I had to watch as his dad turned every morsel of information, every caring action or genuine question Ivor asked into some shaming, hyper-critical insult.

At one point, Ivor mentioned that it was his mum's birthday coming up, and his dad told him in this weird, matter-of-fact way that his mother never wanted Ivor and that it was Ivor who killed her, so he didn't know why Ivor was bothered about her birthday.

WTAF?

She died in childbirth, that's not Ivor's fault. Even having to write that seems superfluous. Imagine living your whole life without your mum and with your dad BLAMING you for her death. It's emotional cruelty beyond belief.

Thinking about it all now, maybe I should have stuck up for Ivor, told his dad what an amazing, kind-hearted man his son has become. Urgh, the more I dwell... I definitely should have stuck up for him. I didn't say a word the whole time. Jeff didn't engage with me once, for his part, but Ivor looked so sad and defeated as his dad rained down blow after blow. It was insane.

When we came away about 20 minutes later, off the site, breathing in fresh, fresh air again, I stopped him in the street and asked what on earth had just happened.

He could barely look at me. I wasn't asking because I was annoyed, I was asking because we have been together nearly four months now (three months and 23 days since our first date!) and I'm only just finding out what a disgusting, bitter, vicious person his dad is. He did try to tell me, I suppose, but I thought he was exaggerating. This is the person who raised Ivor! How on earth has he turned out so sensitive and kind when his only parent is such a beast?

'Why do you go and see him? Why do you go and see him?' I kept saying in a panic.

'Hopefully deep down he appreciates it,' he said. 'Things went down for him after Mum died and I suppose it *was* kind of my fault.'

You could dive to the bottom of the Mariana Trench and it wouldn't be deep enough to find whatever validation Ivor is still searching for from that vile man. I told him over and over again that his mum dying was NOT his fault in any way, but it didn't feel like it got through, if I'm honest.

Why why why didn't I stick up for him? Why do I never say anything? It's the same problem all over again. I'm spineless. Ivor's dad said one mean thing to me and Ivor shot him down. I watch Ivor get eviscerated, the man I love, bullied and abused for no reason, and I have nothing? I feel so so so bad on so many levels.

And what if his dad's right? What if it wasn't a ready-made insult but one he thought of when he saw me – and everyone is thinking I'm ugly and Ivor could do better?

Today has been shitty.

One small lighter note from the visit, I suppose, was that Jeff also says 'agua mineral' instead of 'water'. It's a tiny quirk but I'd never known why Ivor called it that, now I know he gets it from his dad. That's the kind of cute little piece of the puzzle I was hoping to get from seeing Ivor interact with his family, but my word, was it slim pickings!

The colour returned to Ivor's cheeks relatively quickly once we were back in civilisation. I let him choose what we did for the rest of the day. We kicked around at his for a bit, watched some Gordon

Ramsay meltdowns on YouTube, had sex, though it didn't really feel like either of us was in the mood. That side of things isn't really firing at the moment. I blame our parents!

Eventually, inevitably, he suggested we go to the pub. After that he just seemed relieved I hadn't been put off him by the encounter with his dad. Which I do understand because that's exactly how I felt after he'd met my parents.

Of course I'm not put off Ivor. But wow! Finding out your boyfriend's dad – who he went to prison for! – treats him like that... it's A LOT.

We came back to Mum and Dad's late. Sleeping here coz I'm on opening shift at 6.30 a.m. Ivor had to climb through the open back window then let me in because they'd gone to bed and I'd forgotten a key. Nightmare!

Oh yeah, forgot to say... moved out of Cam's at the weekend. It was either sign up for another year or move out and I'm just not saving any money while renting. Ivor is desperate for me to move in with him. I've said I will, but only after he gets the shower fixed, and actually buys a double duvet for his bed so we can BOTH sleep underneath it. Honestly, how do men cope living in such pigsties?! I've mainly managed to keep out of Mum and Dad's way since I've been home, which is good.

Hopefully won't be back with them long, but I'm determined to start saving. There's a Level 2 veterinary assistant diploma I've found at the College of Animal Welfare. It looks perfect. Studying, work experience, contact with actual pets during the training. It's £1,750 and takes 18 months if you do it part time. Told Dad about it, but he's refusing to help with the cost because he doesn't think 'the career path' is well paid enough. Trying not to think about it too much, it makes me too angry.

I've said to Ivor we should go to Sandbanks soon, stay with the Montagues. I want him to see it is possible to have healthy family relationships. I know Wes and Faith aren't technically family, but they might as well be.

I texted Faith this evening and she says we should go before Christmas. Ivor seems keen.

He's asleep next to me now, mouth open, breathing like Darth Vader. I knew he'd pass out as soon as we lay down, he always drinks so much. I'll let him off today.

Did check with Faith that Dillon won't be there and asked her not to mention that we went out.

I don't like thinking about him these days. I was so broken after we finished, but they say it takes the next one to push the last one out. I don't know who 'they' are, but I think they're probably right.

It wouldn't serve any purpose for Ivor to know how serious me and Dillon were. Probably shouldn't even write it in my diary. But I know Ivor. He would never read any of this behind my back. Bless him.

Mum and Dad won't want me to take Ivor to the Montagues'. They'll decide Ivor's going to go there and, like some weird Sherlock Holmes, immediately start putting clues and deductions together about Amy.

Screw my parents.

I should go to sleep. Alarm's set for 6 a.m. Yuck! Definitely not going to be able to sleep though, still haunted by how nasty Jeff was to Ivor.

I'll start Chamber of Secrets again. I love when Fred, George and Ron come and rescue Harry and Hedwig from the Dursleys and whisk them back to the Weasleys' house (called The Burrow, ironically!). That's how I always felt going to the Montagues'. Amy was literally killed there, and it still feels like a sanctuary compared to every waking second with Mum and Dad here. Now, that's saying something!

Another thing that's bugging me. OK... one final thought then I promise I'll read. Ivor's dad, Jeff, is vile to him even though Ivor lied to the police and went to prison trying to protect him. My parents forced me – and the Montagues – to lie to the police to avoid them going to prison and they are equally ungrateful. If I went and told a detective now what really happened, it'd be game over. Yet they never ever acknowledge that. It's infuriating.

19

IVOR

January 2025

'It was always the code!' I yell, thumping the phone down on the
sticky table.

Noz drains his pint, puts his glass down on a sodden beer
mat and brushes a hand over his scalp.

'It's all on here. I know it!' I tell him, whether he wants to
listen or not. 'And the code was always our first date.'

'She musta changed it,' he says.

'Einstein alert!'

'Oi! I'm trying to help!' he bites back. 'I'll get the next round
in, but cool it, yeah?'

He waves over a passing member of bar staff and asks for
two fresh pints, the dim lights from the Joiner's Arms' lamps
bouncing off his empty head.

Oh, Noz, always three goals short of a hat-trick.

I'm a heavy drinker but he's something else. Has he got a
problem? Dunno. But my goodness does he rely on the drink to
get him through every single day. Hence why he was free to

come to the pub at a moment's notice when I got back to Finchley.

Sometimes I wonder if I should kick it for a bit, go sober. Not Dry January, obviously, that's for falafel-scoffing graduates and dads having a midlife crisis. But a few days to reset could be good, give the liver a holiday. Noz would never do that. When he got flu, he filled a mug up with whisky, warmed it up in the microwave, stirred in a Lemsip, then gulped the whole thing down in one. I've never seen anything like it. To be fair, I think he bamboozled the virus too because twenty-four hours later we were back out at the pub and he seemed right as rain.

Any thought of abstaining is put on hold as the barmaid comes back with our two new juicy pints of Heineken.

'Bloody hell, you'd get less head in a brothel,' Noz cries, holding his frothy pint up.

I apologise profusely to the woman for my friend's vulgarity, making sure to leave a big tip before tapping my card on the payment machine she's holding.

As for Noz's T-shirt today – it's pale orange, stretched over his huge stomach with black writing on the front in a hand-written script – 'If the world's flat, so's my belly'. Self-deprecating, at least.

'What should I do?' I ask, more in desperation than hope.

Noz stands up to rearrange himself then plonks back down, the barstool squealing under his heft. 'Hand the phone to police,' he says. 'They can break into it.'

'Too suspicious,' I say, certain what I don't want to do, even if I can't summon the brainpower to plot what I do want to happen. 'They'd want to know how I got it, then either they wouldn't believe me, or they would and they'd arrest me for burglary.'

'The family business,' Noz chuckles with a wink. I respond with my middle finger.

Noz knew my father a bit. Dad and his mates used to drink in the Old Bull & Bush in Hampstead; Noz washed glasses in there. Believe it or not, I didn't drink at all back then. Hated what it did to Dad. But he'd drag me along anyway. I must have been sixteen. Dad used to tank up in the Bull then hit whatever house he had planned for that night. The sickness I'd feel in the pit of my stomach as I sat there waiting was abominable. What would they demand of me tonight? Fit my skinny arms through a letterbox? Scale a trellis? Keep guard out front? Even recalling it makes me shrink in fear.

I'd gone to sit away from Dad, something I often did. But for the first time ever someone noticed – Noz.

'You look like you need a drink,' he'd said, running a disgustingly unclean cloth around the inside of a Guinness glass behind the bar.

I looked at him but didn't say anything.

'What d'you want? It's on me, fella.'

I looked over at Dad, the jokes he was telling, the wheezy snigger, the way he was talking to a barmaid collecting empties.

'Just a Coke please,' I'd told Noz.

He shook his head, walked round the side of the bar and came to hulk over me. I remember thinking he looked enormous but friendly. Shrek, not Godzilla.

And then he whispered: 'Maybe if you seem too drunk, they'll leave you here when they go.'

Noz knew what my dad was, knew his reputation. But, vitally, could see I wanted nothing to do with it.

And he was right, I drank so much that night that Dad's mates convinced him I'd be no good on the job. I'd been saved.

Saved by Noz and six pints of Carlsberg Export. I threw up obviously, but that was no price to pay.

So that was it. I'd sit at the bar chatting with Noz every time Dad went in there after that, making sure to order so many drinks I couldn't possibly be relied upon for any late-night nonsense.

Eventually Dad and his mates moved to another pub, found a new area to terrorise. And by then, they'd given up on me. I don't know why I was too scared to just come out and tell Dad I didn't want to help him. Now I have to live with all that guilt. But Noz helped me get out. So I carried on going to the Bull and stayed friends with Noz.

He met me the day I was released too. That meant a hell of a lot. Actions speak louder than words, and him driving his van to Belmarsh so I'd have someone there to collect me was a decibel-defying act. Yep, like it or not, this Great British beefcake is my best friend.

The first time we fell out was when I met Becky. As fun as it was to have a mate, it never stopped me wanting a girlfriend too, someone to adore, to experience that chaotic mix of lust and love with. It caused friction, the times I couldn't see him, or Becky would want me all to herself. Noz never said it, but I think he was jealous I found that romantic, forever-love with someone.

And now she's gone. No wonder Noz doesn't seem too sad, he's got his best mate back. I'm grasping my glass almost tightly enough to crush it, as he prattles on about starting an OnlyFans where he sleeps with beautiful women.

'You could do a guest video,' he informs me. 'Don't worry about size, stick four inches in three times, it's as good as twelve.'

He guffaws, I don't respond. I can feel my flamethrower turning on him. He needs to shut the fuck up. Becky is dead.

'Ah... you're worried about getting stage fright on camera, aren't ya?' he says. 'Trade secret – pop a couple of blueys, it'll be like a Roman column.'

I sip my beer and exhale slowly. 'Cam said she'd looked up Amy Burrows' death and it was suspicious.'

Noz's smile plummets, eyes almost rolling into the back of his head, he's so bored of the topic.

I don't care. 'Apparently, the police didn't close the case for way longer than would usually be the case if it was a simple fall from a balcony. Phil and Aud stalled over being interviewed. Other stuff too. And why were they hiding Becky's phone? Why was she holding that necklace when she fell? Cam doesn't reckon it's hers. And what self-respecting parents go out to bridge club less than seven days after their only surviving daughter has been found dead? It's not right.'

We sit in near silence, suckling our pints. Such an error asking him to meet tonight, I need someone to take this seriously, he just wants to talk bollocks. But who else do I have?

Definitely didn't need this last beer, either. It's hitting me hard, dragging me down. Maybe I will have a few days off drinking.

Noz's eyes bulge, staring at his phone. 'What the...?'

'Wha'?' I grunt, taking another gulp of lager.

He turns the screen to face me. It's a BBC News alert.

Arrest made over death of 25-year-old Rebecca Burrows

I snatch the phone off him and read the words again. I tap on the link.

A twenty-seven-year-old man has been arrested. Police enquiries continue. No more information at this time.

The words take an age to settle, my booze-soaked brain clunking along in second gear.

'Somone's bin arres'd,' I splutter, the soft lights of the pub roving in my peripheral vision as I fail to centre myself. I am not sober enough for this news.

'Ivor? You...'

I don't hear what he says next, I don't remember making the call, but in a second I am holding my own phone up to my ear.

'Hello?' comes the answer down the line.

I can't find any words. I listen to the voice repeating itself, everything blurring and swaying as I look at it.

'Hello... Mr O'Foyle?' the voice tries again.

'Ivor.' That's the only word I can muster.

'Ivor, this is Tina Schwarz. Did you mean to call?' the detective asks.

'Yeah.'

'OK...'

Arrested. Someone's been arrested. But not the Burrowses. A twenty-seven-year-old. Someone did kill Becky. When I find out who, I'm going to...

'Ivor, I am very busy, what is it?' she snaps, into my silence.

''Oo's bin urrested?' I slur.

'I'm sorry, Ivor, but we're not sharing that with the public at the moment.'

'I'm not public! I'm 'er boyfriend!'

'Ex-boyfriend,' she states.

'No, we were gettin' things back—'

'Ivor, Miss Burrows' parents made it very clear you were her ex-boyfriend. She had been seeing someone else when she died. I know this must be an incredibly hard time, but—'

'Seein' someone else! Who?' I shout. Noz looks uncomfortable as people on neighbouring tables glance at me with their catty, judgmental side-eyes.

'Please calm down,' the detective instructs. 'If you've been drinking, I suggest you—'

'You can't believe a thing Phil'n'Aud say! What else 'ave they said? You've got it all wrong. She wasn't seein' anyone! They're lyin'! Who 'ave you arrested? Who did it?'

'It's late, Ivor. Unless there's anything else, I suggest you sleep it off, OK?'

Hanging up, I swear into my phone screen.

Then I order a double whisky. Then another. And another.

20

IVOR

January 2025

I twitch my neck – a first, brave interaction with the day. The movement only confirms I must stay straitjacket-still. The slightest spasm will buckle my skull.

What happened last night?

The glacial move towards consciousness does not bring solace, only awareness. Lying on my back, the duvet is a furnace broiling me from above. I can't move.

The very act of existing is a cruel, unrequested punishment. Thoughts twist in my head like barbed wire through flesh; the poison still pumping around me; each piteous breath only extending this demise.

My lips pulse, my tongue is wooden and unpliable. I need water. My head, my mouth, my body, shrivelled and dying, scream for agua mineral. But I cannot move. Not yet. I imagine a beautiful gorge with a spring, a plunge pool to dive into. I wouldn't stop gulping until I'd drained the whole stream.

A sharp stab of panic. Someone was arrested. I phoned DCI Schwarz.

She said I wasn't Becky's boyfriend.

I cringe at memories of shouting down the phone in front of Noz and the crowded pub.

The taste of stale Bells rolls out of me. I don't know what the right amount of whisky is for a person to have, but I definitely had the wrong amount. My stomach spasms in terror at the mere recollection of such a mortal enemy.

Plucking up the courage to open my right eye a fraction, I'm comforted to confirm I am in my own room and can see my phone sitting loyally on the bedside table. Next to it are Becky's phone and her bear pendant necklace. Noz said I should hand the phone in. How can I?

I hover a shaky arm towards the table and pull my phone back on to the bed. The roll on to my side is executed with all the requisite time and caution that medics would take to move a paraplegic. I glance down at the screen. There's only one notification, an email from my area manager, telling me to take two weeks' compassionate leave, effective immediately, and that she'll be talking to Trish about her 'stiff management style'. I re-fuse my right eye shut and gingerly roll onto my back.

You know the hangover's bad when you absent-mindedly start drafting up a will in your head. I haven't got much to pass on. I do have Becky's phone now. Although without the password it's about as useful as a kamikaze pilot's helmet.

Another hour is required to summon the courage to scale the great divide between here and the bathroom. Crawling through the hall, still naked, I am awake enough to ponder whether this degrading scene is a new nadir, not just for me personally, but for humanity as a whole. Heaving myself up to the rim of the sink, my knees flat on the floor, I hook my elbows over the porcelain and peer into the mirror.

Bloodshot eyes, hair flat on one side and electrified on the other, bags under my eyes, dark and crinkly as raisins.

Ladies, form an orderly queue.

Turning on the cold tap, I put my mouth underneath and let the liquid overflow out of my mouth and trickle soothingly down my cheek into the sink as I gulp. With the life-giving hydration, today's physical pain reduces... and yesterday's rage floods back.

Schwarz said Becky had been seeing someone else. Is that who they've arrested? Did he kill her? He must have done, otherwise why the arrest?

I take a piss the colour of black tea, then return to bed.

She couldn't have a new boyfriend. We met up before New Year's Eve. She'd texted that she loved me! No way was there anyone else. I feel icky, like I've just found out Becky was cheating. But I know she wasn't. It's her parents lying to the police. It's always her fucking parents.

Shutting my eyes, the next time I open them and check the time, it says it's 4 p.m. Must have dozed off. I feel like a different man. Sleep and agua mineral working miracles, as they so often do.

The Burrowses are lying to police, and I'm not having it.

I open the Uber app. Who cares if Phillip notices me using their account? They can pay for all my travel until they tell the truth, or until they have their assets frozen and are arrested. I tap in their address and have a driver on the way within two minutes, leaving barely enough time to pull on some cleanish clothes, gargle with mouthwash and kick on some trainers.

In a surprise to absolute nobody, the vehicle that arrives is a white Toyota Prius.

'SW19?' the Cockney woman asks as I get into the back.

'Yeah. Can we go left rather than right at the lights though, please? Need to stop off at Greggs quickly, if that's OK?'

* * *

So glad the Uber driver let me devour all three sausage rolls en route. Not my usual order but I need all the strength I can get. And I did at least try to brush away the flaky debris off her valeted seats before I got out.

Knock, knock, knock. The housekeeper opens the door as usual.

'Hello Julie.' I wear a smile so insincere it's a wonder she doesn't lamp me. After years of looking down her nose at me to impress her masters, it feels immensely gratifying to have some dirt on her. Stealing from the bosses. Tut, tut, tut. A stay of execution is called for today, however.

'You are not welcome here,' she states firmly, as if she's a priest, mid-exorcism.

'Are they in? Their car's in. I bet they're in.'

Curiosity kills the chat prematurely as Audrey clippety-clops across the tiled hall in unnecessary heels. She shuts her eyes upon seeing me.

'You told DCI Schwarz Becky has a new boyfriend.'

'Had,' she corrects. 'Rebecca had a boyfriend. She's dead, Ivor.'

The cold, unfeeling words lash me. Like tenses matter at a time like this!

She peers at me, then exhales. 'You'd better come in.'

I'm shown through to the lounge Julie used as her personal entertainment arcade last night. Audrey asks the housekeeper to 'fix a pot of tea', then follows me into the room. It's as old-school shabby chic as the other sitting room, the one with the yummy cognac. But given last night's exertions, a nice cup of tea might sit better.

The room has two custard yellow sofas set next to each other, both angling slightly towards a television set that would be too small for my flat, never mind a fourteen-room mansion. There's a soft smell of old leather coming from the enormous wall of hardbacks opposite, and a candle on a small coffee table offers a scent of cinnamon much more suited to Christmas than dreary January. Is it still January? Every second feels like it's crept by since I found Becky's body, and yet the days all seem to have flown past in a jumble.

The fact I was here only last night, hiding from Julie... it could be weeks ago, so much has happened. In the intervening hours, I've literally had enough beer and Bells to kill a basilisk. Becky would like that joke.

'I'd better get Phillip,' Audrey drawls, her mauve eyeshadow and blow-dried blonde hair looking exactly the same as they always do.

I wait on the sofa furthest from the front door. A photo frame sits on the mantel to the right of the tiny television. Six people standing in a row, leaning up against railings, with the beach behind them. It is the only photo of Becky in the whole house taken after her sister died. No pictures of her at her high school leavers' ball, no pictures of her as a teenager. None of her as a strong-willed, inspiring young woman. The house is almost entirely stuck in a past prior to Amy's death. And even this one more recent photo isn't solely of Becky. Yes, she's in it, giving an unconvincing half-smile, dressed more for a gig than a splash in the sea behind her – ripped jeans, Super Mario T-shirt, her hair dip-dyed blonde, worn down over her shoulders, aged about eighteen. But it also has her parents to her left, then the

Montagues, and on the far right their son, I guess. I've not met him, but he popped up in a lot of photographs at the Montagues' house in Sandbanks. Becky's parents seem about as happy as she does in the snap. If you are going to choose one single picture to encapsulate your whole life post-Amy, why choose one where none of you look like you want to be there? Or maybe that's the point. It would be very Burrowses.

Audrey returns with her husband, forever exuding grey-gammon fury.

'Make it quick,' he barks, not looking at me, pacing up and down the room in dirty khaki trousers, a threadbare checked shirt, brown socks and sandals – gardening attire.

The brass neck of these aristo-twats to make me feel unwelcome, when they are actively misleading the police about Becky. 'The police say Becky has a boyfriend...'

'Had!' Audrey interrupts, shaking her head.

'...had a boyfriend apart from me when she died. That's not fucking true, is it!'

Julie comes in with the tray of tea, as if summoned by my profanity.

'She did,' Phillip states without feeling, still marching around the room. 'She'd dated him before you, she had her...' he flaps an annoyed hand at me as he searches for the words, 'her... foray with you, then they were back together when—'

'Don't you dare,' I snarl. 'What me and Becky had was not—'

'Ivor,' Phillip says, stern, clear and clipped. He never says my name out loud. 'You're delusional.'

'Stop it!' I'm on my feet, up in his face, a fraction taller than him as we come nose to nose. 'You can't erase me. We spent years together. Stop wishing me away.'

'And then you cheated on her,' Audrey snipes, mincing over to provide backup to her spineless spouse.

I clear my throat and lower my voice back down. 'It was a misunderstanding. I would never do that. Never.'

A hot prickly sweat stabs at the back of my neck. 'We were working it out,' I mutter to the floor. 'We'd met up after Christmas.'

They share a minuscule glance.

'I don't know what to tell you, Ivor,' Audrey says, shaking her head but appearing to appreciate the calmer tones. 'She was with Dillon. They were both here on Christmas Day, they spent the autumn together, they were planning a trip away in January.'

'Who's Dillon?' I demand.

'He was her childhood sweetheart, back when—'

'We don't have to tell him anything, Audrey,' Phillip spits, still glowering at this insect in his lounge, desperate to squash me under the heel of his sandal.

'Is he who's been arrested?' I direct the question at Audrey, who looks away, pursing her lips.

'Is it?' I ask again, staring at Phillip now. He meets my eye, but his glare is a brick wall.

'What happened on New Year's Eve? Becky left her phone here and got a taxi to—'

Audrey can't help herself. 'How do you know—'

'Audrey!' Philip cuts in. 'Quiet!'

'She texted me, told me you'd told her everything about her sister Amy. What happened? This Dillon, did she go with him?'

Audrey sits down, head in hands. Are they finally going to... Is this it? The confession? My vision thins in a light-headed haze.

Phillip's forehead glistens in a way it wasn't when he entered the room. He moves an inch closer – garlic breath so potent it could slay a vampire.

Our eyes reconnect and a sober chill clears my swimming

thoughts. He doesn't look vulnerable or upset. He looks fero-
cious. 'Our daughter has died. We are mourning. How dare you
make us feel like suspects!' he growls under his breath, baring
his teeth. 'We will not have our names dragged through the
mud. Not again.'

His words are kerosene to a bonfire. 'ARE YOU FUCKING
SERIOUS! You had the most amazing, beautiful daughter. And
all you care about is your names. All she ever wanted was to be
loved for who she was. But you hated that. You resented it. It
embarrassed you. You're not mourning, you'd have to care about
her to mourn.'

'We loved them both!' Audrey cries, before letting out a
short, pained howl.

'Loved? You despised her!' I say. 'And you despised me for
encouraging her.'

'Get out!' Phillip shouts, pointing at the door.

'What happened that night?' I try once more.

'GET OUT!' he roars, jaw locked, a feral look in his eyes.

I push my shoulders back, tall and broad, take an inch
forward myself and bear down on him, the yellows of his eyes
jittering as his pupils flick from one of my eyes to the other and
then back again. My voice is controlled and calm. 'The worst
thing is, you should have loved Becky even more after what
happened to Amy, but you made her feel like the wrong sister
died. And now look.'

No one speaks as I retreat, passing Julie still holding her tray
of tea and biscuits, and let myself out.

They will never give me the truth. But that's OK, I'm going to
take it anyway.

STAGE 3 – BARGAINING

21

IVOR

January 2025

I did not cheat on Becky. I didn't. I'd remember. Somehow that stupid dating app got on to my phone. But I don't even recall downloading it. Why would I? I was happy, ecstatic, with Becky. I never wanted anyone else, ever. But she found the app, and of course me denying it sounded fake.

I must have added it as a dare or unfunny joke while I was steaming one night. A dense, insurmountable doom descends all around me: the same shame I feel when imagining all those homes I helped Dad burgle. Two deplorable acts so opposite to who I am as a person, so heinous and selfish and awful. And yet those are the only two things people are going to think of when they see me at Becky's funeral today. The Burrowses will have poisoned the well, good and proper.

Was that Ivor at the service? Wasn't he that boyfriend Becky had who'd been to jail and then cheated on her?

Middle-class tittle tattle, perfect gossip over sausage rolls and white wine at the wake.

Still haven't cried. I'd better not disintegrate during the service, surrounded by people I despise who may be hiding something about her death. But if today can help lay to rest that corpse on the cliffs that's haunting me, that would be something.

I check myself in the bathroom mirror. My only white shirt, my darkest pair of jeans and my scuffed work shoes. Is that smart enough? Who cares? They're all going to judge me anyway.

Arriving early for the service, I go in search of a Greggs, but there isn't one, so I'm forced to enter a Gail's instead. A change of scene might be nice, I try to tell myself. Yeah right! A change of scene might be nice? I'm sure that's what passengers on the Titanic said as they swapped their warm bunks for a quick dip in the North Atlantic. Gail's was three times the price and my sausage roll wasn't even warm. Useless.

Ice-cold snack eaten, I then sit in a church Becky never visited, listening to a vicar she never knew, and reassure myself that my attire is the least offensive thing about this thoughtless abomination of a memorial. Hail rattles against the stained-glass windows to my left, making it hard to hear the empty poem and eulogy when Audrey and Phillip step forward to deliver them. A small mercy from God, perhaps.

Despite being punctual, I've plonked myself on the back row in the corner of the cavernous room. Mr Inconspicuous. Which is decent of me – more than decent! I deserve to be on the front row, right next to the coffin, my grief pouring out onto the altar for everyone in the cheap seats to witness. If everyone in this congregation was fairly ranked according to how much they cared about Becky, I'd be leading the world's bleakest conga line.

As it is, I wasn't even informed the funeral was taking place. Becky's old friend Cam had texted me to double check I was coming, accidentally letting me in on the secret. In one sense, I don't blame the Burrowses for not telling me. They despised me already. And then I gave them both barrels in their own lounge. What did I expect? A bereavement massage and two complimentary tickets to the Emirates?

So no, I won't make a scene. I'll keep a low profile, sit with Cam and keep my countless beautiful memories of Becky to myself.

She hated death and funerals. It sounds silly, but I don't think she ever made it through Dobby's burial in *Harry Potter* without crying. And when Marley died in *Marley & Me*, she had to take the next day off work.

Every single detail of this event is so completely not Becky. All the more tasteless for the fact the police still haven't closed her case. That speck of truth sticks in the open wound of my heart, uncomfortable and disturbing. They've released the twenty-seven-year-old man they'd arrested without naming him. But they haven't closed the case either. Was it this Dillon character? Is he here? The thought of seeing him sends a sharp zap of horror across my chest. What if he's handsome and smart and makes me look pathetic and useless? What if I see him and realise Becky was never going to stay with a nobody ex-con like me? I almost don't want to see him. But he must be here.

The organ blares out 'Amazing Grace' as the congregation makes a limp, murmuring attempt to sing along. The last verse reads so beautifully.

> *When we've been there ten thousand years,*
> *Bright shining as the sun,*
> *We've no less days to sing God's praise*
> *Than when we've first begun.*

I've never believed in the afterlife, yet a yearning so fierce it makes my shoulders tense pulls at my insides now. Ten thousand years, then ten thousand more, still with Becky. What if it were possible? What would I give?

Everyone sits and Cam yanks my hand down so I'm not left standing alone. All that's happened, every second since Becky went away, it's rushing forth now, racing into view. Oh no. Not now. Focus on something else. Anything. Margaret Thatcher. Property prices. Global warming. Anything! I can't break, not while they're praying, yet I can't stop it.

I let out a gasp and a groan and keep squeezing Cam's hand. An elderly man in front of me turns round, then shifts back to face the front.

Becky. Ten thousand years with Becky. Or ten minutes. One hug, one inhale of her perfume, one laugh. A sob beats out, then another. I let go of Cam and bundle out, running round to the side of the building and falling to my knees. Head against the stone of the looming Anglican church, I swallow the scream that's desperate to erupt. My eyes are squeezed so tight I'm seeing stars on my eyelids. Fierce, stifled cries wrench out of me, a stabbing pang, like there's a hook caught in my ribs, trying to tear the heartbreak from me.

I miss her so much. I don't know how else to put it.

I grab my hair in my fists, yank at it and bang my forehead into the wall.

The separation from her, the knowing she's not here; the pain is physical, like nothing I've ever endured. Beyond agony, beyond torture, impossible to fathom.

Trying to suppress another scream, I grunt into my neck and let my head bob as I bawl, my stomach aching now, fat tears sploshing onto damp gravel. Pushing my closed fists into the ground, I grind the skin against the rock, anything to distract from my life.

I miss her so, so much.

Punching the ground as another whimper wobbles out of me, I think about the—

'Ivor,' Cam whispers.

I peer up, then immediately back down.

She kneels next to me and rubs my back, like a good friend in a bathroom stall on a night out. 'Hey, hey. It's OK. It's OK.'

I glance up at her again but for longer this time. She gives me the kind of small, comforting smile only women seem to possess.

Placing a hand against the stone wall with its lime green blots of lichen, I get to my feet and wipe my eyes with the butts of my palms. 'Want to find a pub?'

'We're going to the wake,' she announces, as if the decision has nothing to do with me.

'Phil will go nuts if—'

'Phillip Burrows will do what every upper-middle-class man does in a situation like this. He'll ignore you to your face and tell his pals he wishes you weren't here behind your back.'

I gaze at her, wondering if she thinks that is a convincing pitch. She looks nice, with darker, heavier eye make-up than when we met up before. She's also worn an old Quidditch T-shirt Becky once got her as a present, something I really appreciate amongst the hordes of blandly dressed, sentimentally inept mourners.

'You deserve to be there as much as anyone else, Ivor. Don't let them win.'

A flame of contrary desire crackles inside me. I give her a small smile and a nod.

22

IVOR

January 2025

Cam and I give the finger food a miss and find a table to ourselves upon arrival at the Rose & Crown. A wake is the perfect social event for Cam because the family are paying the bar tab. Inevitably, she offers to get the first round in.

For their part, Phillip and Audrey are sitting at a table, both looking despondent. I had expected more of a performance from them, keeping up appearances, brave faces and empty conversations, but at the funeral, and now here, they don't seem to have the appetite to pretend they're coping. Maybe laying her to rest broke something, made them realise what they've lost – or what they've done. Even vipers have feelings sometimes.

'Can I just ask,' Cam starts as she comes over with our drinks. 'Why always Heineken?'

'It's the only lager you can get most places that's still 5 per cent alcohol. Most of the old big hitters have started diluting their ale down. I'm not here to drink dishwater!' I say, putting on an air of indignant superiority that brings her out in a smile.

Glancing back round at the Burrowses, they're still seated, both glazed over, no one even trying to rouse them. I turn back to our table and slurp at my crisp, cool, adequately alcoholic beverage while Cam sips an Aspall. 'I laid into her parents the other day,' I say without any sense of pride.

'How d'you mean?' she asks with wide eyes, ever ravenous for gossip.

'I went round. Said I thought they might be involved in her death, and that they were fake, never loved Becky.'

'At least you held back then,' she jibes. 'So you've still got a bad feeling?'

'I don't know what to think. The police would arrest them if they were involved, wouldn't they?'

'Didn't last time,' she stirs.

I half snort and take a sip of beer. It's nice having it from a glass, with company, rather than from a can, alone, as I have over the last four days. Pubs are where humans are intended to do their drinking. Good old English pubs.

Embarrassing as it was to be caught, I feel pleased to have cried too. Finally! My chest is freer, all guilt over it not happening having now ebbed away.

'You found out any more?' Cam probes, leaning in over the table.

I look around to make sure no one's snooping. My pulse accelerates.

Cam looks confused at my odd, tacit reaction, but waits for the silent film to play out in front of her.

I reach into my pocket and pull out a smartphone, my own one already on the table.

Her eyes bulge. She understands immediately. 'No! How?'

I raise my eyebrows at her, then check the room again for spies.

'Was it... at their house?' she whispers. She wears an expression I imagine most people had when they worked out the twist in The Sixth Sense. Bewildered, confused, impressed.

I nod, maintaining eye contact this time. The daring of having Becky's phone out on the table, which the Burrowses must sorely want back, is exhilarating. There's no other word for it.

'Why don't you give it to the police?' Cam asks.

'I'd have to admit I took it from you-know-who,' I explain, still wanting to avoid saying anything that could be overheard.

'Have you been able to—'

'Nope.' I shake my head and let out a big breath. 'Her password was always the same when we were together – 030721 – the day of our first date. But she's changed it. Can you think of anything else it might be?'

Cam shakes her head too, looking off to the side in a bid to summon a buried memory that could help, but coming up short. 'Sorry.'

'Don't worry, long shot,' I reassure her.

My first pint slides down all too quickly. Cam spots it and rushes back to the bar to keep me hydrated. She probably thinks I'll let more slip if she keeps me well oiled.

Her new-found ability to order drinks – albeit free ones – reminds me of Becky. She actually was generous, always offering to buy her rounds, me always trying to get in first so I could treat her, show her how much she meant to me. That's the kind of couple we were. Both generous, both putting the other person first. We'd have been such good role models to our kids, bringing them up to be honest, kind and big-hearted souls. I always used to tell Becky that. She seemed more nervous and doubtful about bringing new people into this world. But I knew we'd make an amazing team as parents. The most loving, safe family any child could ever have wished for.

A shower of tears drop into my lap in quick succession.

Bloody hell! Floodgates really are open now. I'm going to have to watch myself. What'll set me off next? A Costa cup? A flyer for the zoo? If 'Somewhere Only We Know' comes on the pub speakers, I'm finished.

I wipe my eyes dry and slip Becky's phone back into my pocket before Cam comes back with the latest refreshments.

'What do you reckon's on it?' she says as we chink glasses.

'Dunno, but the Burrowses hiding it means something, doesn't it?'

She agrees.

The hug of the beers softens the barbed edges of this horrific day. It's nice to drink a little slower, too, at Cam's pace rather than Noz's. Lets me bask in that buzzy sweet-spot longer; ideas moving gently, bright and clear like hot air balloons. Unlike full-on drunken thoughts that fire up like rockets and fall like doomed passenger jets.

'Do you know who they arrested?' I probe, bolstered by the beverages.

'Dillon?' Cam guesses, reapplying some lip gloss.

'Why d'you reckon him?'

'Right age, it's always the partner...' She shrugs as if it's obvious. 'Police released the man though. Said he was no longer a suspect.'

Yes, that news update came as a particularly brutal shank in the ribs as I lay in bed drinking, the day after I'd confronted Becky's parents.

'What if they're all in on it, protecting him?' I ask, releasing the thought that's been locked up in my mind for days.

'You should straight-up ask him,' she giggles.

I frown, unsure of the joke.

Cam nods over my shoulder. 'He's at the bar.'

I turn and take him in. That feeling of shredded nerves, of sitting in pubs with Dad, dreading what comes next; it slams into me like a ghost train from my past. Helpless, inadequate, I'm a child cowering in the corner of my mind, begging for a rescue that never comes.

The man at the bar is tall. Tall with a neat, close crop of dark, curly hair. I can't put him together with Becky, he's too... big. I've spent the last few days obsessing over this man, mentally preparing to see him, and yet deep down I don't want to see him at all. What if she did love him? What if he's mourning and feels he's lost the love of his life as well? But then how does that square with being arrested, if that was him too?

I turn back to Cam, who's looking at me rather than the human pylon at the bar. 'You OK?' she checks.

'I... who is he?'

'The Montagues' boy. You must have met him before!'

'The Montagues,' I repeat. That picture on the Burrowses' mantelpiece, the two families, Becky a surly teenager, a weedy boy on the other side of the frame. Is that the same person as this huge slab of granite? She never mentioned him. She'd never had a boyfriend, that's what she said.

What was that stupid nonsense I was thinking a minute ago? Drinking slowly is codswallop! I'm nowhere near drunk enough to confront this man.

'Becky had an old boyfriend and it was the Montagues' boy?' I query again, watching Cam watch me and nod, her head tilted to the side, laden with tender concern.

Turning to look at him once more, I honestly can't get over how tall he is. He's brave to have faced this pub's low ceilings without a hard hat on.

Cam puts a hand on mine. 'You're a good man, Ivor.'

'Don't be nice,' I grunt, knowing I won't hold it together. 'How long were they together?'

'She was with him when I met her, maybe four or five years, from her late teens.'

I sink the rest of my drink. 'Why did they break up?'

'He became too intense, Becky said.'

'What does that mean?'

She shrugs.

Cam's new pint is still pathetically full but this leviathan isn't going to stand ordering drinks forever and I am very much in need of more beer so I sidle up next to him, a sapling next to a mighty oak. He's wearing an oversized green rugby top, looking at his phone. I catch the barmaid's eye with a slight lean forward and a flash of a smile; she comes over. Has this man ever been in a pub before? You can probably see him from space and he still wasn't able to get served before me.

'I think he was first,' I mutter at the woman behind the bar, nodding at Dillon.

He glances down at me and blinks. Becky never had social media, so there's a chance that even if he knew we dated, he wouldn't know what I looked like. But he does, he recognises me, by the pause, the slack jaw, the garble of posh-boy vowels as he scrabbles for his long-lost composure. He knows exactly who I am.

I look away, back at the young, confused barmaid who is still yet to receive an order.

'Two pints of Heineken, please,' I request on instinct.

She goes off in search of the lagers and I shift slightly, leaning my elbow on the well-polished bar as I turn square-on to him. 'Dillon, is it?'

He nods into life. 'Urr, yah yah. Ivor, isn't it?' He's got the

same far-back, plum-up-ya-arse throaty guff that Phillip and
Audrey employ, and the Montagues for that matter, which
figures.

'Yeah.'

In the pantheon of awkward conversations, this is up there
with Prince Andrew telling Emily Maitlis he couldn't sweat. If
only I had such a superpower right now.

'It's good the police released you in the end,' I test, eyes
glued to the barmaid pulling our pints further past Dillon's
shoulder.

'Yah, it sucked. They were never going to charge me so it was
all pretty futile, y'know?'

So he *was* the person they arrested. The confirmation brings
a fresh wave of icy fear. Am I standing inches from Becky's
killer? Should I launch myself at him, rip his guts out?

My pints are pushed across the bar. I redirect one towards
him and move away, back to my table with Cam.

Weird that Becky never introduced us. In fact, the more I
think about it, she must have had to conspire really hard to
make sure we never met, so she didn't have to tell me about him.
But I do feel like we've met. Why? Not a family event. I liked the
Montagues; if I'd known their son was there, I'd have made an
effort to say hello. What then? I rack my brains. That lanky
frame, shiny face and upper-crust accent. I've met him before. I
think. The memory is there, palpable but not visible, a fire in
the room next door, smoke coming under the door.

'Was she still writing in her diaries?' Cam bursts, clearly
excited by the brainwave she's come up with in my absence.
'Could be something in there!'

'Think so, but Phillip would have got rid of them. They
weren't in her room,' I state, having already drunk as much of
my new beer as Cam has of her old Aspall.

'Were you looking for them though?'

I scrunch my lips and nose up as a tacit admission that I wasn't.

She grabs my hand for a second time, even though I'm not feeling in the least bit fragile now I've faced up to Dillon and survived. If anything, all I can think about is that I may have just spoken to Becky's killer and I'm disappointed in myself that I made no attempt to kill him right back.

Cam's still talking but I'm struggling to follow. I can feel myself slipping past that sweet spot of tipsiness, fumbling with the threads of too many thoughts, struggling to hold on to any.

'Ivor, you hear me?' she finishes.

'Sorry, say that again.' I blink hard, wondering if she'll do the right thing and go back to the bar the second she finishes that overly nursed cider.

'You need to keep digging. I think you are on to something,' she implores, leaning so close I can count her eyelashes. She's whispering, her eyes burning with intent. 'I get you can't go to the police with the phone. But you can keep digging. The lies the parents have told, the phone, the history with the sister, that bear necklace... have you got anywhere with that?'

I've started wearing it at home when no one's around.

I shake my head.

She lowers her voice, blinking slowly. 'If they have burned the diaries or whatever, that'd be even more evidence they're involved, yes?'

I nod.

'You aren't going to like this, but you need to cut this shit out.' She chinks her glass on my now-empty one but continues to talk under her breath. 'You're holding yourself back. You've got her phone, you've got her necklace, you know where she died, you know the Burrowses. You could get to the bottom of this if you stay focussed.'

'Drink's got nothing to do with it,' I tell her.

'Oh really? Is that why you left Becky's phone on the table when you got back from the bar and not your own?'

'No I didn't...' I look down at Becky's phone, scrape the handset off the table in a panic, then look back at Cam.

'You are doing right by Becky. Whatever the truth is.' She's leaning in even closer now, the sweat on her top lip ultra clear, barely a foot away from my face. 'But you're no good to anyone sloppy.'

I look away, desperate for another drink but knowing it'd only prove her point.

'Come on, let's go,' she says, motioning. 'Call it a night now and you'll feel OK in the morning.'

We get up and head for the exit. Wes Montague, Dillon's dad, squeezes my shoulder as I walk past him. 'Good to see you, Ivor. You're welcome to come down and see us any time, y'know that.'

'Thanks,' I say, slapping his back. Slipping out my own phone for a change, I ask him to tap in his number as I promise him I'll be in touch about meeting up soon. He obliges then moves back to the circle of old men he'd been talking with. That sums up the Burrowses verses the Montagues. Wes always treated me with dignity, like a real person.

Pushing open the pub doors, we step through the cloud of smokers out front. That scent of cigarettes as you leave a pub is one of the sweetest, warmest hugs you can ever hope to experience.

'You want food before you go home?' Cam asks as we side-step the nicotine addicts, her leaning on my right arm, hiding herself from the bite of the winter air.

'No, bedtime I think.'

She nudges her dainty hand into mine and turns to face me. 'Get a cab back with me.'

I tilt my head down to meet her eyes. They're glassy from the drinks, the dim glow of a streetlamp catching in both and reflecting up at me like an amber pinhead in each pupil. She blinks and those eyelashes beckon me closer.

A millisecond's glance at her parted lips and she's pushing them against mine. Leaning in too, I move a hand behind her head and hold us together, the taste of sweet cider on her tongue, the brush of my stubble against soft skin. Her own hands migrate to the sides of my head, fingers splaying out as they trace up my jaw. I clench the back of her neck tighter, and slip my other hand onto the small of her back inside her parka.

A blast of icy wind howls down the street, making her shiver and we break hold. 'I'll book an Uber,' she says with a smile, biting her nail then slipping the same hand into her coat pocket.

Should I do this? Solace after a harrowing day. She is kinda hot.

Her blonde fringe flicks and dances in the nighttime breeze, still only inches away.

And then it happens. A tiny feather, caught on a gust, nestles in her hair just above her forehead.

She's still peering down at her phone, the Uber app open, the profile picture of the last driver she booked flashing up on her screen.

Looking back at her hair, I pluck the feather off and pop it in my pocket.

'Cam. I'm sorry, it's not...'

She grabs my hand with her free one and tugs at it. 'Maybe we just need to get this out of our systems together, yeah?'

'I... I can't. I'm sorry. I just can't.'

Pulling my hand off her, I stalk away.

'Ivor...' she calls. 'Ivor!'

My feet get faster the further they flee.

'You're pathetic!' she shouts down the street.

I throw an apology over my shoulder without looking back.

'No wonder she left you,' she yells. 'Washed-out freak!'

Let her say what she wants. I'd never do that to Becky. What was I even thinking? Stupid pheromones.

Anyway, a lightbulb's flicked on. Bright and brilliant. I do open the Uber app, but I have no plans to order a taxi.

23

BECKY'S DIARY

Wednesday 17 August 2022

Not written in a while. Things have been fine. What's changed? Not much. Still living at home. Still working at Costa. Still with Ivor. His shower is still not fixed.

Maybe that's why I felt like coming back to my diary. Everything's a bit meh, a bit underwhelming. I'm not in the doldrums but I can see them from here, that sort of thing.

Ivor's desperate for me to move in or get our own flat. Keeps talking about kids too. While I do spend several nights a week at his, he won't accept cash for rent or food until I officially move in. Lovely in its own way... but Tesco ain't paying him megabucks and living in Finchley... well, London at all... is extortion on a level never witnessed at any other time in any other place in the history of the universe. So he never has enough for new clothes or another fun trip to Budapest or even something dull like saving for a deposit. He makes sure he has enough for drinking though. When I do touch on the subject of money, even jokingly, and how much he spends on beer, it's like he's on guard. He doesn't ever quite say it but it's like he's thinking... 'Blimey, you stay and eat my food and order take-aways on my card whenever you want, I get you presents, and somehow you're still not happy.'

I was thinking the other day, why don't I give him an ultimatum on the shower? I mean, I kind of have said I won't move in until it's fixed already. But what if I was serious, and told him so. 'Ivor, fix the shower and I'll move in tomorrow'. If I was that clear, I KNOW he'd get it done. And it hit me quick that the reason I'm not pushing harder, even though it really does bug me, is because then I would have to move in. Give him an ultimatum... he'll rise to it. I'd find it trapping for myself.

Urgh, am I being ungrateful and stupid?

I don't want to fixate on one thing... but I'm going to. How do you continue to live without a working shower? He washes in the sink every morning, it's not a hygiene issue (THANK GOODNESS!) but like... Ivor, how can you not see that a working shower is a basic prerequisite for living in the 20th century, never mind the 21st? I'm not asking for much! But that's why I feel guilty. I'm avoiding asking him. It's more like I'm testing to see when it'll click.

But at the same time, it feels like there's a lack of perceptiveness on his part and it's OK for me to call that out. And that makes me feel like we aren't on the same page. Like maybe he isn't getting me the way I felt he was when we were first going out. And then moving in together feels like a big step.

An excuse I keep giving him at the moment is that Costa won't grant me a move to a branch nearer to his, so it makes sense for me to stay at Mum and Dad's while I'm still working in Wimbledon. But that's a cop-out – there are definitely transfers available if you want them.

Ivor wants to move in together, have kids and get married. But nothing would change. He'd work at Tesco, I'd work at Costa, we'd rent in Finchley, he'd drink. I don't want that – always living one disaster away from not being able to pay the bills. It's not about being rich... I detest that more than anyone... but there's also something fun about living day-to-day when you're first dating someone that isn't so alluring when you've been doing it constantly for over a year.

But then I flit the other way again... coz I'm the one holding us back from taking the next step, being more serious, more long-term together, by not moving in. And making it very clear I am totally against the institution of marriage, seeing as Mum and Dad are so wedded (ha!) to it.

Urgh, Ivor's still so sweet and besotted with me, though. Last month, for our one-year anniversary, he bought me a PS5. An actual brand-new PlayStation 5, because I'd been saying they looked fun, and I could download all the old games I used to play growing up, like *Crash Bandicoot* and *Street Fighter 2*, and that I could play *Hogwarts Legacy* on it when it finally comes out next year. I literally just said it in passing ages ago, and he's secretly saved up week after week so he could buy me a flipping PS5.

That sums Ivor up more than anything else in the world. He can't take one week off drinking to afford a plumber, but he will spend months putting a pound away here, a fiver away there, until he has enough to buy me a huge, ostentatious gift to show me he loves me. If love languages are a thing, his is definitely giving gifts.

I don't doubt for a second that he loves me, and a lot of the time that's enough. But doesn't the fact I'm choosing to stay with my parents rather than move in ever make him think... Hmmm, maybe I need to get my act together?

But that's what I mean, I don't think he sees any problem at all, at least that he can solve. As far as he's concerned, life is one piece away from being perfect, and that last piece is me choosing to move in. He's doing well at work too. I was round there when he had a meeting on Zoom, some sort of review on his progress, and his boss was really pleased with him and gave him a little pay rise. I was so proud, and Ivor seemed shocked, even a bit emotional when we chatted after. But then the rest of the evening is predictable... 'We need to celebrate'. Initially he wanted to run to the off-licence to get some bubbly, until I reminded him I will refuse point-blank to drink that stuff. So instead, he comes back with £30 worth of beer and cider. And any hope of doing anything more exciting or spontaneous, or just not drinking and saving up instead, vanishes.

Then I feel like a complete fraud, like I'm turning into my parents, with their preoccupation with money and high-paid careers.

I love that Ivor doesn't act like that; he lives for today. He loves me today just for being me, and that wouldn't change if I win the lottery or lose my job. I've always railed against my parents' insistence on 'financial security'. Saying those two words out loud would bring me out in a rash.

Ivor has been such a tonic to that toxic world. But what if I'm only with him as a reaction to my other life, as a 'fuck you' to my parents, not because he and I are perfectly suited?

I remember in those early days, when I'd get panicky if he hadn't texted in a couple of hours, how I'd be constantly paranoid he was going to leave me. I don't miss those feelings per se, but they were a sign of how attached I was to him and the relationship, and that urgency, that neediness feels like it's gone. Sure, every relationship has its honeymoon period (look at me acting like I know everything about relationships from the TWO I've had in my whole life, ha!) but things look a bit hazy and uninspiring atm.

Staying at his about six weeks ago, I woke up in the night needing water. Ivor was still up. I was going to get my water then go back to bed, but I heard him sniffling like he had a thick cold so popped my head into the lounge. He was there, slumped on the sofa, can in hand, crying. I sat down next to him, asked what was wrong and he said he was feeling guilty that he was the reason his mum had died. It was heartbreaking. I reiterated the same way I had done tons of times before that he mustn't carry any kind of guilt over the death of his mum, though I didn't feel like I really made any kind of impact. Seriously, the emotional burden Ivor's dad has put on him regarding his mum is beyond cruel.

As Ivor and I chatted on the sofa it was clear he was very, VERY drunk.

But then, out of nowhere, he said something to the effect of... I wish I could stop drinking. He's never said anything like that before. He seemed to get that it was wasting money and making him super unfit and limiting what we could do. I said it was his decision but that maybe we could try doing a few weeks sober together and then spend the money saved on a trip away. He said he loved that idea. It was as if, at the bottom of twenty drinks, he'd finally stripped away all the layers and was being genuinely vulnerable and real with me. I took the half-full can off him, poured the rest away and we went to bed.

Next morning... he had no recollection of our conversation. Zilch. I told him we were taking a few weeks off booze and that he'd agreed to it. He didn't seem convinced, and when he came in from work that night, he had an eight pack with him. Well, seven pack, he'd had one of them on the walk home. The night after that, when I was back at Mum and Dad's for a run of shifts, he called me drunk from the pub, trying to tell me how much he loved me.

He's even turned up unannounced in Wimbledon a couple of times recently. And I don't mean knocking at the front door, I mean him climbing in through the window and surprising me at my own bedroom door. Each time, I'm panicking my parents will hear, but also pleased to see him and enamoured by the fact he'd make such an effort to see me. Then he'll pass out drunk and in the morning, his breath... well, it should come with a biohazard warning.

Urgh, I don't know. They say it takes the death of your parents and the birth of your children to mature you. Maybe if we do move in together and start a family, he'll calm down. But that's not a fair reason to have a baby, in the hope it'll calm your boyfriend down. And is that what I want? With him? Sometimes I think maybe we're too different, and I'm only with him because I can't bring myself to break his heart for no reason.

I don't even know whether I want kids. I do know I want a dog. Mum and Dad would never let me have one here and you're not allowed to keep pets at Ivor's under the terms of his lease. I'd get a rescue from Battersea. Maybe two if I fell in love and couldn't decide between them.

I think about Dillon sometimes, and how close we used to be, and how exciting it was planning our lives together. We were going to get a dog.

I made a fake Instagram account, with a fake name (newtsca-mander_x) and some random fan art of a hippogriff as the profile picture. It felt weird to have an account after never indulging before. I still don't understand how people spend hours and hours scrolling on it, it isn't that interesting. But I used it to look up Dillon without him seeing, and I found him. He posted some pictures from a nice holiday on Santorini with his parents, another jogging on the front at Sandbanks – he appears to keep very fit now – and there was one from a Sunday lunch at a posh restaurant that looked so fancy and tasty. I know he's in finance so that affords you luxuries me and Ivor don't have. But having money doesn't automatically mean you'll turn into my parents.

Seeing those pictures made me miss him.

Plus... he was there when Amy died. That's a big deal. My parents would kill me if I told Ivor, as we've discussed before. But Dillon was there, so I don't have to worry about sharing. Me and Dill used to talk about it all the time. He was my counsellor, and I was his. Two peas in a parentally scarred pod. In an unexpected way, seeing bits of his life again also made me feel that bit closer to Amy, like knowing what he was up to came with a free nostalgia blast, reminding me of all our pasts, when we were carefree kids all together.

Then I flip again and think about Ivor, how much he adores me, how devoted he is. He's a very pure, innocent soul. I hated how paranoid Dillon would get about our relationship, about other men. It was suffocating. That's what his Instagram and my rose-tinted spectacles for the past don't highlight. Dillon had a darker problem than Ivor. The jealousy, the control, the mistrust, the behaviour so off-putting that I – the woman least ready for conflict in the world – broke it off. Have to remember that: he was so anal and obsessive that I broke it off. Ivor's so easy-going and would never check my phone or diary or delete messages on my phone. I don't want white-knuckle love and Ivor is the opposite of that, he just loves me for me. Why would anyone give that up?

So yeah, back and forth, back and forth my stupid mind goes.

24

IVOR

January 2025

The trees are taller than I remember, below the resplendent balcony of the Montagues' home. Shafts of light beam out of the French windows from their lounge high above. My North Star. I can't hide in these sloped cliffs for long, but in the dark and the cold it was the only chance of evading the Burrowses. Do they know the way up from the beach, like me and Becky do? Do they know I've got her phone and that necklace on me? Why did I bring them? Why did I come back at all?

My back to a tree trunk, I catch my breath, trying to keep as quiet as possible so I can hear if they're close. No torch lights coming up from the slippery sleeper steps I've scaled. I spit on the floor and carry on upwards.

What am I going to do? The Montagues aren't going to be happy to see me, they'll hand me over to the police, or worse – Phillip and Audrey. Would they do the same to me? Over the balcony. Their usual MO? Now I'm faced with the sister's monument all over again, the concrete pillars, the bird table and...

Why is Becky still there? They've dressed her in white. Why?

Light from the moon sneaks through tree branches for the first time, landing on her like a stage spotlight. I stand in shock, an audience of one. The air is barbed and oppressive, stinging my eyes, making them water.

'Becky?' I hiss, not wanting to give my position away to the Burrowses who must be catching up behind.

She's getting up, she knows I'm there, she's walking towards me, she's been crying, tears glistening on her silver cheeks. I stand still, she's looking at me. Who cares if her parents catch us? We're back together, it's everything I knew it would be. We'll run away, do whatever we want!

'Becky,' I whisper again, my voice breaking, so overwhelmed I can't think what else to say. I want to throw my arms around her and never let go.

She reaches me but her face changes, sadness flipping to fury. She launches a destructive hurricane of a scream, her defiled, mutilated mouth stretching open twice as wide as it should. Anaconda-like, she lunges forward, plunging her teeth into my neck.

'NO!'

Snapping forward, shaking her off I'm... in bed... alone... shivering under a sheet of icy sweat. I keep my eyes open, panting, trying to fixate on anything except that face, that mouth, that scream.

The room's stuffed with heavy, gloomy shadows, a dim glow seeping through the blinds. I stand up, trying to further remind myself where I am and where I am not. It was a dream. Just a dream.

Staring at the glass of feathers next to my phone is good. When did I bring that in from the lounge? Must have been before bed last night because the one from Cam's hair is sitting proudly on top of the stack.

No one will ever know how noble I was to turn down sex after the wake. I haven't sown my wild oats in well over twelve months. A man – of my virility, in the prime of his life – not even succumbing to Pamela Handerson once last year. It's remarkable! Scientists should be lining up to study my eternal depths of self-discipline. Of course, most of that time was spent desperately and determinedly trying to work out how to get Becky back.

Now she isn't here, though, I should be off the leash. And last night, Cam was all over me. I've earned a break, haven't I? A little one-off treat? Yet I stayed loyal even then. I deserve some kind of award, maybe a medal. Don't suppose the King dishes out many honours for celibate Tesco workers. One of the main reasons I'm a republican.

Checking my phone, it's 8.03 a.m.

There are two messages waiting for me. One from Cam apologising for last night. Meh – she can wait. The other message is far more intriguing. It was Cam who sort of gave me the idea, by accident. Seeing her open the Uber app and it prompting her to rate her last driver, gave me an idea. If the Uber app logs all your drivers from past journeys, surely it would still show which driver took Becky down to Sandbanks on New Year's Eve.

DCI Schwarz said they'd confirmed with the Uber driver that he did drive Becky to the coast that night. But I want more than that.

The app doesn't let you message past drivers directly, but if you report that you lost something – say, your house keys – while en route with them, it will put you in touch.

Bingo!

Initially he'd just said he couldn't find the keys. Then I asked if it was possible to come and have a look myself.

And this morning he's replied saying yes! He's not given me his home address, but says if I come to the taxi rank by East Croydon station at 7 p.m. this evening, he'll probably be around and I can have a look.

What a coup! I message back agreeing to his terms, not sure if my shaking hands are the after-tremors of the traumatic dream or nervous anticipation at the new lead.

* * *

The day drags terribly. I can't bring myself to fall back to sleep naturally in case I meet that awful bastardised version of Becky again. That nightmare is my own fault really. I'd googled how to dream about someone, hoping I'd start reliving my memories with Becky, or maybe have new pretend dates, all while asleep. Sounds pathetic in one sense but I don't care. Google said to think about that person as you fall asleep which wasn't hard, I would be doing that already. But it clearly didn't translate into amorous, heartwarming scenes together, it took me back to the worst sight of my life. My brain's hopeless. So yeah, don't want to fall back to sleep, don't want to drink myself back to sleep for fear I'll still be groggy when I need to head to Croydon, or worse, sleep through the rendezvous time altogether.

The evening does finally roll round though, and I set off. Croydon, by the way, might as well be the Highlands of Scotland, it's such a ball-ache to reach. I don't go south of the river that often, and when I have done, it's usually been to Wimbledon on the nice green District Line, or Brixton on the bright blue Victoria Line.

The London Borough of Croydon is on neither.

My two routes are either via the Overground service which appears to stop at every other house between here and there and still requires me to walk for fifteen minutes at the other end, or a Southern Rail train – probably steam-powered – from Victoria which is more expensive but more direct. I opt for the latter.

I should just use the Burrowses' Uber account again, but I have this awful premonition of taking the mick with another long journey, them noticing halfway through the journey and blocking me from using the app ever again before I've got to this taxi driver, and me somehow missing the chance to speak to him. So I play it safe.

Walking up the ramp at the station, I tap my card and brush through the barriers on to the concourse.

A short female member of station staff in an orange high-viz jacket pushes her hand out and taps me on the chest as I'm walking past her. 'Hey, mate.'

This is not the time! 'Look,' I say, making clear, stern eye contact. 'I'm not over forty and I don't have a spare ciggy. Honestly, why do I always get bothered at train stations?'

The woman looks at me, bamboozled.

'S-sorry mate,' she says, taking a step back. 'I was going to say your flies are open, that's all.'

She glances down at my jeans at the same moment I do.

The humiliation is immediate, my cheeks burning crimson.

'I am so sorry,' I tell her, yanking up the zip. She gives a split-second smile then stalks away.

It's official. I am a moron.

Plodding out of the station, I am met with the strongest smell of weed I've ever encountered. It hits the nostrils like a shovel – heavy enough to floor Bob Marley himself.

Getting my phone out, I open the Uber app and message the

driver again. He replies, giving his car description and number-plate. He's here! I scurry down the sloped road of the taxi rank to his ruby-coloured Hyundai.

Reaching the car, I wave at the driver, who reciprocates. I open the back seat and get in, having rehearsed my opening line.

'Hi, thanks for getting back to me. I know you can't be sitting here all evening. But I haven't lost my key. I need to really quickly ask you about that woman you took to Sandbanks on New Year's Eve.'

He hasn't said a word yet, but he's looking at me gravely in his rearview mirror. He undoes his seatbelt, which I take as a positive sign, and turns to observe me. He looks like he's in his sixties, sides of his head shaved, with an odd tuft of dyed hair left on top like brown candyfloss.

'And who are you?' he enquires in a vaguely northern accent.

'Her boyfriend.'

He searches my eyes. I reflect his seriousness back at him. He nods. 'Five minutes.'

'Thank you!' I sigh, putting my hands together in a prayer sign. 'You picked her up about 12.15 a.m.?'

'Yes, the police came and asked me about it. Told me she'd died. I'm sorry.'

I thank him for his thoughtfulness. It's then that it hits – I am sitting in the exact same back seats Becky would have been in as he drove her to Sandbanks. My head swims, overcome with the eerie proximity of me to her, separated by nothing but time.

'Did she sit...' I point down at my own place, diagonally behind the driver '...here?'

He nods. Nausea builds in my chest and I tense, trying to force my questioning beyond the ghosts of that night.

'How was she in the car? Was she sad?'

'Yes, she was crying, on and off, all journey. I asked her – "what's the matter, miss?" But she just said "Nothing, nothing." I gave her a pack of tissues and I think she used them all.'

'She was alone?'

He nods again.

'She had longish brown hair, to about here, and green eyes,' I say, for some reason wanting reassurance he is definitely remembering Becky.

'Brown hair, yes. I'm not good with eye colour, sorry... She wore a black T-shirt I think, but no jumper, no coat.'

How I found her – jeans and T-shirt. I slap the thought away.

'Did she say anything else? Why she was getting an Uber at that time? What she was doing?'

'No,' he says, turning to look at his phone again. 'Police, they already asked me all this.'

'Sorry,' I say, putting my hands up in front of me. 'Urm...' What else do I ask? The fact she came out in a T-shirt and no other top feels like new information, but it's not huge. What else could he know? This great plan of mine, this hot, fresh lead is wilting under the lights.

'Was there anyone waiting for her when she got to Sandbanks? You dropped her off at 3 Rochelle Drive, yes?' I probe, almost sure I know the answer already.

'The address was something like that, I've never had to take someone all that way before, I am usually just south London. There was no one there to meet her, no.'

I sit up a little straighter. 'Did she ask you to drop her at the gates or down by the beachfront?'

'A gate, a big gate on a road,' he says, gesticulating with one hand to suggest it was a long road.

'You didn't happen to see if she went in through the gate, did you?'

'Yes, she did. I was worried because she was on her own in the middle of the night with no coat. And I could smell drink on her breath. I wouldn't have left if she didn't get in.'

The Montagues have an electric gate, you can't get in unless someone buzzes to let you. Hence why we had to climb up via the cliffs late at night so many times. 'The big gate opened for her?' I check.

He promises this was the case. 'She leaned into something like this...' he pushes his head over to his own palm, out flat in front of his face, '...and then the gate opens and she walks through. So I left.'

'And that was the last you saw?'

'Yeah. I'd made all the money I planned for New Year's Eve, but it was a long way home.' He half-chuckles, hoping I'll understand.

I nod to show I get it.

'You're a good man,' he adds, grabbing my hand. 'You clearly loved her very deeply.'

I smile back but can't summon a reply as my eyes fill with tears. The dam really has burst since the funeral. My bottom lip wobbles as I wave my hand in a silent farewell and get out of the car.

With the fresh air comes a clearer head. Someone let Becky into that house the night she died. She wasn't alone.

Walking back up to the station I google for pubs nearby. The best rated one is The Green Dragon so I set it as my destination. I have so much thinking to do.

And I need a beer.

25

IVOR

January 2025

Someone opened the gate when Becky got to the Montagues'. Up until then I'd assumed she'd gone the sneaky way to get in, the same way we'd used to when we were staying there and got back late.

But the Uber driver was sure. She was let in.

Sitting and supping my Heineken in Croydon's Green Dragon pub, I let my imagination mushroom. Good boozer, by the way, lovely staff, lots of space. I'll come back with Noz if Croydon ever gets a tube station.

Thoughts hover over the Montagues' sprawling, cliff-top mansion like drones, taking pictures, peeking through windows, trying to make sense of Becky's movements that night.

The house was supposed to be empty. The Burrowses and the Montagues told me and the police they were all celebrating New Year's Eve together in Wimbledon.

Becky going all that way does make more sense if she was going to see someone. But it also makes it more sinister and suspicious if she wasn't alone. It also makes it far less likely her parents did it – alone, at least. Why would they be at the Montagues' house and not the Montagues themselves?

Is that why the police arrested Dillon? Was he the one who let her in? Was she going to see him?

But why are they all covering for him then?

And why text me just before she got in the Uber, if she didn't want me to know something?

Mum and Dad have told me everything about Amy. I will always love you.

What had they told her? Did they kill Amy? Did one of the Montagues do it? But the police report had said only Phillip and Audrey were in at the time. Or were they lying about that too? A bit drunk, did Becky decide to go to look for something at the Montagues' home after her parents admitted what really happened to Amy, and they followed her and killed her? But then who let her in? Or was Dillon lying in wait, and killed her on the Burrowses' orders to stop the truth getting out? None of the theories feel quite right. But the truth must be connected to whatever they did to the twin sister all those years ago. It must be. The same spot, the text I got from Becky. It has to be linked.

It takes me about four pints for all the spiralling ideas to settle and for the cream of my thinking to rise to the top.

This Dillon was there when Amy had died too. Not in the house, according to the police report, but the longer I see how the Burrowses have hidden stuff from the detectives with Becky's death, the more I can't trust the official narrative of what happened to Amy either. Maybe those obsessive, weird crime forum people were on to something. I'm certainly on to something. And Dillon is looming larger and larger in all aspects of this.

I had sort of discounted the Montagues as suspects – but both deaths occurred at their home.

Someone was at that house when Becky arrived and I bet she knew it! Otherwise, she'd have got the taxi driver to drop her at the promenade. The only reason she'd get dropped off at the gate – and not bother to take a coat – is if she knew someone would be there to let her in. But who?

* * *

I bet Wes Montague wishes he hadn't made such a loose-lipped offer at the Rose & Crown about me being welcome 'any time'. I texted him from The Green Dragon. They are back in Sandbanks, he replied, and were 'more than happy' for me to visit.

He requests it be no later than midday the very next day, says they're going away after that, probably hoping that'll be too early for me.

Not at all!

Making it to Clapham Junction before 10 a.m. is awful, I can't lie. Rush hour times hangover equals misery. But I'm on the platform with six minutes to spare. Is there an Olympic event for traversing a city when still heavily under last night's influence? There should be. The journey south gives me time to process that brief chat with the Uber driver, having slept on the conversation. It's not the revelation about Becky at the gate that's stuck to my mind like chewing gum though, it's what he said at the end. The way he grabbed my hand, told me he could see how much Becky meant to me. How beautiful of him to spot that and take the time to tell me. It's the first time since she died that someone's genuinely appreciated how hard this is for me.

Noz doesn't care. Cam only cares because she's ravenous for gossip. DCI Schwarz says she cares, but it feels like I'm doing more investigating of this case than she is. And then, in less than five minutes, that taxi driver was able to tell how important Becky is to me, how desperate I am to do right by her.

What is it teenagers say these days, they feel 'seen'? Well, that Uber man made me feel seen, that's for sure. I well up yet again.

Station reached, I get a taxi to 3 Rochelle Drive and buzz for entry. 12.09 p.m., bang on time-ish. It's just as the taxi driver said Becky had done; I lean into the keypad by the large wooden gates, speak into the buzzer, a tinny voice talks back down the line to me, and I am permitted entry.

The Montagues' garden is smaller than the Burrowses' but far better kept, while the house itself is far more modern. If I didn't know the homeowners personally, I'd assume a Bond villain lived here. Lots of the external walls are made entirely of glass slanting at odd angles, making the most of the panoramic views and beachfront below. It would all be very exposed and compromising, privacy-wise, were it not for the carefully grown and manicured 12 ft-high laurel hedges screening the property from nosey-parkers either side and behind.

There's a pristine, polished army green Porsche on the driveway and a Land Rover Discovery plugged into a charging point outside their double garage. To the right, the lawn rolls out like an infinity pool before falling away abruptly, with the sea view beyond. Parallel to the grass is the edge of the house, ending with the patio and balcony. Amy's memorial, where I found Becky, is about 60 ft down, directly below it.

The front door opens before I reach it and Wes is looking at me, not smiling, but not impatient either. Solemn. He's tall and tanned, grey hair never particularly neat. He's got a navy-blue Ted Baker shirt on with the cuffs folded back to reveal a comple-mentary sky-blue pattern underneath. Two collar buttons undone allow a few silvery chest hairs to loll out – white chinos and slip-on deck shoes complete the look. It all seems too summery for a chilly January lunchtime – until I reach him at the door and am smacked hard with the heat coming from inside. Stockbrokers don't worry about heating bills. This man blows his nose on £20 notes, wipes his arse with fifties.

'Hi Ivor,' he says softly, giving me a hug.

It's an odd clash of feelings, being back. I was here, down in the cliffs less than two weeks ago, finding Becky's body. I am here now, unsure whether I can trust this man. And yet I spent so many happy weekends here with Becky. She got on so much better with the Montagues than her own parents and so did I. They are as wealthy as the Burrowses at the very least, but far more generous and happier to spend what they make. One Friday evening we arrived late, went straight to bed, and there was a brand-new iPhone waiting for Becky on her pillow. No real reason other than them wanting to treat her, make her feel wanted. It's almost as if they knew what her parents were like and endeavoured to compensate in all areas. And today feels no different.

Maybe they aren't trying to deceive me or the police. Maybe they're in mourning too, for the closest thing they ever had to a daughter.

I take off my jacket, given the tropical indoor temperatures, and hang it on a coat rack by the front door above two humongous Samsonite suitcases, presumably packed ahead of the trip they're going on.

Wes doesn't guide me through to the usual sitting room we'd use when I came with Becky, he takes me through to the lounge they have facing out to the sea – with the balcony at the end. A chill grips me as I look out to those wrought-iron bars, barely 3 ft tall, protecting the outdoor patio from the drop below. Becky's body tumbling over them plays on repeat in my head. Why have they brought me in here? Becky always refused to come in this room. Not surprising, given Amy had fallen from that same balcony. So we never did come in here. And yet they've specifically chosen to invite me in here now.

Mrs Montague – Faith – sits on a huge elephant-grey L-shaped sofa awkwardly plonked in the middle of the room, awaiting my arrival. A white slate coffee table in front of her gleams. On top of it is a glass tea infuser, sort of like a cafetière but with tea leaves in the top and golden water dripping down into the well below. Three sleek, transparent Pyrex mugs sit around the steeping pot.

That's the thing with the Montagues – everything is state-of-the-art, the sofa looks like it was hand-crafted by a woodworker yesterday, the carpet feels like it was laid this morning. Everything is plush, invested in, cared for. The antithesis of the tight, threadbare principles the Burrowses live by, desperate to save every last penny for a rainy day that will never come.

'Ivor,' Faith says in a pitying, maternal way, getting to her feet and planting a small kiss on my cheek. She smells lovely. Becky would tease Faith for constantly being doused in perfume, but I always enjoyed the expensive cloud of roses and lavender that followed her around.

I can't take my eyes off that balcony, however. My head swims the same way it did as I sat in the back of that Uber last night. Becky was here. The room she always hated. She was on that balcony. And then she wasn't.

The Montagues ask how I'm faring, which I answer with brevity.

'Thanks for seeing me,' I say at the first lull in conversation. Faith nestles in the elbow of the sofa to my right, Wes perches to my other side. I sip my black tea, a fruity, sweet Darjeeling. 'I need to get a few things straight in my head about what happened, and I've never exactly been on best terms with the Burrowses,' I explain, altar-boy innocent.

They don't respond. Phillip and Audrey will most definitely have filled the Montagues in about my outburst at their house in Wimbledon, prior to the funeral. It's a wonder they're still treating me so fairly. Odd, even.

'I never knew Becky and Dillon had a... thing, before I was with her,' I go on.

'Rebecca was very funny about that,' Faith says, pinching the handle of her cup and taking a tiny sip. 'Before you first came here, she made me promise not to talk about her and Dillon at all. She was paranoid. I didn't understand it. We were always going to welcome you, as long as you treated her well. But she seemed to think it would be a can of worms.'

'Over-thinker, under-talker, that was our Rebecca, wasn't it?' says Wes, with a small wistful smile.

They feel so like themselves, so like the couple I myself grew to trust. Becky was totally against marriage, but we'd still sometimes daydream about what a hypothetical wedding day might look like and I'd said I would definitely have asked Wes to be my best man, not because I knew him better than Noz, but because it would mean so much to him and would be a way to say thank you to the Montagues for all they'd done for us as a couple.

Plus... Noz as best man? I wouldn't have survived the stag-do stripogram.

'Were they back together? Becky and Dillon?' I ask, beginning to believe I'll get a sincere answer.

Faith tilts her head, her brown curls shifting as she looks down and then back to me. 'Yeah. Sometime last year.'

The words invade me, disbelief giving way to something much worse, pictures in my mind of the two of them laughing, kissing, getting lost in each other's eyes. A gross, painful alternative universe in which I mean nothing to Becky. There's a picture of grinning Dillon in a mortar board and black gown on the mantel opposite us, making the torturous glimpses of him and Becky all the more easy to imagine.

'She messaged me, the night she went missing,' I admit, trying to distract myself from the heinous images, not even sure if it's wise to divulge such a detail. I suppose, if I want the truth and they are willing to give me honest answers then maybe we can work together, both add our own pieces to the jigsaw. 'She told me she'd always love me.'

'She was very mixed up that night,' Wes begins, before checking himself. 'Err, not that she didn't mean it, of course, but I mean, maybe she was torn on what she felt for who, y'know?'

'You were celebrating New Year's Eve at the Burrowses' in Wimbledon?' I ask. 'Who else was there?'

Wes confirms all six of them – Phillip, Audrey, Becky, Faith, Dillon and himself – were there.

'Were Becky and Dillon acting like boyfriend and girlfriend?'

'Ivor, don't torture yourself,' Faith says, tapping my hand and giving it a little rub.

That's a horrible, painful 'yes'.

I take a bigger gulp of Darjeeling, buying time. 'Why did she come here?'

'Rebecca and her parents fell out,' Faith says. 'You know what they were always like, well, imagine that but with a bottle of bubbly inside each of them. It all got a bit...'

'Becky hates champagne,' I point out.

'Yes, well, we were all drinking bubbly, she was drinking straight rum I think, so even less helpful,' Faith says.

'What were she and her parents arguing about?' I probe.

'Honestly, Ivor, I can't even remember,' Faith says, sounding apologetic. 'We were in the next room, trying to keep out of the way, watching Jools on the telly.'

Hmm, cop-out answers, but not entirely unconvincing.

'And then she got up and ordered a taxi all the way here, to your house. Why?'

'That's my fault... at least slightly,' Wes says, putting his hands in the air. 'Buoyed by the champers myself, I'd wandered in, trying to calm everyone down. Foolish, I know. But I suggested Rebecca could come back with us on New Year's Day, spend some time down here, away from it all. But then she said, 'I want to go now'. Caught off guard, I said she could go when-ever she wanted.'

He pauses, speaks the next words to his wife: 'I should have told her, 'No, we'll go tomorrow.' Maybe she'd still be here if I'd been thinking straight.' His voice cracks under the weight of emotion.

'Oh, Wesley,' Faith whispers, welling up. There's certainly something authentic in their retelling, but is it trauma, love or a profound desire to avoid detection? Hard to tell.

'But if Dillon was there too and they were an item, why didn't he go with her?' I ask.

'She told us all she wanted to be alone,' Wes says.

I nod. It's time to roll out the big guns. 'She said in her message that her parents had told her everything about Amy. Do you know what that would mean?'

The temperature plummets, despite the underfloor heating. Neither speaks. I look from one to the other and back again.

'If she fled here, there had to be a trigger,' I add. 'Something must have made her lose it, and that message would suggest it was to do with Amy. And then she ended up...' I don't say it, just nod at the balcony.

'She was drunk, Ivor,' Wes says.

I cut through the lazy answer. 'She had two hours to sober up in a taxi!'

'Who knows what she did when she got here? She might have kept drinking.'

'OK, but didn't you find it suspicious when you got home the next day and she wasn't here?'

Faith picks up the baton. 'We didn't come home. We messaged her to see how she was on New Year's Day, but didn't get a reply, so decided to give her some space.'

'In your own home?'

'We always made this a home-from-home for her,' Faith says. True enough.

'But didn't Dillon want to go to her either, reassure her?'

'He'd tried ringing her too,' she explains. 'She wasn't replying. He sent messages, offered to come and keep her company, but she was ignoring all of us. We thought it was a bit off, but we decided to go to Dillon's flat in Stoke Newington instead. Talked ourselves into thinking she was just in a huff. Dillon had some decorating he wanted Wes to help with anyway, so we'd thought Rebecca would cool down, come back to London and we'd say no more about it. Then we got the call from Phillip that they'd found her...' She swallows hard and looks over her shoulder at the balcony too. It's so hard to read what genuine grief looks like. Are they playing me or are they heartbroken, or both? Why bring me into this room if not to mess with me?

Tea drunk, we all sit in silence for several minutes. Their story is unbelievable. None of them went after Becky, none of them returned to the house in the days after New Year's Eve, just to give her space. The Uber man was adamant she'd been buzzed in by someone to get through the gates. And the police arrested Dillon for some reason. What am I still not seeing?

'I don't mean to rush you, Ivor,' Wes eventually says, 'but our taxi to the airport's booked for 1.30 p.m. Four days in Catania. So we might have to call it a day, if you think you're ready to head back...'

I get up, apologising for distracting them from packing. All three of us traipse back to the hall. Wes hands me my jacket and we share hugs.

'Last thing... how did Becky get in when she got here alone?' I ask as I'm ushered towards the door.

'Spare key in the Carrera's wheel arch,' Wes says, raising his eyebrows in candour, as if he's an open book.

I persevere. 'No, but at the gate?'

Faith holds the front door open for me, which I walk through, turning back to face them, waiting for their final explanation.

'We've got a new keypad next to the buzzer, you can tap in a code to open the gate manually,' Wes states. 'She messaged asking for it while she was on her way over in the taxi. We sent her the code.'

I nod and give them a small, grateful smile. 'Makes sense.'

'Stay in touch, Ivor,' Faith says. She clicks a button on the wall and the electric gates open for my departure.

I thank them for the tea, then turn towards the driveway, trying not to walk in any way that will give away the jolt of terror that's just struck me.

Becky couldn't have messaged them from the taxi, because she left her phone behind.

They're lying.

26

BECKY'S DIARY

Tuesday 28 February 2023

Hogwarts Legacy is SO FUN! Prescribe it to kids hooked on crack cocaine because NOTHING could be as addictive as this game. I've been meaning to write in this diary for weeks, and yet this is the first time I've found because I've been gaming so much. What a nerd!

I got placed in Hufflepuff (of course!) and have played through the whole game twice. Hogwarts, Hogsmeade, the rest of the map, all you want to do is keep exploring. And you get your own sanctuary where you can look after all these magical creatures. My favourites are the puffskeins – these little fuzzy ball kind of things that bop about and have big, round eyes. I'm so mad, I even found someone making them on Etsy and bought three – a pink one, a blue one and a brown one – as teddies. They're tooooo cute!

Anyway, my *Harry Potter* alter ego is not why I'd been meaning to write in this diary. The update is... I've taken the plunge and moved in with Ivor.

Things came to a head with Mum and Dad in December. They tried to invite the Montagues, including Dillon, for Christmas, but I wanted to invite Ivor and said Dillon couldn't come too. Way too late to tell Ivor about my past with Dill, better to keep things simple and separate.

Dad especially got really weird. Started bringing Amy up, like that was relevant. He kept saying things like, 'Dillon has been very supportive over Amy... more than you'll ever understand, Rebecca,' like she died last week rather than 15 bloody years ago. And why be so cryptic? What could Dillon possibly know that I don't? We went out for almost four years and he never hinted a thing. We used to talk about her and everything that happened a lot, and I never ever got the impression he was hiding anything. Ergh! Typical Dad being a controlling emotionless cyborg.

Anyway, the battle was lost. Dillon was invited. In retaliation, I stayed at Ivor's all through Christmas and New Year's... December 18th to January 4th. Full Christmas. And by the end, I thought... y'know what... it's better to live in Finchley, with no shower, than to stay in the orbit of Mum and Dad. I had made the first step months ago by finally buying him a double duvet and I'm pretty sure Costa will nod through a switch to the Finchley Central branch in like a week. Now we just need to save up for someone to come and look at the shower. Bit annoying because I'm halfway to saving the £1,750 for the vet assistant diploma. Will take longer now. But I couldn't stay in Wimbledon.

So... here I am. We hired an actual removals van and took all my stuff across the Thames. My teddy, my Hogwarts drawings, my desk, my diaries, my wardrobe. The lot.

Mum and Dad didn't offer to help. Mum's face was hilarious when a cheap-ass tatty white van turned up on their drive and an Eastender with an accent that makes Danny Dyer sound posh got out. Looked like she'd swallowed a turd.

Ivor is cock-a-hoop. He insisted on buying a bottle of champagne even though he knew I wouldn't drink it. Said it had to be done as a symbol of how happy he was. So I watched him drink a whole bottle of Moet while I sipped at cans of celebratory cider instead.

And how's it been? Good. I'm not thinking about the long-term. The weird thing is that before the whole Christmas drama blew up, I'd been tempted to message Dillon, see how he is. But then the row with Mum and Dad kind of pushed me back to wanting to get away from them at any cost.

Me and Ivor have enough to pay the bills. I need time to settle, process moving out, save for my diploma, think what else I want to do in the meantime. I mean, I know what I want to do... volunteer at Battersea Dogs Home 25 hours a day, order takeaways every night and play *Hogwarts Legacy* until my thumbs fall off. But like, do I stay at Costa, find a better paid job? But then will that leave less time for studying when I start the course?

Urgh! Getting anxious. Every time I look too far forward, the whole world feels huge and insurmountable. Ivor was really keen to stop using condoms once I officially moved in and I've let him. (Sorry diary... that is QUITE the TMI bombshell, but it's the other thing on my mind.) Him wanting to start trying for a baby is WAY too quick. But I can't bring myself to upset him by putting the brakes on. He is DESPERATE to start trying and I am DESPERATE not to let on we're not ready. So here we find ourselves.

If it was all left up to Ivor, we wouldn't deal with any of the issues facing us, we'd just bring a child into the world on top of all our mess. That wouldn't be fair.

So, I'm taking the pill first thing in the mornings before he gets up. If I dwell on it too long, I feel hideous and icky for not telling him. But it buys us time. We need that. And on the other hand, I am protecting the child we're NOT having, if that makes any sense.

Now you can see why I've been playing so much *Hogwarts Legacy*. The ultimate escape.

What's left, and still bugging me, is Dad... *Dillon has been very supportive over Amy... more than you'll ever understand.*

Have I misremembered something? Has trauma played tricks with my mind? No. There's no way. So what does he mean?

Urgh, he was probably talking rubbish as usual, and it's left me spiralling for no good reason.

Forget it, girl! Fire up the PlayStation. Back to Hogwarts.

27

IVOR

January 2025

It's good that YouTube is free, isn't it? If it wasn't, if you had to pay like, even 5p per video, I'd be billions in debt.

I got the train straight back to north London after my tea with the Montagues. And here I have lain for the forty-eight hours since.

I blame Tesco really. They emailed saying I could have another week off on full pay if I wanted, which I accepted. Think they're terrified I'll take my complaint against Trish higher up. I might. But for now, it's given me time to think. Time spent... in bed, on YouTube.

I've watched someone do a whole game walkthrough of *Hogwarts Legacy* as a Hufflepuff... the house Becky was sorted into; ten videos by a nice Geordie bloke documenting his fall into alcoholism and why he's now given it up; and a lot of angry Gordon Ramsay compilations. Me and Becky used to snuggle up and stick those on all the time, tensing in each other's arms as a gormless chef over-cooked a trout or forgot to reduce the jus, earning themselves a personal evisceration.

And then I stumbled upon these long videos where Americans try Greggs for the first time and film it. I clicked on one, thinking it would entertain me for about three microseconds... and four hours later, I was still watching the bloody things. It's so funny seeing them initially turn their noses up at the cheap prices and the working-class-ness of the bakes and cakes, only to eat their words, along with every last crumb of the comestibles. Then they say things like, 'This is reeely guud, truly!'. Course it is, mate, now get your trap around that caramel doughnut so I can watch you howl with joy over that, too.

Anyway, yes, YouTube... it's been my only company since I got back from Sandbanks. I haven't even drank anything. It feels different to the days I stayed in bed before the funeral. There's a weird buzz in my chest, an excitement about finding out the truth. The Burrowses, the Montagues, they're all lying to me. But none of them know I have Becky's phone or that necklace and they don't realise I know they're lying.

So I've given myself a couple of days to ponder. Nothing could demonstrate better how seriously I am taking my new-found sense of purpose than the fact I have gone two days drink-free. Just me, lots of takeaways and good old agua mineral. I'm sort of like John and Yoko, lying in bed for a higher cause. Unlike their bid for world peace, however, my plotting has gone rather well.

Someone was in that house when Becky arrived in Sand-banks, and she knew it before she got there. I am sure of that. My guess would be it was Dillon. And if she threw herself over the balcony, surely he'd come forward and tell the police that, wouldn't he?

How do I substantiate it though? Getting into her phone

really would be a start. That infernal phone! I've tried hundreds of *Harry Potter* characters' birthdays, scores of dates from our happiest memories and dozens of common six-digit combinations, but nothing cracks the digital treasure chest.

I've found Dillon Montague on Instagram. Can't glean much. Don't like looking at the pictures, if I'm honest, and he hasn't posted since Becky died. I still can't shake the annoying feeling I've seen him before though, don't know why.

It'll come to me.

My next move is decided, however. Another sniff around the Burrowses' house. Last time, I went in looking for the phone, found it and then got interrupted. I need to be more forensic – every room, every drawer, anything. It would be good if I even knew what I'm looking for, but there must be something incriminating. Dad wouldn't always know exactly what was in the houses he hit, but he never left empty-handed.

We're back round to a Thursday again too, which means this evening is bridge o'clock. Of course, Julie could sneak in during Phillip and Audrey's absence again, which would be suboptimal to say the least. But I've come up with a rather mean solution. As I said, it's been a productive couple of days.

It involves Cam. She keeps messaging, apologising for screaming at me at the end of the wake. I've texted her back like three times, telling her to forget it, but now I think about it... there is one thing she could do. If she's adamant on making amends, who am I to deny her such peace of mind? So I text:

> Could you phone the Burrowses, don't say who
> you are, but tell them their housekeeper Julie
> has been stealing from them and using their
> house when they're out. Tell them she's been
> doing it for years, taking expensive wine with
> her when she leaves.

I don't know she's been doing it for years but it gives the accusation some clout. Plus... it'd be extraordinary if the very first time she did it happened to be the time I was also trespassing.

I thought about making the anonymous call myself and putting on a fake accent, but it's much safer if I get a woman to do it.

No way the Burrowses will keep employing Julie after this. Even if she denies it and they don't sack her on the spot, she won't risk swanning in for a tipple out-of-hours now she knows she's been rumbled.

Cam replies immediately. 'Deal.'

Game on.

28

IVOR

January 2025

Noz hands me a Heineken before his rather enormous arse has even hit the wooden slats of the park bench.

He's been wanting his drinking buddy back for days. And to be honest, I am extremely ready to answer the rallying call.

Can't have too much before I enter the Burrowses' house. Need my wits about me. A couple won't hurt though, especially after all my good behaviour recently. I crack open my can and let the froth spill over my fingers.

'How's things?' I ask, clanging my can against his.

'Knackered!' he says with a throaty cough. Today's T-shirt is another tight one. To be fair, a parachute would look tight over his gut. It's a green cotton V-neck number with white writing on: 'Train. Dominate. Repeat.'

Initially I'd told Noz I was busy tonight. Then he demanded I describe in great detail what could possibly keep me away from the pub for yet another evening. When I told him, he decided for both of us that we could have a catch-up in the park before I break and enter. A bromance for the ages.

'What you hoping to find in there now?' he probes.

I take a long sip of lager. Goodness me, that hits the spot! There's something comforting about warm beer on a chilly night. It's very dark in the park, hardly anyone about. I'm in my thick black bomber jacket, black hat, chunky woollen jumper underneath, and I'm still tensing against the cold.

'Dunno,' I admit. 'Look in the safe again. Try to find her diaries, although I'm pretty sure they're the first things her mum and dad would have destroyed. See if there's anything else that feels like it could be important. Didn't get to turn over the whole place last time, was interrupted.'

When we've both finished our tinnies, out come fresh ones from Noz's backpack. We chat Arsenal for a bit then he offers to tell me a joke.

'What's a Freudian slip?'

I play the game. 'I don't know, what is a Freudian slip?'

'It's when you say one thing but mean your mother.'

I snort, bringing my beer up to my mouth.

Encouraged by the reaction, he goes again. 'Copper told me he's been out looking for a thief with one eye. I said, "Well, use both eyes and you might catch him."'

It gets another titter.

Warming to his stand-up routine, he chances a third. 'Met a hottie last night, she said sex was off the table, so we did it underneath instead.'

Glancing at him, I give a that's-enough shake of the head and check the time – it's at least twenty minutes later than when the Burrowses went out last time. Maybe the Julie thing has spooked them... Oh no, they won't forgo the boring bridge brigade when their own daughter dies, but finding out the housekeeper's nicking Malbec, that's a cancel-all-plans emergency!

Noz calls it before I'm ready to. 'They're not going out, are they?'

He's right.

But that's not good enough. I need another look. Keep the line between me and Becky pulsing.

'You need them out the house.'

I grunt in admission.

'What did your dad used to do?' Noz queries. 'This must have happened to him – miscalculating when a family would be out.'

'I'm not like him,' I murmur.

'Ivor! No one's saying you're like him. But it could help. So get over yourself!'

It's odd to see Noz so passionate about anything other than football, beer or ladies he has no chance with.

'There was one time...' I begin, shutting my eyes as the suppressed memory comes surging back. 'He knew the house's phone number, called it, made up that a family member had been in a car crash, said they were in hospital. The couple were out of their own front door within five minutes. Coast cleared.'

Noz cracks a new can and passes it to me as a reward for my breakthrough. 'Right then,' he says. 'So we call them. Make the caller ID anonymous. Get the Burrowses out of the house.'

'Saying what?'

Noz rolls his eyes. 'I dunno, mate. Nuclear attack? Caviar shortage at Waitrose? Anything! You're the one who bloody knows them.'

'Could pretend to be the police, say we've found new evidence, and they're needed at the station.'

'Sounds like a winner,' he states, punching my arm.

'Can you make the call? They'll recognise me.'

He slugs at his Heineken, leaving me hanging, then agrees.

He keeps it brief once he's dialled and they've answered, sounding slightly posher and more formal than Noz ever has before. A light goes out in an upstairs window about fifteen seconds after he ends the call.

Getting up, Noz passes me an extra can. 'One for the road,' he says. I take it, relieved he's not insisting on coming in with me.

I make the walk across the park slowly. Dad used to like returning to houses he'd already hit. The familiarity, the confidence of knowing the layout. It's surprising how often rich people don't update their security after a break-in – telling themselves in hope rather than firm belief that lightning can't strike twice.

I take a slight detour to drop my rapidly finished final can into a waste bin. I may be about to break my own promise to myself and commit burglary yet again, but I'm no litterbug.

Taking a running jump, I haul myself over the wall at the usual place, creep up the side of the house – no light coming from inside – and confirm the Burrowses have vacated the driveway, this time in their own old Merc.

OK. This is happening.

Back garden bench slid across in the heavy darkness, window prised open, I make the familiar, graceless entry.

It's essential to move the garden bench back before vacating the property – as I did last time – otherwise Phillip will know. Learnt that the hard way. He'd spotted it out of place when he got up one morning, guessed what had happened and stampeded up to Becky's room. She'd long since gone to work but he discovered me, intertwined in her lovely warm, fifteen-tog duvet, starkers. I barely had time to reacquaint myself with my boxer shorts before I was out on my ear.

First stop, now I am in and the alarm is off, is Becky's room. It's exactly how it was last time I was here, seemingly down to the creases and folds in her sheets. I collapse on to the bed, head face down on the pillow and notice something has changed. Her scent, it's less strong, her essence diffusing away. Does no one else care? This beautiful, unique woman is gone and the whole world – the police, the press, even most of the people at her own funeral, appear to see it as a sad pothole, to be noted, navigated around and never thought of again. It's a disgrace!

I yank myself away from her sheets. I am now Becky's only advocate in this world, there's no time for futile wallowing. Who knows how long it will take the Burrowses to realise they've been tricked and there's no one waiting for them at the police station.

Back on my feet, I begin.

First: her diaries.

Got to be careful not to ransack her bedroom and leave any clue someone has been in here. That was another, depressingly subtle trick of Dad's – leave a house the way you find it. That way, it will be days or weeks before the families report any theft, if they ever reported it at all, often thinking instead they must have misplaced their cherished heirlooms.

I don't have to ransack anything to see there is no box of diaries in this room. She used to keep them all in a cube-shaped metal box under her desk with a padlock. I knew the code... 9-8-7-6. But I never sneaked a peek. If she wanted space to lay out her thoughts in private, she deserved that. I would look now, but only to help uncover the truth. The point is academic, however. The box isn't here.

My next desperate scan of her bedroom is a hunt for any

lingering detail that could be a clue to the new passcode on her phone. Post-its, dates ringed on a wall chart, marks etched into her desk... What am I even looking for? Impatience soon trumps inspiration. It's impossible. No one has ever left a convenient visual cue to their phone passcode outside of lazy one-hour TV crime dramas.

Move on.

Pushing my gloved hand into my jeans back pocket, I pull out that bear necklace I found on her, open her jewellery box and drop it in. At first, I'd been obsessed with it, one last secret binding us together. But I'm starting to worry it's haunting me, keeping the ghosts of that night alive in my flat. Having her phone isn't the same, I didn't take that from her dead body. But the bear pendant, maybe that was wrong on some deep para-normal level because that terrifying face comes back to me every night. So this is my bid for absolution. Return it to her room, reverse the wrongdoing, the theft. It feels stupid, I don't even believe in that psychic, supernatural mumbo jumbo. But I don't want it in my flat any more. If I find out whose it is, that'll be massive, the fact she was grasping it doesn't change, but the spirits that guard it need not darken my door again now.

I cross the landing, my phone torch the only beam tracing the bald carpet as I go door to door looking for the diaries. It's easy to discount rooms swiftly as the box is too big to easily hide.

I spend a little longer in Amy's old room – the Tigger toy still on the pillow, a Baby Annabell in a small plastic buggy at the end of the bed. I only know that's what they're called because I'd started doing research into kids' toys when me and Becky were trying. Thought it'd be nice to get a baby doll if we had a little girl.

It's important to be even more careful not to leave a speck of dust out of place in here when I leave; it's a shrine to a dead daughter. Dad wouldn't have cared about such sensitivities. But I do.

Nothing useful shows up in there, anyway.

It's not long before I've checked everywhere across both floors. They aren't here.

Where haven't I looked – inside the tumble dryer, bottom drawer of the freezer, underneath the Weathered York flagstones in the garden? Any last ideas seem obscure and frivolous. And nothing else has struck me as potentially incriminating or enlightening either.

Dejection seeping under my skin, I head back to the office and open the safe. It's as empty as a politician's promise.

I swear under my breath; any further ideas for places to search wash away as I lose all confidence in my covert abilities. I lie back on the carpet, my legs either side of the safe.

What am I expecting? A suicide note? A joint confession from the families? Video footage of Dillon throwing her off the balcony? Is this all a stupid distraction to make myself feel like I'm still doing something for Becky? Those stages of grief Cam talked about. Is this 'bargaining'? When in reality, there is no level of effort that can bring her back and no amount of evidence left that could direct me to the truth. What a wasted trip. And to think I've probably got Julie sacked for this futile sojourn.

My dad's voice slaps me across the face.

We don't leave empty-handed! Try harder!

Pushing myself back up, I give a sharp, short exhale, and redirect my trusty light onto Phillip's desk. Bet he's got a membership card for Reform UK somewhere, that would be so Phillip Burrows. I flick through boring letters, bills, a couple of notes with phone numbers on. Googling the numbers doesn't reveal anything. I open the drawers on both sides of the desk, more papers, a phone book, a fountain pen. I sift through it all. No hidden bottle of whisky, no seventies porn stash. How can one man be so vapid?

I move across to a bureau, replete with similarly mundane artefacts but no gold. There is, at least, a key on one of the shelves which fits a filing cabinet in the opposite corner of the room. This is like a weird, creepy escape room. Becky and I were going to do one of those once, a *Harry Potter* one in Greenwich, but we had to cancel. Wish I knew where the clues were and how long I've got left to complete this challenge.

No leads in the filing cabinet, just a meticulously organised row of folders, with file dividers between each wad of paper with names of companies and utilities written in capital letters at the top of each section. I pull out myriad sheets but they all tally – the word 'WATER' on one tab, followed by all the Thames Water bills, same for 'ELECTRIC', 'GAS', 'CAR', 'GARDEN', 'PORTFOLIO'. If this hunt gets any more tedious, I may slip into a coma.

I'm about to shut the drawer again when a tab right at the back catches my eye. On it, clearly written in thick black Sharpie, is the word 'DILLON'. There are several pieces of paper behind it.

I pluck them out and place them on the floor. They look like bank statements. But it's just one name again and again, listed about a dozen times a page – Dillon Montague – with the same date of each month next to every transaction. It looks like payments made by Dillon to the Burrowses, every month, going back years. I turn page after page, seeing just his name, the date of the first of each month and a figure. Going all the way up to this month. But a black marker has swiped through the figure on every transaction. I hold the torch behind the paper, in front of it, at an angle, nothing illuminates the amount of money that's been redacted.

Making sure my phone's flash is on, I take a photo of each page. Dillon Montague is paying the Burrowses for something. What?

My ears are bat-like sensitive tonight, after last time. I hear the clink of the gate at the very top of the drive and the tiniest hint of tyres rolling onto gravel. The spike in adrenaline almost sends me through the ceiling.

Papers put back. Race downstairs. Open kitchen door, through it, shut it. Bench dragged back. I am halfway across the grass over to the park when I hear their car doors slam.

I need a beer.

29
_____

BECKY'S DIARY

Tuesday 4 July 2023

The last two days have been awful.

Not sure why I'm writing this down. It's not anything I'd want to remember or read back.

Yesterday was our anniversary. Two years since our first date. We'd planned to do a *Harry Potter* escape room then go out for an Indian. But as a surprise, I'd made this big effort the night before. It was a Sunday and Ivor had to work but he was finishing at 8 p.m. and I was off all day. The plan was to tidy the flat, prepare a really nice meal and then have it when he got home as a bonus ahead of spending all of the next day together.

I'd bought candles, a new pine air freshener, I'd sneaked out on Saturday morning while he was still sleeping to get steaks from the butcher knowing they wouldn't be open on the Sunday, I'd ordered this black wrap dress from New Look. First dress I'd bought in YEARS.

I prepped some greens and potato wedges, made peppercorn sauce FROM SCRATCH and put the steaks on at about 8.30 p.m., thinking he'd definitely be home by 9 p.m. Nine o'clock came and went. I texted him and got no reply. Ten o'clock. Eleven o'clock. He stumbles in about quarter to midnight, reeking of booze. Steak's cold and rubbery, candles have burned out, my make-up's run. He doesn't even notice I've got my new dress on. Just has this gormless smile, says he's off to bed and that he can't wait for our anniversary.

I didn't get a wink of sleep. He lay there, sprawled all over the place, hogging the duvet I had to bring over because he never bought a proper one, and snoring so loud it shook the bedframe. Like his pneumatic nostrils were boring a hole in his pillow.

I was so angry.

Totally ruined yesterday.

He clocked I wasn't happy when he finally got up around midday and apologised, saying he hadn't known I was waiting up. He seemed a bit sorry and promised not to drink anything all day – a solution to absolutely nothing.

He'd got me this 'adopt a tiger' package where you donate £300 to some charity and they keep you updated on this specific tiger every six months. He said he'd done it because of how much I'd loved the tiger cub we saw when we'd visited London Zoo way back when and he was so excited for us to have a baby of our own.

I snapped, said it was a waste of money. He looked so hurt and deflated. Then I burst into tears and went to bed.

It's all just hit me these last two days... all the things I didn't want to happen by living with Ivor have happened. We still have no savings, I'm still at Costa, he's still at Tesco, he still drinks every night, I still haven't told him I'm on the pill, we're going nowhere. And yet somehow, he thinks life's perfect.

Until this week I was still at least telling myself that we loved each other and that was important to hold on to, but now I'm not even sure I do feel that way.

When I first moved in, I was kind of dreading Ivor having nights out and me sitting at home waiting for him to get home really late, all drunk and annoying. But the longer I've been here, the more I've encouraged him to go out, to give me more time to myself. That's why I couldn't really blame him for coming home late on Sunday. It was totally normal behaviour from him at this point. But how is he OK with that, and how does he think this is a solid, normal relationship any more?

I used to think my love language was spending time together. But honestly, Ivor's over-exuberant, tipsy, lovey-dovey snuggling on the sofa has started to give me the ick. I need space to breathe and feel morose if I want to feel morose. It's cathartic to let yourself be grumpy and down and listen to emo music sometimes. At least, *I* need that. Introverts recharge their batteries by staying in and having quiet time. I didn't like living with Mum and Dad, but being alone in my room was a nice, chilled, restorative tonic to the excitable, OTT, I-love-you-I-love-you-I-love-you fest of being with Ivor.

I'm trapped. I thought about messaging Cam to meet up and talk about it, but she's such a gossip. She'd want every juicy detail about how much Ivor drinks, how much we earn, how often we're having sex. Even *that* – sex – feels fraught and fake now because I know Ivor thinks we're trying for a baby and I know we aren't.

No, Cam isn't a good confidant. Never was.

Ivor was my cry for help, my life raft, my chance to escape Mum and Dad and live without the secrets and lies. But this isn't any better. He is dependent on alcohol, and I don't have the energy left to challenge him. If I said it's me or the booze, I'd have to stay and watch him try to give it up, ruin this lovely life he thinks he has, just so he could stay with a person who is struggling to love him back at this point. Am I selfish? Should I be there for him unconditionally, be his rock? But for what? So I can keep not telling him the truth, and live a sorry, shell of a life with a man who thinks he loves me because he's only spent about 4 per cent of our relationship sober?

I really need a friend right now. I'm so lonely, I'm lost, I'm scared. There's one person I know would listen and cheer me up, the way he always used to. Dillon.

That's why I messaged him earlier today on my secret Instagram account.

He's just replied.

30

IVOR

January 2025

I find Noz in The Rose & Crown, the same pub hired for the wake. He'd given up on the cold, lonely park bench the moment I entered Burrows Towers.

Fortifying double whisky washed down at the bar, I take our Heinekens back to our table and get my phone out to look at those bank statements again.

'Why would Dillon be paying the Burrowses every month?' I ask out loud, as if Noz knows anything about anything.

'Mmdunno,' he gargles, tonsil-deep in beer.

I pinch the screen incessantly, zooming in on each redacted figure – all almost identical except for the dates, and the varying thickness of the black lines.

'Why would these idiots keep hold of documents that make 'em look dodgy?' Noz wonders, trying to engage.

'Phillip hates computers and technology,' I say, confident I've told Noz this before. He never remembers anything. 'So if he wants records, it's hard copies. I mean, it's not like he was broadcasting this for the world. It was at the back of a filing cabinet, redacted. And paying someone isn't illegal. But it's weird.'

'Redacted how?' Noz asks, knocking back more beer and wiping his top lip.

I pass him my phone. He peers for a second, then leans in for a more thorough inspection.

'Use a filter to make the photo black and white, helps with the sharpness,' he says.

My befuddled look is met with an indignant defence. 'Why'd you always act surprised when I say clever stuff!'

'The only pictures you pay attention to are of naked women.'

'That's fair, but on this occasion I'm right. Just make it black and white,' he orders impatiently. 'If the black of the marker is at all different from the printed ink, it might show up better.'

I do as I'm told and zoom in again.

Mouth hanging open, I glance up at my closest friend; his eyebrows rise in smug vindication.

'Black printer ink glossier than the marker pen?' he asks rhetorically. 'How much was this posh fella paying them then?'

'Five grand!' I check the next line down, and the next line, and the next, zooming as much as I can, the bright, white light of my phone's flash bouncing off the printed figure just enough to make it out. 'Dillon was paying them £5,000 – every month.'

Noz's eyes widen. 'How do we get in on this deal?'

Dillon, paying the Burrowses thousands every month – and these statements go back several years. He works in finance, a hedge trimmer or whatever they're called. But that's still tons. And why? The Burrowses have their own money. And why's it coming from Dillon rather than Wes and Faith? He's decades younger than the lot of them. It doesn't make any sense.

Noz has returned with two more pints and two double

whiskies in the time I've been sitting here lost for words. 'Who is this Dillon bloke, anyway?' he huffs.

If this man hadn't just pushed a drink into each of my hands, I'd punch him. 'Becky's ex-boyfriend! The one I reckon was at the house in Sandbanks when she got there! He was at the wake. Size of a lighthouse. I told you about all this!'

He shrugs, so I get Dillon's Instagram profile up and hold it up to him. 'Becky's ex!'

He takes my phone. 'Oh yeah, you said you thought you'd met him before.'

'Maybe.'

He taps on a few pictures as I make a start on my fresh pint. Tilting his head slightly, he makes a small grunt. 'Huh!'

'What?' I bark.

'Stick a condom on your head, mate, because I'm about to fuck your tiny mind.'

I stare back, unimpressed.

Noz sniffs, sips his beer, holds me right where he wants me. Then he says it. 'He's wearing that bear necklace you found.'

I snatch the phone back. Noz has moved on to a picture I hadn't studied before. I haven't really studied any of them. Once it was clear there weren't any of Becky or any from that night, I couldn't bring myself to examine Dillon's grid of middle-class mundanity more closely.

What a fool! Because Noz is right! It's there, nestled on the bare V-shaped skin below his open collar, in one picture taken last year. Becky's bear necklace, it can't be anything else!

And Becky died holding it.

A cold, terrifying image flashes into my mind, him wrestling with her on the balcony, hoisting her over the railings, her grasping for him one last time, missing his neck but coming away with the silver chain and pendant, clutched tight in her fist as she fell.

'You OK?' Noz checks, as all colour deserts my face.

I slam back the whisky and chase it down with half the pint. 'I don't know.'

Do I go to the police now? Admit everything? If they knew she was holding Dillon's necklace, that'd be proof he was there when she died. They'd have to re-arrest him. And it doesn't matter that I've not got the necklace any more. In fact, it now being at the Burrowses' house is perfect – how would a piece of jewellery with Becky's blood on it get there, unless they were all in on this plot together? And Phillip and Audrey don't even know it's there themselves. When the police do get a warrant, they'll find the necklace and it will link Dillon to the scene, and the Burrowses to him. I've only gone and planted the perfect clue by complete accident!

'Noz, I think I know what happened!'

'That's two favours I've done you this evening,' he says, smug.

'Let's go for a hat trick.'

He grunts and burps at the same time. 'Eh?'

'I'm going to confront the Burrowses, but I'm not sure what they might do. I need backup.'

'When?' he splutters.

'Now.'

31

IVOR

January 2025

Noz hasn't ventured into the Burrowses' abode before but I'm glad he's here tonight.

For a change, I approach the orthodox way, through the front gate and down the driveway, my bodyguard stomping next to me. As an additional variable, I have set my phone to record in my pocket, so if they do confess, I'll have it on tape. I should be some sort of MI5 spook, my plan's so good.

It doesn't take long for the door to open – after a few thwacks.

'PHILLIP!' Aud shrieks upon seeing me, fleeing towards the kitchen without shutting the door.

'We need to talk,' I call after her as we enter the hall uninvited.

Nodding over to the library, I lead Noz in and pour a large cognac into one of the cut-crystal glasses. I take a sip and pass the tumbler to Noz, who sees the rest off.

The night's alcohol weighs me down, slowing my words –

I'm past tipsy tenacity, bordering on drunken disorder. But there is enough evidence now. It's time for the truth.

'Ivor, this has to stop,' Phillip says with a sigh, resigned and tired as he appears in the doorway.

It's hard to tell if I'm swaying or not. That's the trouble trying to assess your own level of intoxication, you're not really in the right state to spot the signs. I take a seat instead.

'This can't fucking wait!' Noz yells. He should probably rein in the swearing, but I appreciate the brotherly backup.

Looking up at Phillip, it's a relief he doesn't split into two people as I focus. 'I know someone let Becky in at the Montagues' place.' What else can I tell him without letting on I've been snooping? 'I know Dillon was arrested...'

'And released,' Phillip states for the record.

'I know Becky messaged me saying she'd finally found out the truth about her sister.'

'You can't know someone let her in at the Montagues' because it didn't happen,' Phillip says, peering over his shoulder out into the hall, as if he's only half listening.

'I do know. I checked Becky's Uber account and spoke to the driver who took her to Sandbanks. He said someone opened the gate for her...'

'Wes sent her a code to open it when she got there,' he claims, trotting out the same impossible line he must have agreed with the Montagues when they were getting their stories straight. His eyes are fastened to me now as it dawns on him how deeply I've delved, how dangerous I am to his web of lies. Thank goodness Noz is by my side, otherwise they'd probably try to bump me off right here, right now. They wouldn't try to kill us both, would they? If he's spiked the cognac with chloroform, I am going to be so annoyed.

'That's what Wes and Faith told me too. But they couldn't have, because Becky's phone never left this house.'

'How do you know that? Did you steal it? Was that you?'

I'm ready for the accusation and answer with aplomb, even if I do say so myself. 'Was what me?' Locking my stare to him, I add: 'All I know is I tracked Becky's phone on an app after New Year's Eve and it said she was here. That's why I came round, remember? But she'd already gone to the coast. So she must have left without it.'

Phillip's cheeks begin to colour. He checks his watch. Does he remember? Is he even listening? Is the booze playing tricks or is he really distracted?

'Quit the lies, Phil,' I plead, my voice fragile as my throat thickens. Remembering the phone recording in my pocket, I cast my line and bait. 'Dillon killed her, didn't he?'

'Don't be absurd,' he rebukes, folding his arms in disdain, still blocking the doorway.

'IT'S NOT ABSURD!' Noz erupts, trying to put the fire out with his blowtorch. Still on his feet, he glares at our host.

'Pipe down, you fool,' Phillip mutters at him, his face not as cocksure as his tone.

I yank Noz down next to me and make sure to speak in a low, calm voice. 'Phil.'

'Phillip!' he corrects.

'Phillip. Becky was going to reveal what happened to her sister, wasn't she? You'd told her what happened and she was going to tell everyone. And you couldn't have that. Was it Dillon? Had he killed Amy? So she decided to go and confront him?'

'We were all here, no one was at Sandbanks,' Phillip states, refusing to leave his sinking ship.

'He let her in at Sandbanks. She confronted him. He killed her.'

'You're disgusting,' Phillip snarls.

'Dillon's been paying you for years, hasn't he? Have you been blackmailing him over Amy's death? Did Becky find all this out?'

'Blackmail Dillon!' Phillip scoffs. 'Drink really has eroded whatever limited intellect you ever had, hasn't it?' I feel Noz tensing, ready to gallop in on my behalf again, but I place a hand on his knee. 'And who says Dillon's paying us, anyway?'

'The fact you didn't deny it,' I taunt.

'How do you know all this?' There's an incredulous frustration dripping from every word.

Ha! He's cracked, that's basically an admission. The phone in my pocket will have picked it up too. Noz glances at me, eyes aflame – even the worse for wear, we both spotted it.

'Because I've been digging, Phillip, and I will not rest until the truth is out. I care about her too much to—'

'WE CARED ABOUT HER!' he screams.

'SO MUCH YOU WENT TO PLAY BRIDGE DAYS AFTER SHE DIED!' I fire back.

'No, we didn't,' he cries. 'Of course we didn't!'

'More lies, Phil!'

'We've never been to bridge! OK? We used to say that on Thursdays, but the truth is we've been having counselling – for grief – for years. We weren't coping as a couple, but we didn't want to burden Rebecca, so we said we had a club to go to.'

'Rubbish!' I respond.

'Believe me or don't, but why else would we have gone somewhere less than a week after Rebecca died? We've never needed that emotional support more!'

'And yet you aren't there tonight,' I say.

'Our counsellor cancelled, we'll be there again next week. Ivor, Amy and Rebecca have—'

'Becky!' I attempt to correct.

'Rebecca,' he interrupts even more firmly. 'Amy and Rebecca were our girls, and we loved them both more than anything else in the world.'

It would make sense for why they always disappeared at the exact same time every week, gave Becky such a weak excuse and still kept the routine going after she died. But he's full of bull. The whole time I have known Phillip and Audrey, they have never treated Becky like they loved her. You'll have to wake up earlier than that to trick me, mate.

Phillip's eyes widen. 'How do you even know we were out at counselling last week?' He knows I came in. He knows I stole the phone.

I stare back, tensing as if I'm about to slam into a wall at 1,000 mph.

A muffled voice says something too quiet to hear from the hall. Is that Aud? Is she hiding?

Phillip glances off to his right, to the curtains of the library. 'It's over, Ivor,' he says, softly.

Looking in the same direction, the noise of a car trundling up the driveway seeps in from outside.

'Aud phoned as soon as you got here,' he explains, not wanting to miss his moment of triumph.

'Phoned who?' Noz asks, as I stand, knowing instantly.

'DCI Tina Schwarz. We've been keeping her updated on your little visits, well, the ones we already knew about – to us, to the Montagues. And she told us if you came round again, we were to give her a ring.'

A car door slams.

A small smile edges up the sides of Phillip Burrows' mouth. 'I'm sure she's going to be even more interested when I tell her you've been trespassing too.'

There's a knock on that big front door. Phillip keeps his eyes on me as Aud patters over to open it. She'd been standing out of sight listening the whole time, as Phillip kept us busy, kept us here.

I've got five seconds.

'You tell her I've trespassed, and I'll tell her you hid Becky's phone...'

Aud opens the door.

I whisper the end of my threat. '...and that she died holding Dillon's necklace.'

Detective Schwarz walks into the hall. I can see her over Phillip's shoulder. He is yet to turn round, however.

We stare at each other, years of mutual hatred scorching the air between us. If I'm going down, these monsters are coming with me.

32

BECKY'S DIARY

Thursday 14 September 2023

We met up, me and Dillon. Tonight. It's been nearly four years since we last saw each other, we worked out. He smelled good, he looked better. From his Instagram, I'd already prepared to meet a fully grown man, rather than the boy I'd split up with. And when I got to the bar, there this man was. Still tall, but fuller, more complete. Better dress sense – his old worn-out student hoodies replaced with a denim shirt, open over a grey tee. He's grown up, like an older brother of the former self I'd once loved. His eyes lit up when he saw me, his smile came swooping back. I'd missed that, the way he used to make me feel like simply being in my presence was enough to put him in a good mood.

And his first words? 'Hello, Brown Bear.'

There were enough butterflies flapping in my stomach to carry me up to the moon.

His nickname for me. I'd not heard it in so long. But those three words transported me back to a time I'd forgotten how much I loved. Sixth form, holding hands, sending each other a million texts a day, him passing his driving test so he could drive up to see me more, restaurants, barbecues, walking to a tattoo parlour on my 18th birthday to get matching designs then both chickening out at the door, eating sour snakes until our gums hurt, sunburn on Sandbanks beach, windburn on Sandbanks beach. Everything from when we were good came flooding back, submerging me in long-lost joy.

People say they wish they could bottle up certain feelings and remember them forever. Well, 'Hello, Brown Bear' is proof you can. And the second he said it, he popped open a magnum of our past and I gorged on it.

We'd been messaging A LOT over the last two months, but it didn't feel right to meet up... at first.

But then I'd been forced to go round to Mum and Dad's. I needed my National Insurance number for something at work (how am I managing to make a story about seeing Dillon again sound so boring?!).

Anyway... I was looking around Dad's office and came across all these huge payments Dillon had apparently been making to Dad. Like... thousands, every month.

I confronted Dad and he got angry, snatched the papers off me and told me to stop snooping! Next thing I know, he's got a black marker out and is crossing out each transaction one after the other, which was dumb because I'd already seen how much it was. I asked him if it was anything to do with Amy. He wouldn't reply. But the way he was acting, the complete refusal to engage, it all felt very much like how he is about Amy... like... exactly the same vibe.

I went back to Finchley and thought about telling Ivor, but he was getting ready to go out to the pub to watch Arsenal so I thought... why not just speak with Dillon himself? And it's not the sort of conversation one should demote to an Instagram DM. (That's my excuse and I'm sticking to it!)

There's nothing wrong or naughty about it – he's a family friend, I'm allowed my own social life!

We arranged a date when there was another Arsenal game. I stayed in my pyjamas until Ivor had gone, then whipped out my light blue, pleated skirt – the short one – and my cute white strappy top that Dillon once said looked sexy, and I met him at a bar.

After two drinks, I plucked up the courage to ask about the transactions between him and Dad. He said he's investing some of his income in high-risk stocks and trusts Dad to do it for him since that's what Dad always specialised in. So much less dramatic than I was expecting. Dad will literally hide anything from me, given half a chance.

But the evening... IT WAS SO GOOD!

At one point our fingers touched across the table and we both let them stay in contact, as my insides almost sparked a fire so wild the building burned down.

I know, I know! I'm with Ivor. It ended very badly with Dillon. Those bottled-up feelings washing over me are not the full story of our relationship. I have to remember that! The last year, or however long he'd been doing it... the checking my phone, interrogating me, following me to work. It became horrible, intense, impossible.

But he spent about 20 minutes this evening telling me how embarrassed he was by it all. How driving me away was the worst mistake he'd ever made and that if he could change one thing in his whole life, it would be that. And I believe him. He wasn't trying to excuse his actions or ignore them. He was owning them and seems to have matured. He said he hasn't had any therapy, but he spoke like someone who has, because he seemed so clear thinking and earnest about his mistakes. It's obvious how much he's stewed over it all.

Then he pulled out the necklace he was wearing, which until then had been tucked away under his T-shirt. The bear pendant I got him when he went to uni. He still has it. He says he's never taken it off. I could feel my cheeks blushing as he said it.

I did tell him about Ivor, about how long we've been together. Sure, I also mentioned how much he drinks, but I didn't hint we are on the rocks. That would be a betrayal.

Now I'm home though, Ivor's still out and my mind is obsessing. I miss Dillon. I miss what we used to be, how we were so flirtatious and selfish about needing all of each other as teenagers. Once we had awkwardly fumbled our way through sex those first few times, we had SO MUCH of it. Both our homes, both our gardens, on the beach, a pub bathroom, in his car, a service station disabled toilet after we literally had to pull in off the motorway because we were so hot for each other. I don't know if it's the booze, or a general lack of libido, but life between the sheets with Ivor has never been half as explosive or impulsive. Just touching fingers tonight, it's like…

Damn! Ivor's key's rattling in the door. Better go.

33

IVOR

January 2025

The cognac was really kicking in as DCI Schwarz arrived. It was nigh on impossible to focus. I'm crystal clear on what wasn't said, however.

Phillip and Aud didn't dob me in – about the trespassing, about the phone, about Dillon's necklace. That's how much they want to keep their own secrets.

Noz and I sit in the back of the DCI's posh Audi, my head against the cool window, watching the amber lights flick past. The smell of leather upholstery and pine air freshener are a kind distraction. Is she driving us home or to a police station? Surely, it's home. Noz hasn't committed any crimes and she hasn't read us our rights. I'd remember something as traumatic as that, like when the police raided Dad's flat and arrested us on suspicion of multiple counts of burglary.

Noz is sleeping, his bowling ball head lolling around against the headrest.

The car radio is set to a station playing mellow indie tracks as a wind-down for late-night listeners. 'Yellow' by Coldplay ends. The first chord of the next song is enough for me to recognise it. 'Somewhere Only We Know'.

'Could you turn that off, please?' I ask the detective.

She obliges and looks at me in the rearview mirror.

'You can't keep doing this, Ivor,' she says.

'What?' I grunt.

'Getting drunk and trying to fix things.'

'Nothing to fix. Becky's dead.'

'Trying to solve things, then. Digging, driving yourself mad,' she adds, firmer.

'The Burrowses and Montagues are lying,' I tell her.

'Rebecca Burrows killed herself.'

'No, they're lying. They hid her phone, they paid each other, they made stuff up. Like with her sister.' My eyes are closed. Mustn't throw up on the nice seats.

'Rebecca Burrows killed herself, Ivor,' she reiterates, sounding both stern and sympathetic. 'Would a family who had one daughter who died at a property, really want to kill their other daughter and set it up to look exactly like the first death? No right-thinking person would do that.'

'It's their MO,' I argue. I open my eyes again and look at Noz who's awake again. He nods encouragement. Taking a deep breath, I feel clarity condensing. The detective isn't seeing it, she's argued herself into it all being a tragedy. How do I convince her?

'"Their MO"...' she quotes. 'Too many crime dramas for you!' She gives a tiny, kind chuckle, then shakes her head.

'I think Becky found out what happened to her sister, and that's why they killed her. Dillon Montague has been paying the Burrowses off for years. Phil didn't deny it when I asked him, I've got it on tape.' I sit up straighter. All the things I held back from saying in front of the Burrowses to maintain our fragile truce before, come gushing out now we're alone with the detective. 'I think Dillon killed Amy, some kind of accident maybe, and they've been protecting him ever since and blackmailing him as an adult. Why would Becky message me on New Year's Eve saying she'd found out the truth and she loved me if she was about to kill herself? The Burrowses lied...'

'What did the message say again?' DCI Schwarz asks as we sit at some traffic lights.

'Mum and Dad have told me everything about Amy. I will always love you,' I recite off by heart.

'Ivor.' The detective turns to look at me, the glow of the traffic lights giving her face an eerie red tinge. 'What if that was "goodbye"?'

'Don't you think that'd be the first thought to crop up?' Noz snaps. 'You're not listening.'

I grunt in agreement as the lights change, and the detective is forced to face the road again. 'We've investigated this,' she says. 'The post-mortem said her death was almost certainly caused by her impact with the ground. No obvious struggle beforehand. She wasn't in a good mental state. She was intoxicated. We can't prove anyone else was at the property. I know it's hard to accept. But as a first step, it would be a good idea to stop drinking for a while so you can—'

Noz snorts. 'The drinking isn't anything to do with—'

'Don't you dare interrupt me!' DCI Schwarz bellows over him before adjusting her rearview mirror to look at me only. 'Ivor, the case is closed. OK? I'm going to refer you for alcohol rehabilitation and counselling. I can't force you to do either, but you need help from sober people who care about you.'

'Fucking joke,' Noz mutters under his breath.

'You can get out now, if you're going to be rude,' she informs him.

There's a long, difficult silence.

'Dillon was in the house when she died. I spoke to the Uber...'

'Ivor.' She brakes suddenly and pulls to the side of the road, forcing a black cab behind to blare its horn. Are top police officers allowed to drive like lunatics? They probably are.

She says my name again, then: 'Stop. It's not healthy. And even if she wasn't alone in that house, I still think she killed herself, OK? Please, please try to at least accept the possibility of that, yeah? I know it's painful.'

I shake my head, hot tears burning my eyes. I can feel Noz's discomfort next to me, a one-man audience to an emotional conversation he didn't request to witness.

'It's over, Ivor,' the DCI whispers. 'It's over.'

My tears become sobs.

'You found her body, didn't you?' she asks.

I look up, her petite, pale face now bathed in faint white light from the petrol station further up the road. Her eyes don't look angry or eager, they look sad, moved.

'It's all right, I'm not going to follow up on it. We thought at first maybe the Montagues themselves had made the call, not sure how to report a body on their property. But they denied it, and I've been thinking about it a lot. You knew she'd gone to Sandbanks, you knew she wasn't replying to messages. You strike me as the kind of man who'd be willing to go that far to find her. But when you did...'

Becky's face leaps out of the darkness at me again, her open mouth, her matted hair down in the cliffs, illuminated by my phone. Sobs pulse out of me, high-pitched, staccato bleats as I pinch the bridge of my nose and lean forward to look at the floor, tears pitter-pattering into the footwell.

'We checked you out, ex-boyfriends make good suspects. But there was no way you could have been in Sandbanks in the window of when she... passed. But we found CCTV of you getting off a train at King's Cross on the morning of 3 January. You'd found her in the night then phoned from Bournemouth station, hadn't you? I can't imagine how you must have felt. As I say, I'm not going to tell anyone, but it's time to get help for yourself. You can't help her now. As painful as it may be, you need to accept that Becky wanted to end her life.'

I stay looking at my lap, sniff up hard and clear my throat. 'I was on a work call at Tesco ages ago. Usually, we just talk in the staff room, but they wanted one-on-ones with everyone and decided we should do it with management over Zoom at home.'

I glance up, wondering if I've lost her, but she's hanging on every word.

'I'm expecting this to be a box ticking thing. Five minutes of corporate crap. So I take the Zoom call on the sofa. Becky's just out of frame next to me, messing on her phone. But then my boss at the time, James, starts telling me I'm doing really well, points out a couple of changes I'd suggested, how they'd helped us sell stuff, made life easier on the shop floor. Tells me he's spoken to central office and I'm getting a bit of a pay bump and to keep up the good work.'

I stop again, my mouth filling with saliva, the corners of my lips pointing down.

Deep breath. 'The call ends and Becky is just beaming! She's so proud of me, tells me I'm amazing, that I'm clearly brilliant at my job. Well over the top, y'know. And... I dunno... something just clicked, I just... she was happy, genuinely, because she loved me and something had gone well for me. And in that moment, I realised I didn't need anyone else. Her being proud of me, that was enough. Us, on the sofa, loving each other. That's what a perfect life looks like. And I had it.'

I glance in from the car window, the white light of the petrol station still illuminating the detective's face, a single tear sliding down her right cheek as she tries to hold up a supportive smile.

I wipe my own tears away. 'She filled up my whole world. Now it's empty again.'

DCI Schwarz, already leaning round, undoes her seatbelt, rotates fully to face me and takes my hand in both of hers. Her tone is warm and heartfelt. 'She'd still be proud of you.'

I look out of the window again and nod, silent tears slipping down my cheeks.

She squeezes my hands a little tighter. 'But it's time to let her rest now.'

STAGE 4 – DEPRESSION

34

IVOR

January 2025

It's unclear if the litre of Bells I saw off in my flat last night is still coursing through my system, as I stagger into Tesco on my first day back. But the exceptionally long glug I had from a fresh bottle this morning certainly is.

Snatching mouthwash and ibuprofen off shelves the first moment Trish's Gestapo spotlight is turned, I flee to the staff bathroom. On my knees, head lolling into the toilet bowl, the putrid stench under the rim and the mouthful of Listerine I've just accidentally swallowed conspire to bring up the entire contents of my stomach.

Eyes tight shut, tears of pain bleed across my face as heaves tear at my gullet like broken glass. Catching my breath between waves, my temples pound so hard I beg for death.

After what feels like ten lifetimes, my body accepts there is nothing left to expel. Folding the toilet lid back down, I place my cold, clammy cheek on the cool plastic, quivering. There's a very specific bliss to those few minutes after a hungover throw-up – your body grateful for the respite, before the clouds gather again.

Six ibuprofens washed down with a fresh shot of mouthwash, I lean up against the thin wooden wall of my stinking cell.

My armpits and crotch thrum with heat, utterly disconnected from my shivering limbs. Should have grabbed an antiperspirant off the shelf too. The sweat and stickiness of the T-shirt I've been wearing for the last week is beating out oniony body odour underneath my uniform. Shutting my eyes again, I begin to slip away, only to be dragged back by a colleague banging the door to the cubicle next to me. I move my backside away from the gap between our booths. Whoever it is doesn't bother to wash their hands after flushing. Filth bag!

Leaving the cubicle and tottering over to one of the sinks, I assess the damage. My eyes are black, like I've gone twelve rounds with Tyson Fury and he's landed every punch. What time did I go to sleep? What time did I wake up? The journey here feels like it took ten seconds. Did I have a beer on the way here, along with the whisky at home?

Five days, me and Noz have been out. Like... really out. I'd never touched harder stuff before, stimulants shall we say, but they became necessary. I kept saying to myself... three more hours, then I'll go home. But as the drinks slipped down and each deadline loomed, the idea of returning home seemed like the worst decision I could make. After about thirty-six hours my bank account was dry but I wasn't ready for it to end. I applied for a credit card online, there and then. It was approved and added to my phone's wallet all within an hour, too easy. If there's another financial crash, I'll take the blame. Noz and I have been using that card for all our chemical needs since. Yesterday I finally went back to my flat, just aware enough to remember that today was the end of my compassionate leave. It's hard to know if I got any sleep. I could fall asleep here standing up if I—

'Ivor?'

I whip round and my empty stomach flips.

'Trish,' I croak, attempting to sound normal. Watching her outline sway in front of me, I wish with every fibre of my being that we had gendered toilets.

Glaring at me through lenses so thick they could halt full metal jackets, her expression is not one of annoyance, it's much worse than that. It's triumph.

She peers into the cubicle – the abandoned Listerine and half-popped pack of pain relief – then back to me.

'Oh dear,' she says, only a millimetre away from grinning.

'Stomach bug,' I state.

'Stomach bugs don't smell like a distillery, Ivor.'

'This one does.' I can't be sacked. Sacked and a criminal record? I'll be lucky to get work as a village idiot.

Her amphibian body creeps a step closer. Is her tongue about to shoot out and devour me? 'If we weren't so short on the rota, you'd be finished.'

'Thanks,' I say flippantly.

She snorts in annoyance. 'You're just lucky the new girl's gone, but you are now at the very bottom of the—'

'Sophie's gone?' I ask.

'Was that her name?' Trish shrugs. 'Whatever. Gave her the boot. She was inept.'

'Y'know what, Trish?'

'What?' she snaps, her head flicking up in a come-at-me motion.

'I'm happy for her. You're hideous.'

'I'm your boss,' she spouts, pushing her shoulders back.

'Only because you have no shame and suck up to Central every chance you get. There are packets of Hobnobs out there that'd make better managers than you.'

That feels good to say out loud. A woof of fire bursts inside me. She stares back like she's chewing on manure, which makes it all the more euphoric.

'Insubordination will not be—'

'Trish. I quit.'

'You're fired!' she shouts.

'Looking forward to my exit interview with Central.'

I wink and walk past her. I'd rather never work again than spend another second with her as my boss.

My circuitous route out of the store sees me pick up a crate of Heinekens. Cracking one open the second I pass the threshold, back out into the rainy, dreary bustle of a Finchley rush hour, I cling to the feeling of the liquid sinking down, landing in my empty stomach and being absorbed all the quicker for it. My head swims as I glug and glug until the can is empty.

Opening another one, thoughts turn from liquids to powders and I ring the last number from the call log on my phone.

* * *

I'm on solid floor when my eyes open. Well, 'open' is a strong word... when I unlatch my eyelids 7 per cent to check what room, what property, what city, I'm in. Noz is asleep on a sofa – my sofa. I'm at home. OK.

Shifting into a sitting position carefully, I stare at the coffee table, replete with spoons, foil and a bank card. It's the one other item that freezes my blood, however.

A full syringe.

We'd been looking for drugs and came across a bizarre little man at the back of a pub I can't even remember the name of. He can't have been more than 5 ft 4 in and spoke with an Irish accent. Didn't take kindly when Noz hinted he must be a jockey, even less so when he changed his theory to posit that the man was a leprechaun. But this fella wasn't too offended to allow us a look in the boot of his car when we begged.

What did we find? More pharmaceuticals than Superdrug.

The mind's a weird thing. I don't know what day it is or how we got here, but now, as I look at the syringe, that scene falls into view quite clearly. We enquired about all the stuff we'd gone out there for – uppers, downers, chef's specials. But then I asked a different question. 'What if I wanted to kill myself? Anything for that?'

'No,' he'd said, then paused before adding: 'Not officially.'

'Unofficially?'

Then he'd opened a little metal box with a key to reveal about a dozen syringes. 'Secobarbital sodium. One'll do the job, at this dose.'

SOLD!

I had to go to a cashpoint and withdraw £800 on my new magic credit card to acquire the chemical. Noz tried to talk me out of getting it. But now I have a contraption on my coffee table that could end it all.

Opening my phone, there are several missed calls from an unknown number. Apparently it's 4 p.m. On Wednesday. I quit Tesco, didn't I, but that was... Monday. Shit.

I imagine Dad looking down at me on the sofa and shaking his head. 'Thank goodness your mother never had to see what you turned into,' he'd probably say.

I run my mouth under the tap in the bathroom for a while.

Belly full of nice cold agua mineral, out of breath from slurping so much, I pick up the half-empty – or half-full, depending on your outlook – bottle of Bells by Noz's side and slink off to bed, taking a couple of sips as I go.

Putting the bottle and phone down on my bedside table, I stare at the pint glass full of feathers next to them. That Uber driver comes to me for some reason, the one who took Becky to Sandbanks, how he understood me and how I feel. No one else does. Bless that man! I spin the top back off the whisky and force down three more mouthfuls.

* * *

The buzz of my phone is an abomination. My body needs sleep, endless sleep. When did I even put it on vibrate?

I lean over and hang up, letting my head slam back into the pillow. But the buzzing has been replaced by a small, tinny noise. I try to ignore it, roll over, but it keeps squeaking. What is that? I roll back over and look at the screen. No! I've answered the call rather than hanging up. I put the phone to my ear.

'Hello,' I groan.

'Ah, Ivor. Is that Ivor? Sorry, the signal's bad I think, couldn't hear you.'

I recognise the voice – but why? 'Who is this?'

'Julie! Julie, the Burrowses' housekeeper.'

'Oh.'

'Are you still looking into what happened to Rebecca?' she checks, all the kinds of highly strung and hyper that I don't need right now.

'No, not really,' I mutter, despising myself as I admit it.

'Oh. Could I still speak to you?'

'Why?' My headache is swelling with each fresh second I'm forced to stay conscious.

'I can't go to the police, but I thought maybe you'd believe me. I was there on New Year's Eve, at the Burrowses'. I know what happened.'

35

BECKY'S DIARY

Wednesday 7 February 2024

Excruciating chat with Mum. She called rather than sending a letter though – finally entering the 19th century.

Ostensibly, she claimed she was calling about my birthday.

'If you'd like to pop round on the Friday evening, you are most welcome,' she told me, detached and overly formal, as if I'm the local vicar rather than her own flesh and blood. 'But I don't think it'd be appropriate on Saturday. It is Amy's birthday too, after all.'

I told her they should come up to see ME in Finchley if they wanted to wish me a happy birthday. Stony silence down the line.

I was bluffing, of course. No way I want Mum and Dad to see Ivor's place.

That's not the real reason she'd called though. 'I've got some unsavoury news, I'm afraid, Rebecca... I've been informed by someone I trust that they've seen Ivor with another woman.'

I demanded to know who told her. Because there's no way Mum's friends go to the same places as Ivor. She wouldn't tell me, but said I should be wary of Ivor and his behaviour. Such cheap, nasty games she always plays. The longer she talked, the more convinced I became that she was full of BS.

Ivor – cheat?! No.

I might not be everyone's cup of tea, but I'm no mug. He adores me.

Shame on Mum. It's gross she'd make something like that up, the more I think about it. Gross, but not surprising.

I've got a theory. She knows somehow that me and Dillon have been meeting up – he may have told Wes and Faith, and they'll have told Mum – and now she is trying to poison me and Ivor with her toxic waste, so I can end up with Dillon, as she always planned.

What grates is that I want to be able to talk to her about Ivor. I want a woman's advice. I don't think I love him any more, I want to leave. I want to tell her that.

But I can't bring myself to. She wouldn't be a confidant, she'd use it against me, the way she uses everything against me, to undermine my confidence, to make me feel tiny. 'I warned you so, you stupid girl' – that's what she'd be saying behind every comment and look.

So I told her she was talking rubbish. Ivor would never do that. She should keep her snout out of our business.

Honestly, though, I couldn't have got through the last few months without Dillon.

After that first drink, I tried not to message, which lasted about two days. Now I'm seeing him two or three times a week. Every night Ivor's out at the pub, basically.

We haven't done anything but there's no one I can pour my heart out to like Dillon. Never has been. Because he knows. He knows everything. He was there when Amy died, he was made to keep it all a secret, the same way I was. No one will ever understand what it's like to live in fear of your parents the way we do.

Usually, I go round to his place. His beautiful, cosy terraced house in Stoke Newington. And he cooks for me, and listens, and tells me all these amazing stories about things he does with his work friends, and the city breaks he goes on. And we drink nice wine, or better yet, we don't drink at all. And I think about kissing him on the sofa. But I don't.

I was there two nights ago. He'd made his own ravioli, which was delicious. We watched *Bake Off* and bitched about our parents. It's funny, he feels quite the same way about his mum and dad as I do about mine. Wes and Faith are a dream compared to my parents. But to him, the resentment, the lies, the being forced to live under a cloud – he doesn't blame my parents, he blames his own. I suppose, in some ways, all four of them are culpable. But the Montagues are NOT worse than my mum and dad.

Anyway, then I got an Uber back to Finchley and cried the whole way. Because I'm not with Dillon, and my life is a mess, and I feel trapped with Ivor, but I don't have the heart to finish with him because I know it will ruin him. Is that a justifiable reason to stay with someone forever? So they don't disintegrate upon your departure?

I'm still taking the pill behind his back but I'm not sure why, we haven't had sex in months. He'll suggest it sometimes and I'll tell him we already did it the other night when he'd got in from the pub. And he'll sort of sit there, trying to remember, then realise he was so blasted he can't confirm or deny my claim. That's not a relationship, is it? Me lying, not wanting to be intimate. Him never sober enough to see how lifeless this has all become.

It gets to me sometimes. Why can't he see we aren't happy? What will it take to shake him out of this grey malaise we've got ourselves into?

But absolutely nothing shatters this contentment he lives by. It's infuriating.

I slashed a hole in the bottom of our binbag this morning and put it back in the bin, just to see how he'd react to something going wrong. Would he be angry? Would he snap? Would he feel anything?

He pulled it out and rubbish went everywhere. Coffee grounds, yoghurt, a snotty tissue, all over the kitchen floor. And he just sighed, went to the fridge, plucked out a beer, drank half of it, and carried on with the chore, clearing up as he went, while chatting to me as if nothing was wrong.

He lives for two things: me and alcohol. And he is so drunk on both he hasn't got the sense, ambition or heart to seek anything else.

I wish Mum was right in some ways. If he had cheated, at least I'd have an excuse to leave. Ahh, I can hear you from here, diary... I shouldn't need an excuse to leave. If I don't love him, I should go.

But I feel so guilty. He thinks we're going to be together forever.

He's sitting next to me now on the sofa, drink in hand. I've stopped being cautious with my diary writing in the vague hope he'll find out I've been seeing Dillon and get cross, realise we aren't working. Just ANYTHING.

But he won't. He loves me too much to disrespect me by reading my diary.

So I cry in a taxi home from Dillon's several times a week, and come back to a flat we can't afford to heat, with a broken shower. And I think... I wish I had Mum and Dad here. I wish they called my birthday MY birthday and not my twin's. I wish I could talk to them and cry with them and not have to hide the shit my life has become and even the ray of light that is Dillon, because they'd drench it all in condemnation and smugness and try to control it all, the way they do with everything else.

But if it's a choice between dating Dillon despite my parents' approval or staying with Ivor simply because he infuriates my parents... I choose Option A.

How I achieve that, however – that's a question that has already kept me awake for too many nights. I still don't have an answer.

36

IVOR

January 2025

Café Rouge. Not my usual establishment. You can order steak though. And I've got that new credit card, so it's an 8 oz sirloin, two mojitos and a glass of prosecco please, kind sir. Oh yes, all for me. Who cares about tomorrow? Who cares about today, frankly? That being said, I did force myself to get some sleep and have a wash in the sink this morning.

I had wanted to get a coffee en route for an extra perk-up, but the only one between the station and here was a Costa and I avoid them on principle after how hard they made it for Becky to transfer branches up to Finchley.

Ho-hum, I'm at the restaurant now. Julie sits opposite, a little perturbed at my bumper order of drinks. I did offer to get us a bottle of bubbly but she said she only wanted agua mineral. I think she's under the impression we're going to split the bill and now she's out of employment, she's counting the pennies. But then why suggest a restaurant like this? She's met me enough times to know I'd be happy with a sit-in Greggs. Or even a sit-out one.

I keep insisting I'll pay the whole bill. No way I can let her fork out after orchestrating her dismissal. Plus, what the banks don't tell you about splurging on credit is that it's technically free money if you don't intend on living long enough for them to chase you.

'What happened then...?' I prod as soon as we've ordered.

She looks up at me, tracing a finger up around her ear to push her thick, dark hair away from her eyes. She's not ugly, per say, is our Julie. But – it seems harsh, but I can't help thinking it – it's her personality that's so unattractive. Always stern, no sense of humour. I have never worked out where she gets any joy out of life. Maybe the thrill of stealing from her bosses brought her out in a smirk every once in a while. And now I've taken that from her!

'This stays between us,' she mutters, anxious and intense.

I nod.

'What happened on that night... they're all lying about it,' she says under her breath.

'I know,' I respond, a lot louder. 'You don't need to whisper, *we* didn't kill her.'

'Shhh!' she hisses. 'We have to be careful.' She scans the tables around us, which are certainly tight enough together for eavesdroppers to hear us, if they so wished.

I shrug. 'They can kill me any time they like.' As if to underline my point, my lovely drinks arrive. Putting one of the mojito straws to my mouth, I suck. The cold minty blast of lime, sugar and tart tequila is heavenly. The glass empties in no time, the straw making a big slurping sound as I hunt for liquid amidst the ice. 'Yum!' I cry, puckering my lips then making a kissing noise as they pop open.

Julie frowns. 'You're... I thought you'd be more... I thought you were taking this seriously, about Rebecca.'

'Oh, I did, but I won't be here in a week, so why shouldn't I enjoy things?'

Julie panics. 'Won't be here? Here in London or *here* here?'

'Here London, here here, here anywhere.'

'Ivor. Don't—' She breaks off, staring at me.

'Go on, what happened on New Year's Eve? Let me guess, Dillon was at Sandbanks, the Burrowses and Montagues knew, they convinced Becky to go over there, which proves they lied to the police.'

She takes a sip of her water, a flicker of concern still distracting her. 'Sort of. I knew you'd been digging, the way you stuck it to them when you came round a couple of weeks ago. That was ballsy. You have to be careful with them, Ivor. They are...'

'I'm not scared of them. I told the police my theory and they still say Becky killed herself. It's over.' I take the puny glass of prosecco and see it off in one.

'It was more than that, though,' Julie says, wary again. My ravenous stomach roars, drowning out her whispers. This steak better get here before I collapse. It's several days since I've eaten.

'They were all on the phone to each other,' Julie explains.

'They couldn't have been,' I swat away. 'Becky left her phone in Wimbledon.'

'No... they took it when she was at the door. Snatched it off her.'

That's new. I always imagined she'd got herself into such a state that she forgot the phone and decided it was too embarrassing to go back and get it once she was in the Uber.

Julie continues. 'She was at the door, telling them she was going to see Dillon. That she was done with them. She was waving her phone in one hand, saying she had a taxi on the way, and Audrey grabbed the phone, said she couldn't go. But Rebecca stormed out anyway.'

I make a start on my second mojito.

'Then they phoned who I assume was Dillon and warned him she was coming. Rebecca had definitely told her parents and the Montagues she was going to Sandbanks, and they phoned someone to warn them.'

'Definitely Dillon,' I find myself saying.

'And then...' She shakes her head. 'Well, they thought I wasn't around, thought I was... Well, they probably just forgot about me as usual. But then they were in the library, about two hours later, all still drinking, louder than before. They'd left an awful mess in the evening and the kitchen was taking me an age to sort out. I mean, they'd paid for me to stay over on New Year's Eve, so I didn't mind staying up, but it had been such a chaotic evening, with Rebecca, and the argument, and...'

'Julie. You're rambling.'

'Sorry, sorry. So about 2.30 a.m., one of them says, 'Dillon's calling', so I hang around by the kitchen door to listen in. Mr Montague answers the phone. He's calm. Just says, "right" and "yes" and "no" and "I see" and "OK". Then he hangs up and tells the others Rebecca is dead, she's gone over the balcony, Dillon's there and has checked and she's definitely dead. And there's silence. I was expecting screaming, but no one made a sound. As if they were expecting it, y'know? It was a horrible long silence. Then Phillip says they should phone Dillon back, so Mr Montague does and tells him to stay in the house, not to leave. That they'll drive up to his London flat in the morning, stay there for a couple of days, then drive back to Sandbanks, make it look like all three of them had been in London over New Year's Eve and into the start of January. It was... cold. The Burrowses let Wes Montague concoct this plan to make it sound like their son wasn't at the scene with Rebecca. And then he said...' She shuts her eyes and quivers, a visceral chill so stark it can only have been sparked by a real memory. 'Audrey was sobbing by this point. But then Wes said, "We did it with Amy, we can do it again."'

A sickly dread grips me. Julie's worry at being overheard suddenly feels so much more logical. It's all as I'd feared, as I'd known.

'Tell the police,' I command.

Milk-bottle pale, she shakes her head.

'You can prove they all lied.'

'I'm a single mum with two kids. What if they sue and I lost my house, or they got me sent to jail? They're so much more connected and richer than me. Especially the Montagues.'

'I'll back you!' I point out.

She leans in, petrified. 'What else are they all capable of, if I go after them? I'd be putting my own kids at risk.'

My shoulders slump. Here we are again. Evidence... proof... stuck behind the same immovable barrier. That's why there's no point trying any more. DCI Schwarz told me, it's over.

'Why bother telling me at all if you don't want to do anything?'

'I don't know what to do!' she says, her voice shaky. 'I was hoping the police would just work out what happened. The Burrowses didn't tell them I was even there, so I haven't been questioned. But now it looks like the investigation's stopped and I'm torn because maybe we do need to tell the detectives what we know.'

'There's no "we", Julie.'

'I just thought... you seemed to be the only person left still trying to get to the bottom of it and maybe if you—'

'...do your confessing for you?' I interrupt but then sigh, remembering this woman is scared for her children's lives.

'What was the initial argument about? The one that caused Becky to leave?' I ask.

'I don't know, I only heard the raised voices at the end, when they were in the hall. But Rebecca was saying things like, 'You're all sick, I hate you, all these years, Dillon's nothing like you.''

'Did she mention me?'

There's a pause across the table.

'Doesn't matter,' I assert. 'Dillon's been paying the Burrowses tons of money for years.'

'Dillon has?' Julie checks, wrong-footed. 'Bizarre. Mind you,' she takes another sip of water, 'I do think the Burrowses were struggling for money, more than they let on.'

'How d'you mean?'

'It was always the Montagues who paid my wages.'

'Eh?'

'Ever since I started with the Burrowses,' Julie explains.

Our food arrives and she looks up at the server as if she may be a spy, refusing to say another word. Peering down at my lovely juicy steak, I pick up my serrated knife and shiny fork then look back at Julie once the waitress has walked away again. 'Go on!'

'The Montagues hired me. And I was under strict orders to report everything back to them that the Burrowses said about them... and Amy.'

I look off to one side. 'Surely Phillip and Aud would know you were spying on them. Why would they accept such a weird offer of paid help for so long?'

'I've never got to the bottom of it. All I know is I was paid to do their chores and report back anything they ever said about what happened to Amy. They never said anything that interesting but I didn't want to cross the Montagues by asking questions. Dillon paying the Burrowses though? That is odd.'

My stomach growls again and I find the strength to carve through the meat, red juices pooling on the white oblong plate. 'It doesn't add up. Spying on each other? The Burrowses were surely blackmailing Dillon for money for some reason.'

'They weren't just keeping up appearances though,' Julie states, more confident.

I eat my first piece. Char from the grill on the outside, succulent burst of flavour on the inside. My jaw tenses in glee. If this is to be my last proper meal, I've made an excellent choice. I saw at a much bigger second chunk, then shovel it in. I'm on to my third mouthful when I realise Julie hasn't filled the silence. Glancing up, she's looking at me pensively.

'Wha'?' I mumble mid-chew.

'I'm guessing you don't know they were in cahoots behind your back, do you?'

'Me?' I check, slurping the last of my second mojito, grabbing a passing waiter by the wrist and asking for two more. Noz would be proud. Well, he'd be proud of the pace, he'd make some horrendously homophobic joke at the cocktails ordered. Screw him. This mint and lime are the closest I've come to my five-a-day in several years.

Julie nods. 'Yeah, you. That was another conversation I overheard. Dillon, Audrey and Phillip. They all made a plan to split you and Rebecca up.'

My knife clatters to the table.

Rightly reading my silence as enormous, she continues. 'Early last year, Dillon comes round on his own, already an odd thing to happen, and tells the Burrowses he's seen you messing around with girls—'

'He's lying!'

Julie's hands go up in surrender. 'The three of them sit sipping tea. He says what he says and I linger outside.'

'Then what?' I demand.

'Audrey and Phillip already think you're the devil, a bad influence, bad for her future.'

I can't help shooting the messenger. 'Act like I'm evil but protect her killer? How am—'

She cuts me off. 'The other thing they said is they were afraid eventually she'd tell you about Amy's death. And then they surmised you'd use it against them.'

'What did Dillon say?'

'He was all over the place. Said he didn't know what to do, but he was pretty sure he'd seen you kissing someone else.'

'Which he hadn't!'

'The facts don't matter to the Burrowses, though, do they?' she states, matter-of-fact. 'They're wily. This was a chance to get rid of you. Legitimate or not. They start telling Dillon that if he breaks you two up, he could have Rebecca back. And let's be honest, he's on board. He wouldn't have told them otherwise.' Julie sits back and finally tucks in to her chicken Caesar salad.

'So he agreed?' I say.

She nods, her face full of lettuce.

'Then what?'

'Then Dillon came up with the plan. After all that doubt he feigned, he changed his tune pretty quick, if you ask me,' she says, all needle.

'What plan?'

'Audrey would tell Rebecca they'd seen you cheating, and he'd plant something on your phone.'

'My phone? My... phone.'

Clouds scatter in my mind as the last twelve months of my

life finally, instantly, become clear. I *had* met him before! I knew it!

He handed my phone back to me in a pub last year. Noz and I were in Stoke Newington, we'd just watched Arsenal. Who were we playing? Brentford, I think. That's right, we beat Brentford 2-1. Havertz scored late. I check my phone now for the date of that game... Mid-March!

Me and Noz got quite lairy after. And then some tall bloke had passed my phone to me, said I'd dropped it. That was Dillon!

'He handed my phone back to me,' I repeat out loud. 'Becky found that stupid app on there two or three weeks after that. The one for people wanting affairs. I'd never even heard of it, and then...'

'That's it, he'd said he'd do that!' Julie cries, before clamping down on an extra crunchy crouton.

'He...' It's hard to get the words out as I blink in astonishment. 'He said he'd plant an app on my phone?'

She nods.

'And then what? Did he say he'd managed to do it?'

'I don't know, that was the last I heard of it,' she says. 'Sorry.'

I stand up from the table just as another waiter arrives with my fresh drinks. I sink one and plonk the other in front of Julie.

'Sorry. I've got to go,' I tell her. 'That's just... you've just... Sorry. I'm...'

With that most eloquent of explanations, I stalk out. There's a cash machine over the road. I withdraw £1,000 and march back into the restaurant where Julie is still seated, shell-shocked.

Slapping the absolute wad of notes down, I touch her on the shoulder. 'That's to pay for lunch – and help you get by until you find a new job.'

Glancing up at me, mouth open, she doesn't get a chance to respond before I'm heading off again.

Back out into the fresh air, the world feels gigantic all of a sudden. Like everything's too big and I'm too small to handle any of it.

I didn't download that app. I didn't cheat! It was all lies and gaslighting. Becky was tricked. We both were. We didn't break up, Dillon broke us up.

37

BECKY'S DIARY

Monday 15 April 2024

It happened so quickly. It was over a week ago now and I still can't get my head around any of it. I've left Ivor, I'm back at Mum and Dad's. They're the headlines.

How do I feel? Sad, obviously. Relieved, certainly. Confused, definitely. Hurt, deeply.

Part of the struggle is that I didn't see it coming. I thought he was besotted with me, too besotted. I had him down as a lot of things: problem drinker, clingy, unambitious. But cheater? It's taking a lot of time and headspace to redefine him, to repaint the picture of the man I've been with for almost three years, to imagine that he could do something like that.

What makes it worse is that Mum predicted it. That weird call around my birthday. She still won't say who gave her the heads up about Ivor. Now she tells me every five seconds that I should have known he would be that sort of man, that his drinking and criminal record pointed to a life of instant gratification.

I'm so embarrassed, I'm such a fool!

How can men commit to a football team for life and never cheat, but fail to stay faithful to their girlfriend?

I had initially tried to forget about Mum's claims. But then she kept saying it, told me he'd been seen again... kissing a woman, groping her, them leaving a pub together. Again, I told her she was an idiot, a fantasist, especially when she still wouldn't tell me who'd seen all this alleged infidelity. Despite everything I was and wasn't feeling for Ivor at this point, I stuck up for him... he was a morally good man who had a horrendous past and didn't need judging and having spurious rumours spread by a bitter, meddling matriarch. I said other things too, really went for her.

She held firm though. Told me to check his phone, how she'd read in the Telegraph that more than 75 per cent of cheating partners now use apps to facilitate adultery.

I assured her I would not be doing that and that I trusted Ivor implicitly.

I spoke to Dillon about it the next time we chatted. At first, he said I shouldn't check Ivor's phone as it would be an invasion of privacy (see, he really has changed!). But the more we discussed it, the more he couldn't think of any other way for me to have peace of mind.

Once Ivor had conked out that night... I looked. Literally grabbed his dead-weight hand and pushed his thumb against the sensor to unlock the thing, he didn't wake even a little bit.

I didn't know what any such apps would be called but guessed they wouldn't be titled 'I want to cheat on my partner' in big capital letters, so I looked up what some more popular ones were, then flicked through all Ivor's apps, and there it was. More The Merrier, it was called. He'd not even tried to hide it (can you hide apps? I'm not sure). But there it was.

I was in shock. I didn't sleep a wink. And it's weird, but a large reason I couldn't sleep was excitement. The hours flew by as I contemplated life again, life outside this relationship. Travelling, saving up for the diploma. Dillon.

Most self-respecting people would have ended it months ago, maybe years. But I'm not most self-respecting people, as you well know, diary. You could make me a latte sopping in cyanide, I'd gulp it down and use my last breath to tell you how delicious it was. Much rather that than endure the crushing, unfathomable anguish of hurting your feelings.

But this was different. This wasn't me airing my feelings or rejecting Ivor, this was grounds for anger, pain and, ultimately, release. This was an escape rope – so I tied myself to it.

I'd planned to confront him about the cheating app as soon as he woke up, but my pathetic, spineless impulse to flee from conflict saw me wave him off to work as if nothing was wrong. I spent the day talking to myself in the mirror. I literally put on a Spotify playlist of motivational songs ('Lose Yourself', 'Eye of the Tiger', that sort of thing... so cringe, I know) and stared myself down. I must speak to him tonight. End it. End it now.

Ivor had gone to the pub after work so didn't get back until after 11 p.m., by which time I'd had about a bottle and a half of wine myself, Dutch courage helping much more than the songs had. And then I told him.

That was horrible... his face, when I first explained. The bewilderment, the sight of him seeing everything crumbling in front of him. He promised he hadn't downloaded it, he promised he hadn't been with anyone. Part of me believed him. He got more and more upset, more and more insistent. But then I asked him how many nights in the last week alone had he lost his memory from drinking? He couldn't answer – because it was almost certainly every night. And there lies the flaw in all his protestations.

I don't know how much Ivor genuinely wanted to cheat on me, but out at a pub one night, plastered, lots of attractive young women around as temptation, it doesn't take much imagination to see him downloading the app or snogging some random girl, and then forgetting about it by the morning. Or just lying to me.

We rowed for about two hours. It was awful. Just going round and round about his drinking, mainly. Him still in denial. Eventually I slammed the bedroom door on him, made him sleep on the sofa. But then, farcically, maybe inevitably, he woke up in the morning and could barely remember what we'd rowed about. He kept making arguments as if bringing them up for the first time, said he didn't have login details for the app I'd found, that I could go check CCTV of any bar he's been in this last month and how I wouldn't see any cheating whatsoever. It was sad how starkly he was underlining the biggest problem… he loses his memory when drinking.

He said he would quit booze, that he'd do anything, but I was so close to getting out that I stayed the course, told him a van would be over to pick up my things the next day and got a taxi to Dillon's.

Mum was smug AF when I returned to Wimbledon with all my belongings the day after, which boiled my blood. I pretended I was heartbroken and that seemed to pierce the leathery hide around her heart for an evening, long enough for me to get from the porch to my bedroom and shut the door, at least.

I've barely left the room since. Ivor keeps trying to call and text. He's visited five or six times, with Mum, Dad and Julie acting as gatekeepers, telling him I'm not in.

Urgh, what a mess. I do feel bad for him, in one sense. We'd been in love. Genuinely. And if he still feels that way now, the same way I did for him at the beginning, then I get it, he must feel like his world's collapsing. But then… don't cheat, and don't get so blotto you don't remember cheating.

He's got a drinking problem, that's my other concern. He was barely in control of it when we were together, I don't think a break-up is going to steady the ship. I tried mentioning this to Mum and Dad, suggesting that maybe as a final gesture, we could pay for him to have a few days in rehab. I even found a place that I think would have been good for him. Dad took one look at the price and told me to stop being soft.

It hurts that my boyfriend was playing away. That, I don't deny. But the beautiful thing about all this is that my head wasn't with Ivor towards the end, it was back with Dillon. And now we can be together again.

I'm going round to his for dinner tonight. And finally, FINALLY, I can say yes to staying the night. It's been a wild few weeks. A wild few years. But maybe... just maybe... things are going to be all right.

38

IVOR

January 2025

Why hadn't I thought to speak to Julie before? She was at the Burrowses' most days. But therein is the charm, I suppose. The Burrowses got so used to her, she was part of the furniture, rather than a living, breathing, wine-pinching human being – with rather sensitive hearing. And I fell for it the same way.

But it doesn't change the truth. Dillon broke me and Becky up. Julie couldn't have lied about that, she had her side of the phone-tampering tale and I had mine. Neither knowing that the other held the dovetail joint to the story. He broke us up. Then he got Becky back. But still, he was paying the Burrowses for something? Was that money for killing Amy? But why would he have killed her? And why would the Burrowses accept his money all these years later, rather than reporting him straight away? And why were the Montagues spying on the Burrowses through Julie? Whatever the answers, I bet Becky got to the bottom of it on New Year's Eve. She confronted her parents. She went to Sandbanks to confront Dillon too. He killed her.

But then why are the Burrowses still in league with the Montagues, if he killed both their daughters? That makes no sense.

Sunken costs, dear boy. Sunken costs. They are the bleak, heartless words that come to mind in Phillip Burrows' curt, posh voice. He's so obsessed with money and, let's be honest, they'd always treated Becky more like an unwanted pet than a beloved daughter. Maybe all the money they'd taken off Dillon Montague, and the agreement to protect him, became more important than going to the police. Otherwise, they'd have to admit too that they'd been protecting this hideous family for all these years for profit, at the expense of their own daughter. Their precious reputation would be in tatters. No wonder Becky was so upset when she texted me.

Mum and Dad have told me everything about Amy. I will always love you.

It makes so much more sense now. Oh, Becky... Why, oh why, did you go to confront him, rather than running to me? You'd still be here if you'd come to me!

I mustn't blame her. She was brave. She sought out the perpetrator, someone she'd been out with, someone she'd trusted.

Dillon.

He broke us up.

He murdered Becky.

And got away with it.

He can't! He can't get away with it.

Wait.

He hasn't. He hasn't got away with it at all...

Because I'm going to kill him.

STAGE 5 – MURDER

39

IVOR

February 2025

It's weird to have quit Tesco. But it was the right decision. Killing Dillon, that's my full-time job now – no room for distractions, least of all Trish.

I did look up the new girl, Sophie's, number as it was still saved on our rota system and I still had a login. I messaged her and told her I was very sorry she'd left, that it wasn't her fault and that Trish deserved locking up. Said I'd be happy to do her a reference for her next job if it would help. She seemed grateful for the offer.

But aside from that, my thinking has become utterly focussed on one thing. Deciding to commit murder is profound. It feels so right, so obvious, so pure an endeavour. Pure in the sense that it has given me crystal clarity, rather than pure in the whiter-than-white sense.

I've never felt the impulse before, never contemplated it, but that made it feel all the more correct when the epiphany did land. I'm not some weird recluse inspired by a twisted TV show.

It isn't a flippant, knee-jerk act of rage. It is the most logical solution I could possibly come to. Those stages of grief Cam introduced me to, the last one is supposed to be acceptance and in a sense that's what I've reached. I've accepted that murdering Dillon Montague is the only way to achieve a tiny modicum of justice for Becky.

I've stared at that deadly syringe on my bedside table countless times, daring myself to use it now, end it all. But why should I die, and leave those two families to get away with their lies? The police aren't punishing them, they aren't punishing themselves – maybe the universe is using me for that exact reason. I am their karma.

As I say, it's been a profound few days. And with such heavy thinking has come patience. It's odd. A calm has settled, like a fresh bedsheet falling on me from above, the warm waft of air and soft fabric of the idea reassuring me that I am doing the right thing. Sometimes it's hard not to imagine what life could have looked like if Dillon hadn't interfered. We'd surely have had a baby boy or girl around by now. A little family. A life full of love and joy. Then I get angry again and return to plotting Dillon's demise.

With no job and a lot of planning to do, I told Noz I couldn't go cruising for a boozing around town any more. Far too expensive and time consuming. Not that it stopped him wanting to meet up and drink, of course. Knew it wouldn't. Instead, we've been sitting at my flat of an evening, polishing off a lot of Polish lager – it's cheaper than Heineken, and stronger.

Noz knows about my plan. He didn't react the way one might expect. No remonstrations, no shock, more looking to advise, trying to help make sure I do it right and don't get caught.

'You don't want to end up inside again, mate, making toilet wine... mug's game.'

He's the only person I'd trust not to blab, and it has been useful having someone there to bounce ideas off. I don't drink when he's not there though, I need to be thinking straight, making rational, intelligent decisions about this.

As Noz says, I need to make sure I don't get caught. Otherwise, what's the point? I might as well stab Dillon, his parents, the Burrowses all in the street and get it over with.

No. This needs to start and end with Dillon. It was one of the first blocks of my plan to fall into place. I'm going to kill him at his home and leave the note he should be writing himself, admitting to killing Becky. Two birds, one clever stone... A note makes it look like suicide so they won't be looking for a suspect, and having him admitting to the murder will finally allow the world to know what he did.

So, I had my goal set early. But I didn't know how to get into his house, how to kill him, how to write a note that looked like it came from him, and – critically – how to avoid detection.

I needed to know more about Dillon, about the act of killing, about whether Belmarsh has updated its rules so you can get Greggs ordered into custody now... just in case this all goes tits up.

But I couldn't use my own phone and laptop. I may be studied closely after his death, regardless of how careful I am in advance. DCI Schwarz knows I think Dillon did it, I mustn't leave her any suspicion to cling to. So I buy a tablet computer, cash in hand, from a bloke with one arm at Camden market, no names, no receipts. Then I've been hotspotting Wi-Fi from the cafe over the road rather than using my own internet for all my stalking and searching, in case the police can track what you search for via your internet provider or something.

Honestly, I've been so careful and clever, if I do change my mind and decide to keep living on the other side of this little project, I think I'll join Mensa.

The social media digging I've done into Dillon has revealed the company he works for, his date of birth, a tattoo he has on his right shoulder and, most importantly, where he lives. Stoke Newington. Then I checked the Uber records for Becky's journeys over the last few months – and there was one address in that part of town she'd travelled to multiple times. It's his house, literally backing on to Clissold Park, not far from where me and Noz do our R.A.C. pub crawl. It makes sense. We frequent those bars a lot.

I did wonder how he knew what I looked like, given Becky didn't use Facebook or Instagram. Then I remembered the Montagues had taken a photo of us while we were down there once, put it in a frame and left it in the bedroom Becky always used at their house. He'll have seen that picture, for sure.

Then he must have spotted me in one of the pubs one night and come up with his plan on the spot. Took my phone, downloaded the app, went to the Burrowses pretending he'd seen me cheating, let them think they were all plotting in real time, when in fact he'd already carried out the deed.

A blaze for extinguishing this vile man roars afresh.

I want him to suffer, I want all the parents to know he suffered, since they don't seem to care how long they all made Becky suffer and how much they're making me suffer.

But it needs to look like suicide, no hint of foul play. That's fundamental. So sadly, Dillon will escape the torturous demise he deserves. His parents' anguish will come with the world knowing what he did.

And with that settled, the next bolt of inspiration struck. What's the best method of killing to make it look like suicide? It's the exact method I'd planned to use myself. My syringe –

purchased in the slough of despond, behind that pub from that tiny jockey man. Maybe that was the universe, again, making good life choices for me, or should that be 'death choices'?

All I need to do is get him unconscious, then inject it and leave the implement in his own hand. Any coroner will conclude it's the suicide of a man with a guilty conscience.

Everyone wins! Except Dillon, obviously. And his parents. And the Burrowses.

Perfection.

40

IVOR

April 2025

Living off benefits is no fun. Finessing my plan has taken longer than I'd expected, and I've maxed out my magic credit card. I applied for another, but with no job, no repayment yet made on the current card, and more than £16,000 spent in nine weeks, I was denied.

So I've been picking up dole, sitting in soul-sapping rooms, convincing soul-sapping staff I'm looking for soul-sapping work, and the whole time thinking about nothing else except how I can get home with enough money for food and beer, and get back to my masterplan. I say masterplan, if I pull this killing off, it'll be more like a masterpiece.

But as with all great works, it requires great respect. With the early building blocks falling into place quickly, part of me expected everything to be concluded within days. But the more I've pricked and prodded at the plan, the more exacting I've realised it needs to be. It's not just about me getting away with it for my sake. It's about others being convinced that Dillon has confessed, resetting the narrative of what happened to Becky. That's more important than anything else, and that won't happen if there's even one iota of suspicion he's been murdered.

So I've taken my reconnaissance to the next level, watched him from the park his house backs on to, from the bus stop down from his front door, I've lingered during the day, the night, dusk, dawn. But to do all that without arousing suspicion has taken many weeks. Can't be turning up around the property on CCTV ten days in a row. But I do now know his movements, his habits, his timings, when he'll be there, when he's likely to be out.

And after that has come even more self-discipline. I've waited another three weeks without going anywhere near his home. This operation needs to be beyond the investigative abilities of the world's greatest detectives – Sherlock Holmes, Hercule Poirot... even Coleen Rooney. It's got to be ironclad.

I've ascertained where all the public surveillance cameras are in the vicinity of his street, and plotted a route that can get me all the way to the park behind his house from Stoke Newington station undetected. As I mentioned previously, if I do choose to continue living after this, I will be joining Mensa, probably as its president.

The cherry on top of this plan will be staying in the park overnight the evening before I do it. That way, even if police were looking for someone arriving at the local station in the hours before his death, they won't find me, I'll have been there for a lot longer than that, out of sight of the digital spies in the technology-free Clissold Park. Keep a low profile once in the park and no one will remember or even notice me there.

It brings us to where we are now. Noz getting another warm-ish can out of a thin plastic bag from an off-licence, us both sitting on a bench, as the sun goes down this fine April evening.

'We've done a lot of sitting on park benches recently,' Noz observes. He's been rather invested in my preparations for this, asking me lots of questions about how I'm going to do it, sometimes coming along to keep me company when I've been watching Dillon. His loyalty is touching, if a little tragic. I wonder if I'd be as trustworthy and devoted to him if he was contemplating such a thing.

But here we sit, at the end of it all. And he's still with me. Over the last few weeks, I've wondered if his friendship alone might be enough to convince me to stay in the land of the living. Not sure. But I couldn't be doing this without him. Even after everyone else stopped listening, he's never doubted me. He rescued me from my dad, he picked me up from prison, and he's still here now. He might not be able to join me at Mensa, but he's a true friend. And those are rare, for me, at least.

'What time do you reckon you'll stay until?' I ask him.

'Until my beer jacket runs thin, or you fall asleep,' he mutters, his teeth already chattering against the cold in his thin grey unzipped jacket and jeans. On a navy-blue T-shirt underneath, white letters read: 'I'm no lawyer, but I'll get you off.'

My black parka and woolly hat do a much more admirable job of fighting off the elements.

We don't speak too much. Dusk turns to night, the amber glow of a distant lamppost in the park is the only light to see by as we work our way through the beers.

'I don't know anyone else who'd have stuck by me like you have, mate,' I say into the silence, ability to communicate amplified to almost female proportions by the growing boozy haze.

'Stick with me, Ivor,' he says back, almost in a whisper. 'You don't need anyone else.' With that, he downs his last suds, slaps me on the back and tells me he's heading home.

I nod, lay my head down on the park bench, cushioning my

cheek into the warmth of where he'd been sitting, and shut my eyes.

* * *

Next morning, my black trainers and then, inevitably, my socks drink up moisture as I cross the dewy grass towards Dillon's house.

I open his stiff wooden gate with minimal noise, the same way I did a couple of times at night when I was scouting the place out, then keep to the far left of the path in his garden so as to avoid being seen from his kitchen window.

Round the side of the house and up to the front door with my black leather gloves on, I ring the doorbell. This is not going to be a break-in, I've known that for weeks.

This is going to be a friendly visit.

Until it isn't.

41

IVOR

April 2025

What if Dillon sees me in the gloves and assumes the worst? The seconds waiting for him to answer the doorbell provide too much thinking time. A plan I've been perfecting for months suddenly feels flimsy and amateur.

The gloves disappear into my jacket pockets, hands emerging again as the door swings open.

'Ivor,' Dillon says, perplexed. He's in pyjamas – a tight-fitting maroon T-shirt and checked cotton bottoms. He even looks suave in sleepwear.

He puts out a hand the size of a dinner plate, ready to shake mine.

That's why you needed to keep the gloves on, Ivor, you moron. You can't leave any DNA on him!

I peer down at his palm, then back up at his sleepy eyes. 'Can I come in?'

He scowls at the snub but nods silently, turning on his enormous haunches and leaving me to close the door behind me.

I kick my shoes off and leave them on the doormat outside so as not to leave footprints or mud indoors – one detail I have remembered to do correctly.

Don't deviate from the plan again, numbnuts!

We wander down a narrow hall with bare pine flooring. The home is warm, central heating as constant a luxury as it is for his parents. Fresh coffee and warm toast linger on the lazy morning air. The walls are pristine magnolia, as if freshly painted, with unimaginative pictures of a vineyard and a European cobbled street leading the eye onwards.

Turning left into the lounge, there's a television in the corner so large you could lay it down flat and play five-a-side on it. The far wall is heaving with books. I spy the *Harry Potter* series at easy reaching height and imagine Becky plucking copies off the shelf. Where else is her trace? Best not to think about it.

I made the decision not to do a scouting trip to familiarise myself with the inside of the house. I probably could have got in while Dillon was out at some point, but couldn't bring myself to do it. It won't be a problem, though it does leave me noticing and processing this man's tastes and choices in real time. All new to me; yet Becky would have known it so well.

'Take a seat,' Dillon says, walking into the lounge. The set-up is open plan. I plonk down on to a sofa facing the bookcases; he loops right to the back of the lounge and through an arch that opens up into the kitchen. There's a large counter and cutout space in the dividing wall that allows me to watch him as he potters to the kettle.

'Tea or coffee?' he calls out in that stupid posh voice.

'Got anything stronger?'

He laughs, looks at me, then frowns.

'Tea's fine,' I mutter.

This is going to be tricky. I have something to drop in his

drink, but I'd planned to get him out of the room while I did it. With the kitchen and lounge so open, that's not going to work. At least he's pouring himself coffee in a mug. My biggest fear was him having a glass of very tasteless, very transparent agua mineral, which would have made any kind of drink spiking nigh on impossible.

I use his time getting the drinks ready to unzip my bag and put the downers into my trouser pocket.

Dillon comes back in with two steaming cups in one hand and his toast in the other. Putting my tea on a low, square Ikea-basic table next to me, he retreats to the sofa on my right, the back of which sits flat against the wall underneath the kitchen counter.

He places his own drink down on another identical plywood coffee table and shuffles so his back is flush with the cushions. At home but not relaxed.

Looking down at his toast, he picks up a slice and takes a big crunchy bite. 'Mmm... So surry,' he splutters, mouth still full. 'D'you want some too?'

Too easy, fella! 'Yeah, go on then.'

He gets back up, wanders back around the sofa and into the kitchen. I get up too, drop four tabs into his coffee while his back is turned, then follow him.

'Nice place,' I say, standing in front of him as he pulls a half-sliced loaf out of a metal bread bin, grabs a knife and saws off two fresh slices. My heart is pounding, but the deceptive doping went well. Those cute pink pills will be dissolved by the time we go back in. I practised at home, making sure they disappeared in most drinks but didn't leave a tell-tale scum on top, even without stirring. And let me tell you, once I drank a cuppa with just two of those bad boys in, I conked out and inhabited a completely different realm for the next eighteen hours. Highly recommend giving them a go, if you've got a spare weekend to yourself. When I finally woke up, it felt like I'd enjoyed a sabbatical back in the womb.

'Yeah, I love it here,' Dillon replies, placing the two pieces of bread into one half of his four-slice, black Dualit toaster and pushing the lever down.

He opens one side of his double-door Siemens fridge-freezer and gets out Lurpak butter and Bonne Maman Strawberry Conserve.

My head's in overdrive, taking in too much. But as I look around, everything feels poignant. Every decision he's ever made, his choice of kitchen appliances, the brands he uses on his toast, his style of freezer, they all seem to matter, as if committing them to my memory will let his spirit live on in some minute way, somehow mitigating the total removal of life I am about to inflict on this man.

There's a well-stocked drinks cabinet with charming bottles of Jameson, Grey Goose and Tarquin's gin all cooing at me. They might quell the firecrackers snapping in my mind.

Don't you dare!

Dillon turns to face me, the move feeling quite confrontational. But he doesn't look angry, he seems weary.

'Ivor, is there something specific you're here about? Because I need to be out of the house by eight and...' He twists his wrist up as if looking at his watch, though he isn't wearing one.

The fact he's got a short-sleeved top on is good. Focus on that! Another concern was how I'd get the needle into his arm if he had a shirt or tight jumper on. All these variables, all these unknowns I've been playing out in my head for weeks – little answers are popping up left, right and centre now as the wheels turn irreversibly.

Dillon glances up at the clock on the wall, aware of how silly his watch-look mime came across. 7.08 a.m.

'I'll be gone before eight,' I reassure him.

Bread toasted, buttered and jammed, he hands me the thick porcelain plate and I take it in one of my uncovered hands. Maybe it was right to take the gloves off, still wearing them at this point would have been weird. Going to have to clean the shit out of this plate before I go, though.

Walking back towards the lounge, I look out of the front window, the room concealed from the road by a large laurel bush in his front garden, another useful detail when plotting where to carry out the deed...

I stop in the archway between kitchen and lounge.

'Are those Becky's diaries?'

Dillon flashes his eyes in the direction of the TV, at the cube-shaped, metal trunk behind it, then back at me as I glare at him over my shoulder. 'Err... yeah. Her parents wanted to chuck them after she died, so I said I'd do it. But I haven't had the heart to...'

'Have you looked at them?' I demand.

He shakes his head, retaking his seat as I stand, still staring at the box. 'Don't know the lock code. Suppose I could break it but not sure I'm mentally ready.'

I know the code, I think to myself.

For now, I too retake my seat.

Dillon fidgets, taking a bit of his toast, chewing for an age then having to force it down with a sip of his coffee.

Good. Drink up, fella!

We hold eye contact for several seconds, neither wanting to blink. 'What really happened to Becky?' I eventually ask.

'I told the police everything,' Dillon states, gentle but certain.

'Did she love you?'

He stops and takes another sip of his drink, clearly not noticing any difference in taste. 'I think so.'

'Think so?' I ask.

'She told me she loved me.'

'When?'

'Plenty of times,' he says.

'Why do you pay the Burrowses five grand every month?'

Biting his lip, he looks away, then sighs. 'Suppose there's no point asking how you know that.'

'Were they blackmailing you because you killed Amy?'

His eyes lock back on me but I can't read them. 'I was paying them back.'

'Back?' I repeat.

'They paid my parents a lot of money after Amy died.'

'Why?'

'If you don't know, I won't tell you,' he says, taking another sip of coffee. 'Suffice it to say, I didn't feel it was right my parents had taken the money, so I'd been trying to pay it back.'

'How much are we talking?'

He looks away furtively. 'About three-quarters of a million.'

'Pounds?'

'No, potatoes,' he snaps. 'Yes, pounds.'

'Amy dies at your house, and the Burrowses pay your parents all that. Why?'

'Look, I'm here to be honest and open but these are not my issues. You need to speak to the Burrowses.'

'But Becky found out about all this money changing hands behind her back,' I say.

'Sort of.'

'So you all decided she'd left you no choice...' I growl, fury narrowing my vision until all I can see is his smug, petulant pan of a head.

'No choice but to what?' he replies. 'But to...? No, Ivor. If you've come for some sort of confession, then... no.'

'What did happen?'

'I was in London!' he cries, patronising yet defensive.

'You let her in. Cut the fucking shit and tell me what happened!' I'm as loud as I dare be, knowing this house is only semi-detached.

He pauses, finishing off his last ever coffee. 'She was super-upset, inconsolable.'

His eyes fill up.

'Don't you dare,' I tell him, the order overwhelming me, causing my own tears to splat against my trousers. 'You don't get to cry.'

'I lost her just as much as you,' he hits back. 'More even.'

'Fuck you! You killed her.'

He's indignant, voice much louder than I'd like. 'She killed herself. She came to Sandbanks to kill herself. To do it exactly where Amy died. I tried to talk her out of it but...'

'She was holding your necklace, she grabbed it as you forced her over...'

'She was on the wrong side of the balcony, swaying, holding on with one hand, telling me she was going to do it.' Squeezing his eyes shut, he shakes his head for a second in a feral, exasperated figure of eight. 'I'd gone to get her some water, came back into the lounge and that's where she was.' He's not looking at me now, he's looking straight on, out of that front window, as if reliving it. 'I ran over and hugged her. She held me for a second and then leaned back, grabbed the necklace, and told me she loved me. I thought...' He pauses, the words catching in his throat. '...I thought she was saying she'd come back over... and then she let go of the rail...' He stops again, re-shutting his eyes, a volley of sobs barrelling out of him. His chest shudders, his hands are clasped to his face.

I watch the performance, unmoved. 'Thing is, Dillon. You've all been lying to me for so long, I can't believe a single thing you say.'

He sits back again to take me in, his eyes beginning to droop. 'I'm tellin' the truth dough,' he slurs.

'None of you cared about Becky. Not like me. And you...' A lightning strike of anger brings me to my feet. I should throttle him, that'd be better than an injection, more satisfying, more painful – repay one tiny per cent of the agony he's put me through. I wipe my eyes and nose and clear my throat as I stand over him. 'You broke us up. You planted that app on my phone, lied to her, got back together and then killed her anyway. You fucking—'

'Am sorree, twas...' He tries to take a deep breath but his head is beginning to loll to one side, making it hard to focus on me bearing down on him. 'I shouldn' uv...' He burps, his arms limp by his sides now.

I kneel down in front of him – revenge suppressing rage. 'You and your family are vermin. So that's how I'm going to treat you.'

His head twitches, eyes closed. 'Am not lyin'...' Another deep exhale and he slumps sideways on the sofa, mouth lolling open.

I return to my seat, put on my gloves and eat my toast.

He's breathing heavily.

I look past Dillon, through the kitchen and out into the garden, over the fence and into the park beyond. You can just make out the bench I'd slept on. My route of retreat.

I should just finish the job then flee. That's the plan. But something stops me. Instead, I go over to the TV, pull the trunk from behind it and plonk it down next to me on the sofa. The same old padlock is on it. I always knew the code but never betrayed Becky's trust by trying it. Until now.

9-8-7-6. Click.

Open Sesame!

Is this wrong?

I've gone rogue.

He's still technically alive.

If I leave my gloves on and put the diaries back before I leave, no one will ever know. He'll be out for hours from the pills alone. Quick read, administer the injection, send the text, leave. The plan still works.

I pull out the diaries. Years and years' worth, all scribbled in plain red jotters like the ones you'd have at school.

I know exactly where I'm going to start – the day we first met.

42

BECKY'S DIARY

Friday 16 August 2024

It's been weird being back with Dillon. Good, amazing, fantastic! But weird.

Hello, by the way! How rude of me! Sorry, diary.

Living with Mum and Dad yet again is a dragggg. But I am out with Dillon, or at least sleeping at his, most of the time. And his house is... chef's kiss.

It's weird (need to summon better words... can't describe literally everything as weird!). It's... a head-scramble being back with him because in one sense we've settled back into the old dynamic, so comfortable, chat so easily, laugh at the same things, remember the same TV shows, mock the same parents. It's as if we never broke up, five years gone past in five seconds.

But in another sense... he's changed a lot. Not his character, but his circumstances. When we split, he was at LSE doing economics, failing to land an internship and contemplating whether to do the MBA his parents were adamant he should do.

Now... I think he might earn more in a morning than I've earned in my lifetime. He's still goofy and laid back and modest. Thank goodness! But instead of both eating Pot Noodles, spiced up with Asda's-own chilli sauce, we have moussaka from M&S. Instead of finding a dodgy online camcorder recording of a new film, he pays to stream it on Sky Cinema. And best of all, instead of washing myself in Ivor's cold, tiny, cracked sink, I take long, luxurious, steamy showers in Dillon's pristine bathroom, letting the water pelt me, the pressure so strong it almost bruises the skin. I stand with my back to it and let it hammer my shoulders, working out the knots, with the temperature cranked so hot I come out pulsing like a radioactive tomato... but feeling fantastic. Then it's into a fluffy dressing gown, flopping onto a duvet plump with duck down, listening to a chilled, jazzy Spotify playlist Dillon plays through his expensive bedroom sound system.

And that's before we get to Dillon himself. I'm pretty sure he did complete his MBA, if MBA stands for majorly beautiful abs! (OK, sorry, that was cringe, but I couldn't resist, ha ha.) He is definitely more... what's the word... sculpted than when we were together before. He goes to the gym every lunchtime at work, apparently. He said we should start going running together, and I laughed so hard I almost choked on my doughnut.

No thanks, Dill. You do the exercise, I'll do the grabbing your thighs of steel every time you sit down next to me on the sofa.

Not usually one to kiss and tell, but since we have done SO MUCH kissing, maybe I'd better just say that the sex has been dynamite too. That's the only word for it. We crave each other, we lose ourselves in it. With Ivor, we were both – not just him, to be fair – always so drunk by the time we did it that it was all a bit numb and shoulder-shruggy. I've already gone over this, so won't dwell. But back with Dill, we're both so present, every sense on high alert. It's a different act all together. Like we're making up for lost time, missed opportunities and forgotten desires, all rediscovered. As I say, dynamite.

One thing I can't help being a tiny bit wary of, though, is his jealous streak. He still gets a bit weird (Urgh! Last time I use that word, promise!) with other guys around. I've played down the Ivor thing, told him it'd been dead for ages, that we'd only still been together so I could move out of Wimbledon. It's not that far from the truth. But in general, he doesn't like talking about him. And he gets very cold if any other guys try to talk to us while we're out in public. It's subtle, but leaves me a bit tense. It's far less pronounced than it used to be though. I have found myself setting a passcode on my phone that he'll never guess... better not write it down even here, in case there are any prying eyes on our private conversation, dear diary.

No, but in general, that annoying, untrusting side of him does seem to be mostly in the past. He's probably growing out of it. He says he is. Now he's got an excellent job and has had time to reflect on how destructive his behaviour was before, you'd hope he would have matured.

Sometimes I get sad, trying to figure out why he's still in love with me. He says he never stopped loving me, that he never found anyone who made him feel the way I do. I tell him the same.

I'd never admit this to him, but for those first few months with Ivor, I think I did have someone else I truly loved. Reflecting on that relationship since, maybe that's why I stayed with him too long... always hoping against hope we'd rekindle that initial spark. But in the end, Dillon and I were always destined to be together. I'm his brown bear. Thank goodness I nabbed him when he was still a confused teenage boy. If he'd met me for the first time now, with his muscles and his money and his magnificent shower, he wouldn't look twice. But that history, both the good... and the not so good... has bound us together forever. And I kind of love that that's our story.

One annoying thing is that he's off working in New York several times a month and that's delayed my full invasion of his home, my clothes in his drawers, my *Harry Potter* books on his shelves.

I'm still round there, scalding my skin and eating his middle-class dinners several times a week. But he says he'll be doing less travelling by January, so we'll probably keep things as they are through the autumn, and I'll carry out the full military coup of his living quarters in the New Year.

It's all so happy and positive. Saving money at home and knowing I'm about to move in with the richest under-30 in the Western hemisphere has allowed me to cut my hours at Costa and I've been making up the difference volunteering at Battersea Dogs Home once a week. Actually doing it! LOVE LOVE LOVE! And Dill says he's easily got the money for me to do the vet's assistant diploma next year. And not part-time either. He reckons I should do it full-time, get it done sooner. Ooh ooh AND he's agreed we can get a dog! There's one at Battersea called Hoppy because he walks a bit funny, a grey mongrel. I am PRAYING he is still there come January, because he is everything I want in life.

It puts in perspective how bad things had got with Ivor, flipping from the last day of that relationship quickly into the throes of this one. We'd been flatlining. He's messaged a lot since we split, insisting he never cheated. Still don't know if I believe him. But it doesn't really matter at this point.

One grain of annoyance with Dillon, and definitely with Mum and Dad, is all this money he's paying them. When I asked Dill a second time about him giving Dad money to invest, it sounded like bullshit because he couldn't tell me any specifics. And then he tried to be patronising, like, 'Oh you wouldn't get it coz you're not into finance', like I'm a three-year-old and he's holding an abacus.

That's the tiny bit that's weird (Damn! Note to self... look up synonyms for weird!) being back with Dillon. We're in love again, we're happy, and yet these payments to Dad make me feel like they're all lying to me. Hot showers and endless gourmet food can only stave off the gnawing misgivings for so long, because I can't shake the thought that it's all got something to do with Amy, in some horrible way.

43

IVOR

April 2025

Becky was on the pill. She had no intention of starting a family with me. And she genuinely still thought I had cheated. It's too much to take in.

Why did she want to rekindle things before New Year if she was so out of love with me and so in love with Dillon? What changed over that last autumn?

Finishing the last page in the diary I've been reading from, I shut the book and slouch, staring at the tears in my lap. It hurts how much she lied to me, and how happy she was with him. Yet also I'm so pleased she was volunteering at Battersea. I never knew that and imagining her interacting with the dogs makes me miss her all the more.

There's only one more recent diary left to read, but checking the time, I've already been here an hour and a half – mustn't risk that downer wearing off. I know I gave him four tabs, but he's so big, he'd withstand a dose that would floor a thoroughbred.

I retrieve the syringe from my backpack, ease myself down

next to Dillon and hold one of his arms in the air, letting it fall back on to his meaty, broad torso. Mr Muscle is out cold.

Fuck his working shower, fuck his easy life and job that pays too much, fuck the fact he tricked Becky into leaving me. It cuts so deeply, reading how disconnected we'd got as time went on, but one thing I did notice, she never tempered what she wrote when we were together. She trusted me not to read her diary, always. Whereas with Dillon she was already hiding stuff, like not writing her new phone pass-code down, for fear he'd check. That doesn't sound perfect to me.

Staring at this unconscious colossus, no part of me regrets what I am about to do.

I've envisaged it a thousand times, fantasised about it more than all other parts of the plan put together. Of course I have. This is the moment.

I pin his arm against his thigh, palm facing upwards, and thread the needle into a vein at a flat angle like a plane coming in to land. Pushing the plunger in until it won't go any further, his croaky breaths grow shallower and shallower. Then I take his other hand and rub it all over the syringe before placing both arms back down gently, so as to leave the offending article stuck in his thick, tanned forearm.

Quiet snores ebb away.

Dying isn't a crescendo, it's an unimpressive slip towards remarkable silence.

I pick his phone up off the table, next to his empty coffee cup, use his fingerprint to open the handset and use the same index finger of his non-needled arm to open WhatsApp. The contact 'Dad' is high up on his recent chats. I tap on the conversation with Dillon's finger and use the same digit awkwardly to type in the words...

I killed Becky. Goodbye. I love you.

Send.

Then I send it to a random name halfway down his contacts too, just so there's no chance his family try to cover it up – their forte.

Locking the phone again, I place it back on the coffee table.

My plate and untouched mug of tea are taken back into the kitchen, the drink poured away, and both objects washed up with bleach from under his sink. Drying them thoroughly, I place them back in their cupboards – my trusty leather gloves covering my tracks the same way they covered so many before.

I should leave. Now the message is out there, his dad will know something's up. Back to the official plan.

Although...

Honestly, what on earth happened in the autumn that had Becky doing a complete 180?

I linger in the kitchen, staring at Dillon's drinks cabinet, then take the bottle of Jameson back to the lounge.

I pick up the last book, it only looks like the first four or five pages are filled in.

Read it quick, then depart before his family see his message and rightly assume the worst.

Spinning off the top from the bottle, I take a huge gulp of whisky. My shoulders relax, my cheek muscles loosen, my mind is a notch less wrought. I'll have to take this away with me, even if I finish it, so as not to leave a trace. But that's fine.

I flick to the opening page of the last diary – Friday 27 December 2024. The day we met back up!

44

BECKY'S DIARY

Friday 27 December 2024

Saw Ivor today. First time since we broke up, so what's that... April...
eight months. Wow. He looked terrible. He's been pestering to meet
up ever since we split, usually trying to call or leaving me a
misspelled text late at night when he's obviously drunk.

But I have been feeling bad about how abruptly it ended, and he
was making it very obvious he was still upset, so reluctantly, I agreed
to one last coffee. Thought it best to do it before New Year. If I am
going to move in with Dillon, the start of the rest of our lives, then I
wanted the slate to be totally clean. And I thought maybe some
closure for Ivor would be helpful. For him, yes, but also so he'll stop
texting. At the moment, I'm having to hide the messages from Dillon
so he doesn't get suspicious or angry. Not that I think he would
particularly, these days, but it's just, I know what he can be like, even
now. So it's better if never the twain shall meet.

I felt too mean to simply order Ivor to stop or change my number.
That'd be too high school. So we met at a coffee shop called Fuckof-

fee. I suggested it, sort of as an inside joke to myself – let's meet one last time, Ivor, but I'm afraid it's time for you to…

It wasn't very satisfying, to be honest. I'd insisted on a coffee shop to avoid him drinking his way through proceedings, but it was obvious he wasn't sober.

I remembered how honest I'd been when I left him, when I'd psyched myself up for him getting home and confronted him. I wanted to bring that energy again. But then, looking at him, asking him how his Christmas had been and realising he'd spent it alone… Asking him what he'd been up to apart from that and hearing him list the same old pubs, and how much his boss at Tesco was bullying him… His life is exactly where I left it. Apparently, his dad died in the summer, which for most people would be a big deal, but if anything, he seemed relieved. Not to speak badly of the dead but… I don't blame him. Ivor said there was literally no one else at the funeral. Bleak.

He told me he's kept my saved games of *Hogwarts Legacy* and 'your PS5' as he called it. I said it was his now. My word, that did make me sad. All those hours invested in exploring Hogwarts on that game, never to get them back, in a lame attempt to show my ex-boyfriend we're truly over.

He also said he'd been collecting birds' feathers and filled up a pint glass of them for me. He really needs a new somebody so he can move on… and to do a lot less drinking. But that's not my problem now.

In the end, I didn't have the heart to be callous, I didn't tell him to shove off or tell him about Dillon. Obviously, I didn't lead him on or arrange another time to meet, but I shied away from the brutal realities I'd planned to hit him with. He's such a lost soul.

Seeing him, and feeling my own reticence to hurt him, it reminded me how bad things had got between us and how trapped I'd become by always trying to put his feelings first. He's so fragile. I don't know when we went from happy, carefree couple to unhealthy dependence. Is there a world where we could have worked out? Not really worth dwelling on.

Found myself thinking about his dad's funeral again later. Then my mind jumped to what my own funeral would look like. Started tearing up thinking about how sad Dillon, Wes and Faith would be during the service (and hopefully Mum and Dad too!). Then I caught myself. What kind of morbid narcissist wells up contemplating people's grief at their own funeral? Lol. Lunatic!

Didn't tell Dillon about seeing Ivor. It's not a big deal, but he'd have made it into one.

Brought my new diary round so I can write in it while Dill's out with some work mates tonight. I bet he doesn't come home steaming, the same way Ivor used to. Stinking the place up, singing, slapping me with sudden sloppy kisses. Maybe if I text him now, he could pick me up a kebab on his way home.

Urgh! Scratch that! He's coming through the front door. Damn it! Now I've written it, I really want a kebab. Anyway, better go...

LATE UPDATE:

Hmmm. Weird. Can't sleep. Sitting in the lounge writing by the light of my phone because I sneaked out of bed and don't want to wake Dillon.

When he came home, he wouldn't look or talk to me, then started crying. Told me he hadn't been out with friends, he'd met up with both our parents. Said he'd asked to meet them to talk about something and that they'd reacted badly, not how he expected.

I asked if it was about this money he's been paying Dad, and he said it was. I asked if it's to do with Amy, and he broke down again and wouldn't say, but seemed clear it was. He said he wanted to tell me everything but Mum, Dad, Wes and Faith had made him promise not to. He said he felt so guilty not telling me. I said he should ignore our parents and tell me anyway, that he'd feel better. He said that wouldn't help at all.

Then he flipped completely... tried to get ready for bed. And I was like... 'Oi, drama boy... we can't leave it like this,' and he went all quiet and said he had nothing left to say and that I should speak to my parents, not him.

Like... what the actual fuck?! I'm so stressed. I feel sick.

I've been pulling and twiddling my hair so much since I came downstairs that it's formed a ringlet. A literal dreadlock!

Genuinely. What the hell is going on?

45

BECKY'S DIARY

Monday 30 December 2024

I'm numb. I don't know how else to describe it. All the hope of these last few months – gone. I've never felt so alone.

Dillon's been spying on me. Again. I thought he'd matured. But he hasn't.

He's been checking my phone. He knew I was meeting up with Ivor and followed me. Worse, he's then gone into my phone and changed his and Ivor's numbers round. What was he thinking? As if I wouldn't notice!

We were sitting watching TV at his tonight, and I'd decided over the last couple of days that I was going to send Ivor one last message, tell him there were no hard feelings but that this would be the last time he'd hear from me and I'd appreciate him not contacting me again either, because he'd sent a long soppy message after we'd met for coffee. I spent ages crafting the text to be clear but kind, if that's possible. Not brutal, at least. And then I pressed send and Dillon's phone lit up between us immediately. I didn't mean to, but I happened to glance and noticed it was my message to Ivor, flashing up on the wrong phone.

Then I looked back at the messages above the one I'd just sent Ivor on my own phone, and they weren't from him at all, they were ones between me and Dillon.

I looked at him and he broke down, the same way he did two days ago when he'd been out with our parents. Said he'd been checking my phone for weeks, had worked out my passcode.

He kept apologising in this frantic, panicked gabble. I kept asking him why he'd swap the numbers and he said he wanted to see if I'd accidentally send something incriminating to him instead of Ivor, and that way he'd catch me out.

WHO DOES THAT? WHO DOES THAT?

My boyfriend. Who did this before, who I love and trust and thought I was finally going to be with. He hasn't changed. And right there again, I'm trapped. Back in the same relationship I left five years ago.

How could he do this? Why would he still not trust me? How can I ever trust him, now I know he never changed? The pain and disappointment are too deep to describe. I just want to end it all. I was finally happy. Not love-drunk, not in a honeymoon phase... just excited and happy.

It's ruined. Over the last few months, I'd realised I couldn't be with anyone else – because of Amy. It had to be Dillon. He knew it all and yet he was still here, wanting to get back with me, still in love with me. Even with Ivor, there was always that nagging feeling of what if he found out... what if he knew.

But Dillon was the one person in the world that didn't apply to.

And now he's broken everything. Me. Us. Everything.

I will never fully love. And I can't tell anyone why. My secret. That I try to forget every single day. But haunts me every single second. The reason my parents hate me. The reason I am a shell of a person.

It's over now. I don't care if my parents die of shame or disown me. They basically did that the day she died. I have nothing left. I'm done. I can't deal with the guilt and self-hatred any more. I want to admit it. Tell the world, then leave it forever. I just want to go outside and scream...

I DID IT! I DID IT!
I KILLED AMY!!!

46

BECKY'S DIARY

Tuesday 31 December 2024

My whole life has been a lie. Ever since she died, what my parents have done, what the Montagues did, it's all more horrible and grotesque than I could have imagined.

We were seven! WE WERE SEVEN! Mum and Dad let me have that glass of champagne. Literally put it in my hand because they were already so tipsy themselves. Tried to give Amy one too but she refused.

They left us playing on the balcony, Amy showing off as usual, saying she could climb it, Mum and Dad too busy inside trying to impress Wes and Faith. All of them blotto. Then Mum spotted her standing on the rail. Told her off, told her to get down. And Amy blamed me. 'Rebecca did it first,' she lied.

So I pushed her.

A flash of sibling conflict. An impulse from a child plied with alcohol she should never have been offered. I didn't even like the taste. It was bitter, like off Appletiser. And I've sure as hell never drunk it since.

So they all watched as Amy screamed and disappeared over the railing.

That was it.

We had to wait about five hours before we could phone the police, let the booze sweat out of all our systems. I remember sobbing, not being allowed to go down and see Amy's body, Wes and Dad coming up with the story we were all to stick to.

My parents never forgave me, would rather die themselves than admit to the world what happened. Reminded me whenever we were all alone that if I said a word, they'd both be sent to jail for child neglect and illegal supply of alcohol. I'd be alone, and it would be all my fault. Beyond cruel.

But the Montagues. After Amy's death they'd truly parented me; they were the ones who loved me, cared for me, didn't make me feel guilty and ashamed every second of every day, simply for still having the capacity to breathe.

And that's what makes this all so impossibly twisted. THEY... Wes and Faith... blackmailed Mum and Dad after Amy died. Demanded hush money, threatened to tell police, and the world, what I did. The four of them have just told me everything.

They were all sipping champagne (CHAMPAGNE OF ALL THINGS!) and laughing as I burst into the library and demanded they tell me what was going on with Dillon's money. Three of the four held the line but the drink had gone to Faith's head. She started crying and blurted it all out before Wes could stop her.

The Montagues had witnessed my family in the darkest moment of their whole lives, and saw nothing more than a chance to profit. They literally put a price on Mum and Dad's silence.

And my parents agreed!

They were forced into massive debt by their best friends... and they're STILL all friends! Like it's no more than another transaction. Everything's just money and status. And using one to protect the other. Mum and Dad probably also think they have to stay friends to avoid Wes and Faith changing their minds and going to the police anyway.

IT'S SICK! THEY'RE ALL SICK!

Dillon's always known, apparently. He'd vowed to pay it back as soon as he was working. Faith said it's the only reason he took a job in the City, so he could earn more to pay Mum and Dad back.

AND STILL HIS PARENTS DIDN'T HELP REPAY THE MONEY!

AND MY PARENTS DID TAKE THIS MAN'S MONEY, WHEN HE DID NOTHING WRONG!

THEY'RE VILE! THEY'RE ALL SUB-HUMAN RAPACIOUS SCUM!!

I've locked myself in my room, alone, with a bottle of rum. Happy New Year to me! Julie has knocked on my door a couple of times to check I'm OK. Wish she'd fuck off with the rest of them.

I keep flitting between anger, heartbreak and desolation. But it's mostly the latter. What is the point? My family has been lying to me my whole life.

And yet, I still have to keep this horrendous secret. Not just for them, but because I've spent so much of my life hiding it now – made to feel like nothing because of a momentary mistake I made as a child of seven under the influence – that the conditioning has worked. I can't bear for anyone else to know. So my parents will get their way. And I will exist as nothing more than a pathetic, useless worm. No one I can ever tell the truth to, no one to leave all this behind with, just a lifetime of eternal shame tied to my ankle like a hulking anchor as I flounder in a pitch-black sea.

It's not like I don't feel indescribably guilty without them burying me underneath it. I loved Amy SO deeply. We were twins, best friends. I think about the woman she would have become, the memories we would have made. She preferred babies to animals. Maybe she would have become a nurse or a midwife. Would she have married? Would I have become an auntie? I think these things over and over again, half-trying to bury them, half-basking in them because they keep her alive in a horrid, empty sort of way. They didn't have to MAKE me feel guilty.

I tried getting away from this world. Ivor. What if we'd worked out? What if I'd never seen Dillon again, come back to this life, this family? I wouldn't have known the truth, but that would have been a blessing. Maybe the second it broke down with Ivor, maybe my fate was sealed then.

Because then I turned back to Dillon. But he can't sustain an adult relationship either. Should a grown woman really have to hide her phone passcode as the date she broke up with her ex-boyfriend, just so her new man won't decipher it? That's what I've become.

And as soon as I left Ivor, it was back to Mum and Dad, to the lies, the secrets, the shame. I'm trapped again but worse because there's no way I can stay with these people in my life any more.

This rum is going down quickly.

How dare my parents make me feel like the only one to blame, all this time. THEY should have been looking after their seven-year-old daughters rather than giving them bubbly as a stupid joke. THEY shouldn't have allowed us to climb a frigging balcony 60 ft up. THEY should have protected me afterwards, rather than treating me like I'd ruined their lives.

All they think about is Amy. Amy Amy Amy. What they don't realise is that I died that day too. Because they have not treated me like a human being ever since. Instead, they've left me to rot, to cower, to never develop, so I'm too scared to move out, too scared to tell a boyfriend or a colleague or even myself how I truly feel, spending every waking second dancing on eggshells, because of the way they made me feel and the desperation to save their own skin.

They would rather accept a blackmail from THEIR BEST FRIENDS than admit they screwed up, that they should have taken better care of us, and risk their peers knowing what truly happened. Oh, they're happy to crush me, but will never accept one iota of responsibility for what they did to both me and Dillon forever onwards.

I've finished the rum and thrown the bottle across the room. I hope they hear downstairs and worry about me. They won't.

I'm going to text Dillon.

I know we've broken up, but I can tell him I'll always love him and that I know the truth about Amy. He was at least trying to do the decent thing in all this. Yeah, one last text.

There. Done.

Wish I could tell him in person though. Before I end all this for good.

Actually! Why not? Why not see him one last time? He's at Sandbanks. I'm going to order an Uber. Fuck the cost, fuck the time, fuck them all.

There. Ordered. Four minutes away.

I going to tell him he's the only person who ever knew the truth about Amy and accepted me anyway. That still means something. I want to tell him that one last time.

Then I'm going to do it.

Mum… Dad… You wish I'd died instead of Amy. You abandoned me the moment she fell from that balcony. Now, at least, you can leave us both there.

47

IVOR

April 2025

Turning the page, it's blank. That was her last entry.

I get Becky's phone out of a side pocket in my bag and turn it on. I know the date we broke up as if it was tattooed on my eyelids.

050424.

The screen unlocks.

Opening WhatsApp on the phone, I tap on my name. There's no message. The night she died, New Year's Eve... she texted me... I've literally read it ten million times on my own phone... but there's nothing. Just a string of messages from me to her that I don't remember sending.

The realisation destroys me.

Hand still shaking, I go back and find Dillon's name instead. And there's her message...

Mum and Dad have told me everything about Amy. I will always love you.

And below it... all my frantic replies.

She'd texted Dillon. She'd wanted to text Dillon. He'd switched our numbers, she'd forgotten at the end. Drunk and spiralling into oblivion, she'd forgotten.

I tap on his contact details and my hell is complete – my number comes up.

She never meant to message me at all.

Glancing across the silent room, I take in the pale corpse of the man I've killed.

Dillon is still, mouth and eyes both a crack open, lips purple, torso twisted, collapsed sideways on the sofa as his feet stay planted on the floor.

What have I done?

I pick up the Jameson to take another sip, then stop myself.

I've killed an innocent man. An innocent son. The one other person who did care about Becky.

And I'd made her so unhappy. How? The one thing I cared about in life, I'd managed to ruin without even realising. How? HOW?

Looking at the bottle in my quivering grip, I slowly, shakily twist the cap back on and slip it into my bag.

Boots on at the front door, I march zombie-like round to the back garden, then into the park. My whole body is trembling as I find myself sitting back down on the bench I called bed last night. Hands gripping my knees, I stare between my legs at the floor.

What have I done?

You killed your own mother. Now you've killed an innocent man. Dad's voice tears me apart.

I shake my head. 'NO!' Whimpering, I put my hands to the sides of my sunken head, banging the palms into my temples. 'No, no, no...'

This was justice – for Becky. I did this for Becky.

You wanted revenge, Dad cuts back in. *You sick, unlovable runt.*

'Stop it!'

You thought you were better than me, you were never better.

'I'm nothing like you,' I whisper as tears roll down my chin and splat on to the floor. Getting back to my feet, I gaze out towards the edge of the park – my route of escape.

What are you waiting for, you idiot? Get out of here!

I turn around. I'm not going to flee.

Because I refuse to be the one thing my dad always was – a coward.

Heading back towards the house, I know exactly what I have to do.

48

IVOR

April 2025

Traipsing through Dillon's garden, out to the front of his house and on to the main road, I pass one surveillance camera, then a second – two digital spies. I am blowing the alibi I'd so carefully plotted and navigated to preserve, step by step.

My whole life, there was only one person I ever truly loved and who loved me too. And I wrecked it. She was looking for a rescue. She was desperate to leave them behind, and I somehow drove her back to them. How could I be so blind, so insensitive? What if I'd been better? What if I'd loved her like she wanted to be loved? She'd still be alive. She'd still be here, happy, with me. Oh, Becky, how did I get it so so wrong? How did I let you down so deeply? Why didn't you tell me? I'd have changed anything – everything – for you.

But you hid so much. About Dillon, about Amy, about you. Why? WHY? I would never have stopped loving you. I'll love you forever.

I was fighting for you. And now Dillon is dead. The

Montagues have lost their only son because of me! It's been harrowing knowing you're gone and this pain now is excruciating, my soul is being cleaved into two.

But I still need you, if I'm going to do this.

Reaching the street I've been to so many times for the R.A.C. pub crawl, I reach The Red Lion first. Peering in through the window, I see Noz at the bar with two pints. Maybe I should go in. Tell him what's happened. He might know what to do. He might calm me down.

But as I watch, he stumbles into a stranger at the bar, knocking the man's beer over him. Half apologising, he makes a quick escape and finds a table in the far corner of the bar to himself.

No. Leave him be.

I walk on.

Next, I come to the The Auld Shillelagh, the Irish pub on our route. The door happens to swing open as I'm passing and I spot Noz in there as well, sitting with two pints and two shots of whisky, interrupting a couple on the next table, trying to tell them a crude joke. I should go in and stop him, down one of those beers for him too, knock back a whisky. We could spend the rest of the day in there, like we did all those times he was helping me avoid Dad. No judgment, no demands, escape everything. C'mon! Let's do it!

NO! I mustn't.

I continue my walk.

All those thoughts and memories Becky wrote down, how much I missed, how much I ignored. How could I possibly do that to the only person I loved?

I adored her, yet made her feel so alone. I don't deserve to live.

The Clarence Tavern comes into view. Against my better

judgment, I glance in through the open door. Noz is at the bar, eyes locked on the plethora of spirits on the back wall, slinging a sexist comment at a young timid barmaid, who looks like she'd rather be anywhere else in the world.

He continues gabbling away, completely blind, deaf and dumb to how he's coming across.

The end of my nose prickles with heat; shame and self-hatred grip me so tight I could pass out.

I don't think Noz has been quite as good a friend as I thought he was.

He spots me snooping on him. 'Mate! What you having?'

I stalk away, knowing where I need to reach – but he follows me out.

'Ivor! Come on, come inside, let's get a drink.'

I don't speak, just keep walking. Almost there.

'Ivor!' Noz says again, more aggressively.

I can see it now, stay strong!

'Where are you even going?' Noz asks.

'In here,' I say, reaching the police station.

'No mate, come on, let's go back to the pub, yeah?' He matches my pace as I ascend the steps up to the entrance. 'Don't do this, I'll protect you.'

Ignoring him, I yank open the door and we both march up to the reception booth.

But as I stare at my solitary reflection in the glass barrier between me and the young police officer, it's clear it's only me here and it always has been.

'You need to arrest me for murder,' I tell the officer.

'Wha... err... who... who did you kill?' he asks, his eyes roving up and down me in panic.

'Dillon...' I say, voice wobbling under the nerves.

Taking a deep breath, I shut my eyes for a moment and imagine she's next to me, holding my hand. 'I murdered Dillon Montague... and Becky Burrows.'

EPILOGUE
IVOR

Seven years later

Sophie visited today, which was kind. She knew it was the anniversary, which is always a tough one for me.

Seven years to the day since I was taken into custody, since I learned what really happened to Becky and, let's not ignore the elephant in the jail cell... seven years since I killed a man who did not deserve to die.

Where's that time gone? In one way, it does feel like an age, like remembering a film about a completely different person. And yet it also feels like it happened yesterday. I suppose that's the weird trick your brain plays on you when you're inside. Life's on pause – you're aging but not progressing.

Actually, that's not quite true. I do think I've grown a bit in here. Not in a boastful way. There was a hell of a lot of room for improvement on the version of me that handed myself in to the police. But maybe that's when the growing started.

Sophie, as I say, is an enormous support. She contacted me pretty much straight away after I confessed, before the full story was out in the press, before the sentencing. Apparently, it meant a lot to her the way I'd helped her at Tesco. And then when she did go for another job, I'd sent over a very complimentary reference and she was hired off the back of it. If I'm brutally honest, I barely remember anything that happened in those last few months after Becky died. But Sophie did and she wrote to me saying that no matter what I'd done, she'd always be grateful because I cared when no one else did. It's hard to put into words how much that meant to me, especially at the start, when I was getting a lot of heat in the newspapers and whatnot.

She's been visiting regularly ever since. She confided in me when she first started dating her now husband, Paul. I'd initially been sceptical – he's a Spurs fan – but he treats her right and it was obvious she was head over heels. They both came to see me the week before their wedding, and Sophie gave me a copy of the invitation along with one of the little cookies she'd made as a wedding favour. It wasn't as delicious as a Greggs one, if memory serves, but that thoughtfulness and time she has put into staying in touch has been enormously powerful.

Then, about four months after the wedding, she came and whipped out a black and white baby scan photo as a surprise. Twins! There were tears in both our eyes that day – 80 per cent joy, 10 per cent shock, 10 per cent terror, I think.

Holly and Alfie – they turn five next month. Sometimes she brings them to see me too. They call me 'Uncle Ivor' which melts my heart every time. And they bring me drawings of their dog and their house and their holidays that I stick on the wall of my cell.

It was just Sophie today though. Paul is taking the kids to their first Tottenham game. I offered to call child services.

I've also had a lot of help from the prison chaplain who comes in on Tuesdays and Thursdays. I think his name's Clive, but the first time I met him I asked him if his name was Charlie – like Charlie Chaplin – and he thought that was hilarious. So he's been Charlie ever since.

What I like about Charlie is that it'll always feel like we're just catching up, and yet he'll say deep things or be brave enough to call me out on something and I'll find myself dwelling on it late at night in my bunk. He's a clever man, is Charlie. He was the first person I ever truly admitted the extent of my drinking to, and he said the fact I'd compartmentalised it as a separate person wasn't helpful, that I needed to take full responsibility. It was direct, but he was right. I also had so much pain and anger to deal with, it took a while but through all our chats Charlie eventually worked out that while, yes, I was distraught about Becky, a lot of my anxiety and self-torturing was down to guilt over Dillon too.

I'd pleaded guilty immediately, done everything I possibly could to minimise the trauma for the Montagues but at the end of the day, I'd still taken their one and only child from them. It's such an extraordinarily hideous thing to take ownership of, that I tried to bury it for the longest time. But when I was crying about this depressive mood that'd been hanging over me for so long, Charlie asked if I'd truly come to terms with what I'd done. I said I had, but again – he was right. I'd got my head around Becky dying and my role in failing her. I mean, I was adamant I should be charged over her death when I handed myself in but was told by prosecution and defence alike that it was out of the question, given I was over 100 miles away when she died. But what I hadn't let myself fully accept was Dillon. It took a long, long time, but Charlie has helped me come to terms with that too. I can't undo it, which is what I realised I really wanted to do. But that doesn't mean I should punish myself every second of every day by making sure I'm miserable.

I wrote to the Montagues in the end to apologise. Obviously, that was of no comfort to them, but Charlie said it was still important to demonstrate my contrition and that one day that may be helpful to them.

I wrote to Phillip and Audrey as well, though I have less sympathy for them. I've beaten myself up so much for my own role in contributing to Becky not feeling able to continue in this world. I wonder if they have. I asked if they could send me the diaries from her time with me, I would absolutely love to have the entries to read from our early days. London Zoo, Budapest, kisses on the sofa. The good times. But they haven't replied either.

The two families tore each other apart, by the way, in the aftermath of Dillon dying. It all came out. The Burrowses dobbed the Montagues in over the blackmail. In return, the Montagues gave statements describing how Phillip and Audrey had given their seven-year-old daughter alcohol before she pushed her sister. No custodial sentences handed down between them, but the kind of reputational damage that is so fatal to any social future in the middle classes.

My only other visitor is Becky's old mate Cam, which is distracting in a very immediate sense, but I always get the feeling she's just showing up to hear the jail gossip. Like, she's more interested in the latest fight I've witnessed on the wing and being able to pass on those types of stories to her pals than she is concerned by how I'm doing. Ho-hum; it's still nice to see her.

And jail? It's fine. My duty solicitor was in touch recently, trying to be nice, pointing out I'm already almost halfway through my minimum term, suggesting that if I keep my head down, I should be able to start preparing my application for parole in just another seven years.

But I'm not sure I have the appetite to leave.

As I walk around the prison yard now, enjoying the April sunshine, is this so much worse than the outside world? For someone like me – who fears they might walk straight into a pub the second they're released, undoing all the good work that others have helped me achieve – the limits of jail are actually a blessing.

Being released won't bring Becky or Dillon back, so what's the point?

Reaching the chain-link fence at the edge of our outdoor space, I glance down to see a little feather on the floor.

Crouching down, I pick it up.

That's it, you see. All I want is to be back in those early days when we were in love, when nothing else mattered.

And I can do that as well in here as I could in the outside world. Better, even.

The only time I've ever felt complete was with Becky and in here I have the time to recollect those moments, where we are eternally happy and back together.

So that will do me, thank you, just getting part of Becky back, every day, forever more, the two of us as one again.

Somewhere only we know.

* * *

MORE FROM TAM BARNETT

Another twisty, witty, razor sharp crime thriller from Tam Barnett is available to order now here:

https://mybook.to/TamBarnettBook4

ACKNOWLEDGEMENTS

First, I would like to thank God, who is with me everywhere I go.

Every book has a specific dedication, but at the same time all of them are for the same two people – Hannah and Harlowe. There'd be little point in writing or enjoying any of this without you here to share in it. I adore you both far, far beyond words. My happy place is the three of us playing together in Harlowe's room (with the baby gate locked so our resident explorer doesn't charge out at the first opportunity, obviously).

Dad and Paula, this book is for you. Your belief, enthusiasm and support is key to me as a person, to us as a family and my writing as an endeavour. Dad, your commitment of time, thought and excitement to all my writing has been, is, and always will be invaluable.

Mum, thank you for all the friends you've sent books to, given bookmarks to and have told about my writing. But much more importantly, I'm so excited for you and Harlowe to become thick as thieves, scouring charity shops together, hunting for bargains. As long as it's no carriage, I guess it's ok...

Given this book spends a lot of time in pubs, I'd like to highlight the heroes who I have spent time frequenting public houses with... i.e. my best friends. I'm going to limit this to one happy memory with each of you, just as a tiny attempt to thank you for what you mean to me.

Phil, Emma and Connie – The six of us, at The Salutation,

beer in hand, watching the F1 qualifying in our own private booth.

Mike and Beth – Our first visit to the Hackney Wick flat and a delicious introduction to whipped feta.

Nick, Abbie and Boaz – Our sunny picnic in St James's Park (we were all technically there).

Ben, Ellen, Freya, Leif, Fen, Juni and Flint – You guys letting me stay last-minute during Covid, sleeping in Freya's room while Ben worked and chatting Pokémon with Leif.

Ben, Val, Sully, Imogen and Joy – Coming to visit you, Sully tearing around the lounge and a lot of tasty homemade pizzas.

Josh and Charlie – Getting a huge takeaway when you guys met Harlowe for the first time (even if we did have to banish the talking Yoda...).

Tom, Liddy, Delilah and Otis – All of us playing in your lounge in September, embracing the chaos.

Spizz and Carrie – Catching up over a pub lunch in a lovely beer garden before we went off to Silverstone.

Doug, Jo, Alice and Aaron – You all coming to the hospital to meet Harlowe the day she was born.

Ben – Driving back from seeing The Killers in Manchester, blasting some Girls Aloud.

Nat and Maddie – My introduction to Ely and watching you use the Avada Kedavra curse with wanton abandon on *Hogwarts Legacy*.

There are so many more family and friends who have been super supportive through buying the books, sending me messages or sharing posts on social media. I'm massively grateful to you all.

Huge thanks to Euan Thorneycroft from AM Heath for representing me and Francesca Best at Boldwood for being my editor. The advice, help and encouragement I get from you both is deeply appreciated.

Finally, thank you to anyone who has picked up this book, or the previous ones. It still blows my mind that these stories exist anywhere beyond my computer screen. But if you've made the effort to buy one of the books, then the least you deserve is to enjoy it. So I hope you have! And I'll now crack on with trying to ensure you'll enjoy the next one too.

ABOUT THE AUTHOR

Tam Barnett is a journalist, living in London. His debut with Boldwood was *How To Get Away With Murder*, a darkly comic thriller set in the Wirral.

Download your exclusive bonus content from Tam Barnett here:

Follow Tam on social media here:

facebook.com/TamBarnettBooks
x.com/TamBarnettBooks
instagram.com/tambarnettbooks
tiktok.com/@TamBarnettBooks

ALSO BY TAM BARNETT

How to Get Away with Murder

How to Read a Killer's Mind

The Last Stage of Grief is Murder

THE *Murder* LIST

THE MURDER LIST IS A NEWSLETTER DEDICATED TO SPINE-CHILLING FICTION AND GRIPPING PAGE-TURNERS!

SIGN UP TO MAKE SURE YOU'RE ON OUR HIT LIST FOR EXCLUSIVE DEALS, AUTHOR CONTENT, AND COMPETITIONS.

SIGN UP TO OUR NEWSLETTER

BIT.LY/THEMURDERLISTNEWS

Boldwood

Boldwood Books is an award-winning fiction
publishing company seeking out the best
stories from around the world.

Find out more at www.boldwoodbooks.com

Join our reader community for brilliant books,
competitions and offers!

Follow us
@BoldwoodBooks
@TheBoldBookClub

Sign up to our weekly
deals newsletter

https://bit.ly/BoldwoodBNewsletter